THE METEORIC RISE OF SIMON BURCHWOOD

a novel by

SCOTT SEMEGRAN

MUTT PRESS

Austin

Mutt Press
Austin, Texas
http://www.muttpress.com
info@muttpress.com

ISBN 978-0615753355

Photo of Scott Semegran by Lori Hoadley
Cover by Alchemy Book Covers and Design
Illustrations by Scott Semegran
Edited by Brandon R. Wood

Books by Scott Semegran:
Sammie & Budgie
Boys
The Spectacular Simon Burchwood
The Meteoric Rise of Simon Burchwood
Modicum
Mr. Grieves

Find Scott Semegran Online:
https://www.scottsemegran.com
https://www.goodreads.com/scottsemegran
https://www.twitter.com/scottsemegran
https://www.facebook.com/scottsemegran.writer/
https://www.instagram.com/scott_semegran
https://www.amazon.com/author/scottsemegran
https://www.smashwords.com/profile/view/scottsemegran

What Reviewers Are Saying About Simon Burchwood:

"A clever and surprising twist... cutting observations of the writerly demeanor."
-- *Kirkus Reviews*

"Simon is such a character that I couldn't wait to find what he did next."
-- 5 Stars / *Great Books Under $5*

"A very good novel that was humorous throughout." -- 4 1/2 Stars / *Red Adept Reviews*

"Simon Burchwood Is A Genius, It's True!"
-- 4 Stars / *Bitsy Bling Books*

"Cracked me up! Overall a very good and funny read."
-- 4 Stars / *Ashton the Book Blogger*

"Verdict: An ambitious, enjoyable read with a superb ending that changed my interpretation of the entire text."
-- *Indie Reader*

"This book will have you rolling in laughter at a man who cannot or will not realize who and what he is. Nonstop laughing from beginning to end."
-- 5 Stars / *Free Book Reviews*

"Strong, funny, and very well executed."
--- 4 Stars / *Book Stack Reviews*

Table of Contents

To my wife and kids - my inspiration, my everything

1.

"I have become wildly more successful than I ever could have dreamed." Listen to me blab my goddamn head off. That sounds pretty stupid but it's true. The cabbie kept *looking* at me in the rearview mirror like I was crazy or something, the bastard. "My new novel, THE RISE AND FALL OF A TITAN, will be published in the next few weeks, barring any printing glitches of course. But I am already receiving unbelievable press. The hype mill is churning. According to a source at the New York Times, I am the new Kurt Vonnegut. And according to another source at the Los Angeles Times, I will dethrone Charles Bukowski as the torch bearer of the lowly and disenfranchised." Listen to that. I was just blabbing away. Sometimes I just need to be slapped in the face because I just blab too goddamn much.

The cabbie kept staring at me in the rearview mirror. He was one of *those* cabbies (you know the ones?), the ones that scare the shit out of you when you give them a good look once they start to drive you to where you want to go. The ones that *could* be crazy with the strange last names and the cabs that smell like vomit and cigarettes and exhaust and body odor. The ones that constantly eyeball you from the rearview mirror and don't watch the road. He wouldn't watch the goddamn road. He was too busy looking me up and down to watch where he was going. For a minute, I thought he was going to crash and kill us both. He kept swerving in and out of our lane. But he never did crash. I guess he was used to driving that way, what, staring at his passengers and not watching the goddamn road, the crazy cocksucker.

"Vonnegut? Didn't he write that Slaughterhouse book?" the cabbie asked. Man, his eyes were really red and bloodshot. He must have been on crack or something. Most of those cabbies are on *something*. It's true. Something to kill the pain, something to make the dreary day go by easily, something to help them forget how terrible they got it. And this guy had it bad.

"Yes, of course," I said, trying not to sound too snooty. "Now, I know what you are thinking. That is an odd pairing of sorts, mixing the time-twisting tale-telling of Vonnegut with the in-your-face simplicity of Bukowski. But that is exactly what I did, using my two heroes' styles as a blueprint for my own. I took the best of both worlds and rammed them together, creating something utterly original and new and very post-modern; a stylistic pastiche, you could say." I found myself pressing my hands together as if I was *really* ramming those two ideas into one. I hate when I talk with my hands. It really gets on my nerves but I do it all the time. I have to work on not doing that so much. "That's what you have to do these days to come up with something original, borrow from the masters, because everything has already been

1

done. Every angle of every idea has already been examined and explored and expounded." The cabby's red eyes were glazing over, like I was talking about astrophysics or macroeconomics or some shit like that. I kept trying to think of something he could relate to, some kind of simple analogy. I thought of a good one. "It's like hip hop music and sampling. I'm like a DJ taking bits and pieces of music and making it my own, my very own, but with words and phrases instead. You'll get to read my new novel in due time and make your own judgments."

"I look forward to it," the cabbie said. "I like to read when I'm on the crapper. That's the best time to read. You got a good twenty, maybe thirty minutes of down time." A big smile slid across his face when he started talking about taking a crap. I guess he really liked taking a shit because I hadn't seen a smile that big on his face the whole time I was in the cab. Henry Miller liked to read on the toilet too. He felt that was the best way to express how he felt about what he was reading. I like to read in the can, except I like to read gossip magazines and shit like that. I don't like to *think* too much in the can; it interrupts what I'm trying to do in there in the first place, which is to take a crap and get the hell out. If I get all riled up, then the turd won't come out. And there is nothing worse than being all riled up in the bathroom with a turd that won't come out. It's true. He kept staring at me though, with his blazing bloodshot eyes. He kept looking at my backpack on my lap, I could tell. And for the love of God, he kept talking about the crapper. "The reading helps me relax. I need to relax to ... you know? I get constipated easily. Sounds like your book would be a good one for the crapper."

"That's interesting. Anyway, in the meantime, I've generated most of my buzz through the internet. I have a web site where I have posted samples of my work and snippets of reviews and letters I've received from publishers and editors. I have garnered a small following of rabid, devoted fans who read everything I write and support me artistically as well as financially. They give me gratuities and buy small chapbooks printed by my publisher. You can read my work too by going to www.simonburchwood.com."

I was really tearing it up, blabbing as if he was the last fucking person on earth. Man, wouldn't that be my luck, stuck on earth *alone* with that red-eyed cocksucker. But I knew the cabbie was listening. He couldn't keep his goddamn bloodshot eyes off me. He kept staring at me and my backpack. It made me a little nervous, especially when he almost hit an old lady walking across the street. Man, I've never seen an old woman *move* so fast. She about started sprinting when she saw our cab heading for her. I bet she hadn't moved like that in decades. But I think I got him interested in my book. Maybe that was why he was looking at me so intently. Or maybe he was just crazy. I'll bet you a hundred dollars that he was both.

"There I go again, always the shameless self-promoter. But go and check it out and enjoy my work, give me a gratuity, and support the arts. There is not a nobler endeavor than to lend a supportive hand to an artist!"

"I don't have a computer. Can't afford one," the cabbie said. Can you believe that? Who the fuck doesn't have a computer? That's like saying you don't have a TV or a microwave or a fucking telephone? Who the hell doesn't have a computer? I'll tell you who doesn't have a computer; those crazy cabbies, that's who. They're too busy staring at you and shit to be a part of a modern society, a society of TVs and microwaves and computers. That's pretty sad.

"That's too bad. Because I am very grateful for all the support and notoriety I receive from my fans. My life's dream is to become somebody known and read. I don't think that there is anything more important than making your name in this world. Otherwise, who are you? A schmuck who works from eight to five and brings home a check that will last until the end of next week? What kind of existence is that, you tell me?" I could tell what I said really got to him. For once, he stopped staring at me. He kind of looked off into the distance, contemplating something. I bet he hated his job. I bet he had really bad hemorrhoids. I bet they stung his ass all day long and made him crazy. "That was my life for ten years, a hard life at the grind; a thankless job that beat me down. I would wake up an hour early every morning and write until I had to go to work. Then I would write some more on my lunch breaks. The rest of my daylight hours were owned by my wretched employer."

"I know how that feels, buddy. My boss is a real dick!" he said. I knew it! He hated his job. That must have been it, why he stared at me all fucking day long. He must've been wishing he was somebody else right then, what, with his burning hemorrhoids and his stinking cab driving him mad. He eventually turned on Airport Boulevard, obviously in la-la land. He made the turn fast and hard, sending me into the door. I wasn't ready for that so I kind of fell over and shit. I felt pretty stupid for falling down but I wasn't ready for him to do that. He caught me off guard, you know, with his looking away from the rearview for once. I mean, he was staring at me the whole time and then he looked away and made that crazy turn. I almost broke my neck with that turn and the way I fell over. But I caught myself and propped myself up with my elbow. He started staring at me again but I wasn't going to let him know that I was caught off guard by his turn. My elbow was planted steady and hard. No turn was going to knock me down this time. I started blabbing again like I had never stopped.

"Now, the night time was my precious time, time owned by my family. My loving wife and doting children deserved all they could get from me. So I didn't dare write in the evenings. Instead, I would play with my children and spend quality time with my wife. But my life's dream always called to me and I desperately wanted to be a famous writer. So five o'clock every morning, my typer would be rapping and my fingers would be tapping furiously. Thankfully, it all paid off. Thankfully, my dreams will be realized soon, really soon." I started to feel like I was talking to myself. I was hoping that he would understand what I was saying but I don't think he did. He was too busy staring at me to care. I would've stuck him in the eyes with a red-hot poker, if I could. That would've really given him something to stare at.

"What's your name again?" the cabbie asked. He pulled up to the curb in front of the airport terminal and stopped the car. He turned around and really gave me a stare. Man, his eyes looked like they were going to start bleeding, they were so goddamn red. He was freaking me out. "I'll look out for your book."

"My name is Simon Burchwood. Here's my business card."

I had a small stack of business cards in my shirt pocket so I gave him one. I had them made up the other day. They say: *Simon Burchwood, best-selling author.* I am not a best-selling author yet but I expect to be soon. The feedback I'm getting from my publisher is really positive and they expect me to move hundreds of thousands of units. Can you believe that? That's quite a lot of eyes reading my work. Anyway, he seemed quite impressed with my card. There's something about a nice looking business card; people really seem to be impressed by them. Don't ask me why, they just do. Especially ones like mine. I mean, I paid extra attention to the type of paper and the particular font the print shop used. They say people who use the font called Verdana show a strong sense of character. So that's the font I chose. And I selected a nice off-white, sturdy card stock. Pretty fucking fancy if you ask me.

"I packed a case of these business cards for my trip along with as many pens and pads of paper as I could, in case I have the urge to write on the flight. I will be flying first class to New York for my literary debut at the Barnes & Noble flagship store. But first, I will stop in Montgomery, Alabama for a brief visit to an old friend. His name is Jason. I haven't seen him in sixteen years."

The cabbie quit staring at me long enough to get out of the cab and unpack my luggage from the trunk. I stood behind him, holding my backpack, and placed my foot on the rear bumper. But it was a little wet from a drizzle earlier in the day and my foot slipped off and I almost fell smack on my face. That would have been pretty impressive, huh? I could see the headlines in the newspapers: *Simon Burchwood, best-selling author, maims himself with wet bumper; career and intellect in jeopardy.* I'm glad he didn't see that slip. That would have been pretty embarrassing. And I bet he would have laughed to, the crazy cab-driving cocksucker.

"Jason knows all the success I've come upon even though I moved away after the eighth grade. He and I remained in contact through letters and later e-mails. He followed my entire career through clippings I sent him in the mail and then in more detail through my web site. I'm looking forward to finally seeing him again face to face. And I'm looking forward to hearing his kind words of support in person. Undoubtedly, he is my biggest fan."

Without warning, as if immediately possessed by a demon, the cab driver turned around and gave me the evil eye. His bloodshot eyes were flaring. He kind of started to freak me out. It's true.

"Wha'cha got in the backpack, Simon? That is your name, right?" the cabbie asked. His demeanor was quickly upgraded from scary cab driver to *really scary* cab driver. I thought for a second that his head was going to explode, his eyes and cheeks as red as they were. He was pretty scary looking. It's true. "You're holding on to it like you have something illegal in there, like a bomb or drugs or something. Wha'cha got in the bag?"

"What do you mean?" I asked. I guess I was holding onto it pretty tight. I hadn't really thought about it. Who thinks about that kind of stuff anyway? Do you think about stuff you hold onto and how tight you hold onto it? Most people with any sanity don't think about that kind of shit. But this cabbie was crazy, I tell you. He was a crazy cocksucker. He was really starting to scare the shit out of me.

"It's a simple question. You been holding onto that bag with your life. Care to tell me what's inside? In a way, I have a right to know. You could be endangering lives or something."

"How could I be endangering lives?" I asked.

"Like I said, you could have a bomb or a weapon in there. You're holding onto it like your life depended on it."

I *was* holding onto my backpack pretty tight but I think that was because I was nervous about flying. I really hated to fly. I wasn't looking forward to it at all. I have a really deep fear of being in the air in that plane, especially when the plane hits those air pockets and it drops suddenly, sending my stomach right into my throat. God, I really hate that! It scares the shit out of me. I think what scares me the most is that I'm not in control of the plane, you know, because I'm not actually flying it *myself*. I think if *I* was flying the plane that I wouldn't be so nervous. I asked the publishing company to send me to New York by train but they refused. They said it would take too long. I guess they are right. Trains are pretty fucking slow. And they go off the tracks all the time. I always see news stories about trains that go off the tracks, at least once a week. It's true.

"Oh, this is just the original manuscript for my book in here. Like I said, I'll be reading from it at the Barnes & Noble flagship store in New York in a few days. This is the only copy I have of the manuscript and I'm quite protective of it."

The cabbie looked at me from head to toe with his goddamn bloodshot eyes. I really wanted to jab them with a stick or a poker, anything long and sharp. I guess it took a minute for his pea-brain to register that I wasn't a terrorist or a criminal or anything. I mean, look at the way I was dressed for Christ's sake. I looked like a fucking dipshit with the khaki pants and pastel Izod shirt that my wife made me wear. I mean, she didn't *force* me to wear it but she kind of did force me to wear it since she does all the clothes shopping. Man, she sure does like to shop more than anything. And she's a sucker for department store fantasy bullshit. I mean, she wants me to look like those goddamn mannequins in there, all Ivy League and preppy and stuck-up. She can dress me up all she wants but that will never be me. I mean, I love her more than anything but I'm kind of pudgy and losing some of my hair. You never see pudgy mannequins that are going bald. Who'd want to look like that?

"Well, sorry about that. You can never be *too* sure these days," the cabbie said, leaning forward to shake my hand like he was really sorry or something. Man, he was creeping me out, what with his bloodshot eyes and sweaty palms. It was like he ran his hands under lukewarm water before shaking mine. It was disgusting. "Good luck to you, Simon. And if you have anything going for you, it's definitely your ability to tell *long* stories. *Very long stories*. Have a safe flight. And good luck being a famous writer."

The cabbie hopped in his car and sped away, off to scare the shit out of another fare no doubt, the creepy bastard! I didn't give him a tip because of his bloodshot eyes and the staring, of course. His mother should have taught him that it is rude to stare. A civilized cabbie would know that.

A black fellow came over to help me with my luggage. He was definitely a nice change from the crazy cabbie. He had pleasant eyes and a kind smile and he smelled like Old Spice.

"Can I help you with your bags, sir?" he asked me. He was very nice. It's true.

"Yes, you can. Thank you."

"Where are you going?" Man, he was really nice and all, almost *too* nice.

"New York via Montgomery." He quietly followed me all the way to the ticket counter.

2.

"I can't believe those cheap bastards at the publishing company! They said I would be flying first class." The woman behind the ticket counter stared at the computer screen. No matter what I said, her demeanor was unfazed. She wouldn't even look at me. It was a big change from the nice black fellow who helped me with my luggage. I could really tell that she hated her job, just like the cabbie hated his job. What airline employee doesn't hate their job, though? If I was an airline employee, I would hate my job too, what, with the terrorists and the raging passengers and the bad airline food and the constant fear of crashing to my death. But I'm not, thank God. I'm a writer. Who would want to work for an airline anyway? I guess she probably gets cheap tickets to exotic locations but it's obvious that she doesn't *go* anywhere. And she didn't care one bit about what seat I was *supposed* to have. All she could probably think about was getting off work and drinking a quart of vodka with her other miserable airline girlfriends and smoking a pack of cigarettes and meeting a pilot who smells like cigars and scotch and grabs her ass when no one is looking. "Seriously, there must be some kind of mistake. I'm supposed to be in *first class.*"

With the exception of her scowl, the ticket lady was cute in a *Janet from Three's Company* kind of way. Seriously, she had that jet-black hair and it was cut in the same style. Well, kind of. I mean, she looked more like Janet in the *face* than by the hairstyle. She was a drop-dead ringer for her, only if you looked at her face. Coincidentally, her name was Janet as well. It's true. This made for an interesting segue.

"Has anyone ever told you that you look like Janet from Three's Company?" I could feel the shit-eating grin stretch across my face. I mustered as much sincerity as I could into it. And I was *sincere.* She *did* look like Janet from Three's Company. Pretty crazy, huh?

"No, that's a *new* one," she replied sarcastically. And she was really *sarcastic* about it. She kind of ruined it for me, with her sarcasm, you know. I hate sarcastic people. Sarcastic people can stick their sarcasm right up their sarcastic asses.

"Seriously, Janet. My publisher said I would be flying first class. Is there anything available?"

"Did you say you were a writer?" she asked. Bingo! It worked every time. I don't know what it was about being a writer but it sure caught people off guard. It's not like I wrote the Bible or The Catcher in the Rye or Hamlet for Christ's sake. But I do like the attention, I guess. Well, sometimes. I don't like *too* much attention, just enough.

"Why yes, I am. My new novel, THE RISE AND FALL OF A TITAN, comes out in a few weeks. Maybe you've heard the prepress? Or seen my web site?"

"What was your name again?" Can you believe it? I didn't know exactly how hard my publisher was working on promoting my name but it sure wasn't helping me too much. I might as well have been just some ordinary schmuck. My business card should have said: *Simon Burchwood, ordinary no-writing schmuck.*

"Simon, Simon Burchwood. But you can just call me Simon."

"Your name does sound a little familiar. Wow, a writer," she said, her demeanor becoming a little brighter. A true look of admiration shined from her face. I could tell that she admired me, at least a little. "I've always wanted to write, you know."

Ask anyone famous what they fear the most and it is having to listen to people's failed hopes and dreams of becoming a writer or an actor or a singer or a baseball player or a ballet dancer or some shit like that. For me, it was no different. I didn't necessarily *mind* talking to people about writing for a career. I just didn't like talking to people *too* long about it. But I was prepared for this moment. I pulled one of my business cards from my shirt. Her eyes damn near popped out of her goddamn head, she was so impressed. The business cards never failed to impress for some reason. They really *never* failed. They're fool proof.

"Wow, what a cool business card!" she exclaimed. She was all excited like I gave her a gold bar or some shit like that. "If I could have your autograph, Mr. Burchwood, I'll check the system for any cancellations."

"Call me Simon. Mr. Burchwood is so *pompous* sounding."

I signed the front of the business card as she checked the computer for cancellations. I think it's strange that people want somebody famous to sign something of theirs. I guess it's their way of proving that they met the famous person that they will be bragging about later to their friends over beers and chips at their favorite bar. I remember this time when Jeff Arms told me that he met George W. Bush and I didn't believe him. Jeff Arms was this guy I worked with at TechForce, the company I worked at before I got my publishing deal. We were at happy hour one day and he told me this story about how he bumped into George W. Bush at a gas station. He tried to tell me that Bush was pumping his own gas and that they struck up a conversation between the pumps. He told me how Bush was tired of being chauffeured around and that he wanted to pump gas like a regular guy. I told Jeff he was full of shit. He said that Bush made his chauffeur run in and pay for the gas and buy him a six-pack and some beef jerky while he pumped his own gas. Jeff said he thought about asking Bush for his autograph to prove that he did actually talk to him. But how did Jeff expect me to believe that he had the signature of the *real* George W. Bush? Jeff was the kind of person that would sign a piece of paper and say it was the autograph of some goddamn famous person. Jeff was a real lying cocksucker like that. He lied about everything. But it's true what they say about famous people getting away with murder. It's absolutely true. I came up with gold.

"Luckily, there *is* a cancellation. I switched your seat for theirs. There is a small fee for the switch, though."

"Do you think you can waive it?" I asked.

She looked a little distressed at my request but she found the courage to please me. I could see that she really *wanted* to please me. That made me feel really good. It also inspired me. Maybe I'd write her a poem on the flight and mail it to her. You have to show your appreciation when *ordinary* people do things for you. It's true. Otherwise, they can get really ugly because they'll assume that you're a pompous asshole or something like that.

"Sure, why not. I didn't get my raise like they promised." She typed away furiously, entering some bogus claim into some comment field in the system. She had a devilishly content look on her face, as if she had just swindled thousands of dollars from her employer and thinking her deed would go undiscovered. She handed me my new ticket, looking around for onlookers with the authority to fire her. "Here you go. The flight will be boarding in an hour."

She sure was nice. I felt bad about saying that she looked like the Janet from Three's Company, especially since it's such a crappy show. I mean, to be honest, that show really sucked. Most of the shows from the seventies sucked except for the Jeffersons. The Jeffersons was a good fucking show. Any show where they had a black guy calling a white guy a honky was a good show in my book. Good old George Jefferson wasn't sarcastic about it at all. He really *thought* old Willis was a honky, even though they were *friends*. Now *that's* brilliant. The writers for that show were geniuses. But I felt bad about associating Janet with *the Janet* from Three's Company. I'd have to make it up to her since she's really a nice person and not a jaded airline employee, like the rest of them. I can be such a jerk sometimes, but it's not on purpose. It's true.

"Thank you, Janet. I'll wait in the bar."

"And thanks for flying with South Texas Air."

"Janet?" I asked. I had to make it up to her for being so nice to me. I just had to.

"Yes, Simon. Is there something else I can help you with?" She was really sweet. She really did want to help me with *something*, I could tell.

"Janet, would you like to have a drink with me? You know, over at the bar. You have any time to join me for a cocktail?"

"Well, that's very nice of you Simon. But I am *on duty*." I guess she was right about that. What was I thinking anyway? She looked down at my hand and kept staring at it. "And you are married, Simon. Aren't you?" She was right about that too. I *was* married. She was a real fucking genius, for sure. But I wasn't trying to hit on her or anything. I was just trying to make up for being a jerk and saying that I thought she looked like Janet from Three's Company. "I don't think that would be appropriate, would it?" She started to get all preachy and condescending and shit. I was sorry I said *anything* to her at all. I was sorry I opened my goddamn mouth in the first place. She didn't seem so sweet to me anymore, just annoying and condescending and jaded. I imagined her at the bar right outside the entrance to the airport, getting drunk with her fellow airline employees, blazing through ultra-light cigarettes and draining cheap vodka shots, draping her goddamn leg over the lap of a drunken pilot, in town briefly from Seattle or San Francisco or Boston or wherever he left his real wife and family behind. I was quite sure that she fell for the James Brolin-like pilot, I was quite sure of it. It seemed to me that the bitterness she had stemmed from the recurring rejection she probably faced from the unfaithful pilot, even though he promised to divorce his wife and whisk her off to Antigua or Cancun or Bermuda or wherever his bonus airline miles would take them. It seemed to me that she had clearly mistaken me for someone else. It's true.

"I guess you're right. Please forgive me." I gathered my things together. "Thanks again. Thanks for switching my seat. And don't forget to buy my book. That would be great."

"I won't, Mr. Burch... I mean Simon."

"Or you can leave me a tip by going to my web site at www.simonburchwood.com and clicking the Submit button on the gratuity web page." I was such a fucking shameless self-promoter. It's true. I wrote the web address on the back of my business card. "I take Visa, Master Card, Discover, debit cards, you name it. Support the arts!"

She thanked me and told me she'd leave me a big tip the next time she was online. As I walked toward the bar across from the boarding area, I turned and waved. She politely waved back.

Actually, I take everything back I said about Janet. She *really* was a nice young lady. It's just too bad she looked like the Janet from Three's Company and was a little annoying and jaded and bitter. It was just *too* bad. But it's amazing what a little notoriety and a smile will get you. Hopefully, it will get me a couple of *free* cocktails at the bar.

3.

"Do you know what the most undervalued punctuation mark is?" I asked the barfly sitting next to me. He was a real winner, he was. He sat there all pathetic-like with his left hand attached to his beer and his right hand practically shoved up his goddamn nose (you know the ones?). See, he had been picking his nose ever since I sat down at the bar and I thought asking him a question would interrupt his incessant picking at least for a few minutes. It was like his car keys were up there or something. It was making me sick to my stomach. "The ellipsis."

"What the hell is an ellipsis?" he asked, lifting his crusty finger in the air and waving it to the bartender. I guess that was some kind of code for serving another beer because the bartender brought one right over. The barfly didn't even have to say what kind or size or nothing. The bartender just served it up and brought it over. Now that's what I call service. But with the exception of the crafty, secret hand signal, the barfly was dumb as a bag of toenail clippings.

"Dot, dot, dot. You know what I mean?" I unsheathed my special writing pen and began to write this on a bar napkin:

Four score and seven years ago...

I pointed to the *dot, dot, dots.* The barfly took a swig from his fresh beer and wiped the foam from his lips with his grubby hand. He was a dirty fucker, smelling like he hadn't taken a shower in at least three to four weeks, if not longer. One thing I really hate is smelly people. I go out of my way to take at least a shower a day, sometimes two showers a day, depending on the physical activity I exert. And then I pile on the deodorant, the cologne, the talcum powder, the mouthwash, the foot powder, and anything else I can get my hands on to cover the stink. You *have* to cover the *stink*; it's a moral imperative. It's what separates us from the chimpanzees. You know, they say the difference between human DNA and chimp DNA is less than one percent. Well, that one percent is the I-gotta-cover-my-stink DNA that us humans have. This guy was closer to chimp than I was because his stink-covering gene was obviously deficient. Again, I pointed to the dot, dot, dots.

"That, my friend, is a powerful punctuation mark. It indicates something that does not have to be put into words, an understanding the author has with the reader, something so powerful that it has no equal within the syntax." I didn't really think that the ellipsis was *that* important but it sure sounded good. Talking about grammar always makes someone sound good. It's true. If you're ever at a party and are at a loss for words and everyone else is talking about evolution and lunar landings and stock options and politics and the economy, start talking about grammar. I guarantee you'll sound like a fucking genius. You know why? Even though English is the predominant language in our society, *everyone* failed grammar courses in school. You never hear someone say that they did *well* in English class. So when you talk about grammar, someone always says that they did poorly in English which, of course, means that they won't know what the fuck you are talking about when you start blabbing about ellipsis and conjunctions and past participles and all that shit. It's guaranteed.

"That's very interesting," the dirty barfly said. And then he stood up and just walked away. He walked away like *I* was the one that stank to high heaven. I'm glad he walked away though, what, with his god-awful stink and all that incessant nose-picking. He was a maniac about picking his nose like there was some lost money up there. The bartender walked by and I decided to try the secret hand code. I lifted my finger and when he saw me, he turned around and whipped up my favorite drink. He filled the glass a third of the way with whiskey and splashed a little cola on top with the soda gun. He seemed like a real professional bartender.

"That's pretty interesting, what you were just explaining to Ernie," the bartender said. He was pretty sincere about it too, I could tell. It's hard *not* to be sincere about grammar.

"You think so?" I asked. I was holding onto my backpack pretty tight and I still must have been nervous about the flight or something. That cabbie really got me going about my nervousness. I couldn't stop thinking about it.

"What are you, some kind of professor?" he asked.

"Why no, I am a writer. My book, THE RISE AND FALL OF A TITAN, comes out in a few weeks. First in hardback, then in soft cover a month later."

"Well, congratulations there. What was your name?" He held out his hand to greet me. I extended my hand and he shook it firmly.

"Simon. Simon Burchwood."

"Nice to meet you, Simon Burchwood. That drink's on the house," he said, pointing to my cocktail.

"Thank you for your generosity." Can you fucking believe it? Wow, he *was* a professional, a real topnotch bartender. I have known many bartenders in my time but he was one of the slickest. The bar wasn't full at that particular moment but I knew that he probably did pretty well on most nights. He *had* to, he was that *good*. Most bartenders do pretty well, even in slow bars. You know why? Well, no matter what's going on in our society, everyone wants to drink alcohol. I'm serious as a nuclear war. If the economy is great, everyone wants to celebrate and drink booze. If the economy is bad, everyone wants to drown their sorrows and drink booze. Bartenders can't lose. They have a steady customer base, no matter what. In college, I was a bartender at a saloon right outside of campus. It was packed every single night like fucking clockwork. Sorority girls, fraternity boys, geeks, weirdos, athletes, musicians, artists, sluts, you name it. They were all there, every night, Tuesday nights, Friday nights, Mother's Day, and even fucking

Christmas. And I made pretty good money too. I didn't have medical insurance but I didn't care. I always had cash in my pocket even though I wasn't *that* great of a bartender. I mean, I didn't have secret hand codes and all. I always had to *ask* someone what they wanted. I envied this guy just a little though. He must have been pulling in pretty good money. He was that good.

"Don't mention it. Being that I work in an airport, I meet lots of famous types. Singers, actors, politicians, reporters, disc jockeys, athletes, porn stars, you name it. But I ain't never met no writer before. Come to think of it, I don't even know what writers *look* like. I might be able to pick Stephen King out of a criminal lineup but that's about it."

"That's a shame. Writers should be like rock stars in our society. They should be revered," I said. And I meant it too.

"That's funny. That's like saying everyone should recognize chess masters or cyclists or physicists or inventors. Nobody *cares* about writers just like nobody cares about those other types. No offense."

"None taken." Actually, that really pissed me off. I mean, who the fuck did he think *he* was anyway? I was the one with a publishing deal. He was stuck in an airport bar serving swill to his high-class clientele, the nose-picking barflies. But I didn't want to start anything. I had just gotten the hang of the secret hand code and was on a roll for more drinks. Uncharacteristically, I kept my mouth shut. Can you believe it? It's true.

"I'm just speaking the truth," he said. "Who has time to read anyway when you can see the movie? You're in and out in less than two hours."

"Movies and television are the scourge of literature. They cheapen and demean our imagination and they limit the range of our creative minds," I said.

"Maybe. But they're fun and I get a no-bullshit story in two hours. I'm in and I'm out. Reading a book can take weeks, months. I once tried to read a book and it took me over a year."

"Did you ever finish it?" I asked. He was starting to sound like a real fucking genius. I began to miss the turd-loving cabbie. At least he *liked* to read.

"Nope, never did."

"What was the book, if you don't mind me asking?"

"The Bible. Now that's a long book. But I saw The Ten Commandments on TV one night after getting off a late shift. It's a good movie even though it's three hours. That's kind of pushing it for me," he said. Now I kind of agreed with him there, you know, since The Bible is all about letting this be and letting that be, and people begetting people and more people and more people. It just goes on and on and on. All you really need to know is the Ten Commandments and a few essentials about Jesus, Moses and a few other main characters, like God. And that movie *was* a good one, what, with Charlton Heston kicking ass in the name of God and impressing the shit out of the Jews. He was right even though the movie was a little too fucking long. I like short movies, an hour and a half tops. And I like short books, 250 pages long, tops. My new novel is exactly 246 pages. Exactly. Can you believe it? It's true. I decided to let that comment about writers slide. You know, the one about what they look like. I'd hate to look like Stephen King anyway. He looks like a real dumbass. I mean, did you see that movie he was in called Creepshow? What a fucking piece of shit movie! Well, (if you didn't see it) Stephen King was in that movie. He played a hillbilly that finds a meteor that falls from the sky and he thinks he can make some money off it by selling it to the local college. Well, the college jips him and he eventually is eaten by a green, fuzzy space fungus that was living in the meteor. Man, what a piece of crap movie! And it's two fucking hours long! But that's how I think of Stephen King, as that dumbass *hillbilly*. I know he was just playing a character but that's how I think of him; that's what I picture him being like in *real* life. I don't know why, I just do. It's *my* mental image, you know? If I was in a movie, I wouldn't play a role like that. There's no way I'd want someone's mental image of me to be tainted that way. I'd play someone tough and manly, just like Robert De Niro. Think of your mental image of Robert De Niro. He's a pretty cool motherfucker, huh?! That's how I'd want to be.

"I see," I finally told him. I was kind of at a loss for words. I mean, our banter was hitting a pretty low point by then, even though I agreed with him. I was really ready for another drink. I kept raising my finger and waving it all over the goddamn place but he wasn't making any more cocktails. It seemed his professionalism was shot out the window. He just stood there wiping his bar glasses clean, wine glasses, lowball glasses, shot glasses. He was wiping all kinds of fucking glasses. Man, I was ready for a drink and all he could think about was cleaning.

"Hey Simon? How long 'til you board your flight?" he asked.

I checked my watch for the time.

"About forty minutes," I replied. I was still waving my finger all over the bar but no response. He was not sympathetic to my needs anymore. His tip was really in *jeopardy*. And I *was* going to tip him pretty good too.

"Forty minutes, huh? Want to *burn* one with me in the beer cooler?"

He kind of caught me off guard with that question. I remember feeling like my brain had been sucked into a vacuum or something after he asked. I just kind of sat there like I had been kicked in the nuts, really speechless for some reason. How often has someone asked you *that*? That's what I thought.

"You *know*?" he asked, raising his hand to his mouth and pretending to take a hit off a marijuana joint, making a sucking sound as he inhaled. Man, he sure did look like an idiot there, sucking on his fingertips with his lips all puckered up like he was kissing his mother but with the air going in reverse. And, what, did he not think I knew what *burning one* meant? Did he think I was a fucking idiot? "It hits harder in the cooler. Come on, we'll only be a few minutes."

"Well, I'm not sure..." I didn't really know what to say. I never was much into smoking pot. It always made me really stupid and paranoid. I'd say things I would have never said sober and I'd eat every piece of food in the goddamn house. I once made a ketchup sandwich and ate ice cream with coffee grounds on top when I was high. I'm not kidding. It made me act that *dumb*. And I met my wife when I was high. When we talk about the night we met, she says I was *charming*. But all I remember was thinking that someone was out to get me. You know, like spies and shit. I kept seeing shadows out of the corner of my eye and I kept thinking that they were coming for me. Pretty stupid, huh? But it gets better. She also says that I told her that I was going to marry her. Can you believe that? I don't remember saying *that*. But that's how stupid I get when I smoke pot. I try, to my best ability, to stay away from that shit.

"Come on. I thought all famous folks smoked herb? Don't you?" he asked.

You know, you really can't argue with that. He was right again, first with the thing about The Bible and now about smoking pot. He was a real fucking genius. And a professional bartender too. He made me a quick drink and asked me to follow him. So I did. I grabbed my backpack and followed him through a door behind the bar.

4.

The bartender unlocked the door to a walk-in refrigerator in the storage room behind the bar. It had a big padlock on the front, one of those Master Lock padlocks like I had when I was a kid, the ones I used to lock my bike up at school so no one would steal it. I imagined it was locked because the nose-picking barflies would probably sneak back here and try to steal all the beer and wine and shit. That was a pretty funny *thought*. As the bartender unlocked the door and pulled it open, a whoosh of cold air rushed into the warm room. Inside, the interior walls of the refrigerator were lined with cases of different kinds of beers and exotic wines, stacked from the floor to the ceiling. There was enough room in there for the two of us to stand in the center, at arm's length. But I wasn't sure if I wanted to be stuck in there with *him*. I mean, I didn't even know his name and he wanted me to go in *there* with him. What if we got locked in or something? What a thought that was. I could see the headlines in the newspapers: *Simon Burchwood, famous writer, dies inside a refrigerator. Nose-pickers mourn.* I wasn't sure I wanted to go in anymore.

"After you, kind sir," the bartender insisted.

"Aren't you afraid that your customers will try to rob you while we are back here? Or lock us in? Anything could happen, right?"

"No way. I installed a camera in the bar and there is a monitor here inside the cooler. See for yourself." He was right. He pointed to a small television monitor hanging in the back of the cooler. I could see all the nose-pickers sitting at the bar and at their tables. The camera had a fisheye lens so I could see the entire place. I didn't feel one hundred percent safe but it helped. It helped a little bit. "We're safe as kittens," he said.

The bartender directed me to step in, bending over and waving his arm like a maître d' in a fine restaurant or something. I was kind of nervous. I didn't know exactly why, I just was. I slipped my backpack over my shoulder and secured it snuggly to my back. Then I said *fuck it* and stepped in. The bartender followed after, shutting the door behind him.

It was cold as a polar bear's dick in there. My nipples were standing at attention and mist was shooting out my nose. I rubbed my arms to keep warm but I wasn't getting any warmer. It was so cold that I forgot I was standing in a goddamn refrigerator. You can rub your arms all you want but you aren't getting warmer in *there*. The bartender pulled a silver cigarette case from his shirt pocket and opened it. Ten perfectly rolled joints were inside, lined up in a perfect row, like little white sardines or something. He pulled one out, flicked it into his mouth, and lit a Zippo with a snap of his fingers, like a magician lighting fire from his fingertips. He was pretty masterful with that lighter. You had to be when you were a bartender as good as he was. When the ladies came into his bar, he had to be prepared to light their cigarettes. Women always want men to light their goddamn cigarettes at bars. It used to drive me mad when I was bartending because I didn't smoke at the time. I never had an excuse to buy a Zippo. I should have bought one anyway, especially since I picked up the goddamn habit after college. I might have made better tips if I had one to light ladies' cigarettes with. He sucked the joint until his lungs were full. He was like a fucking vacuum cleaner. It's true. Not a bit of smoke leaked out of his mouth. He then exhaled with a wheeze and a violent staccato cough. He coughed like his fucking lung was going to fly out of his goddamn mouth. His face turned bright red and tears kind of rolled down his cheeks. For a second, I thought he was going to choke to death. I really did. And I wouldn't have known what to do. I probably would have left him there, called 911 anonymously, and boarded my plane as soon as possible. Nobody would have known I was there except Ernie the nose-picker. I didn't know what I would have done about him. He would tell the police about me for sure, the bastard. After a minute of wheezing and coughing, a smile crept across his face. He looked very happy in a *distressed* kind of way.

Then he wanted to give *me* the joint. He put it in front of my face, coughing a little more as he did. He looked to me to take it. He really wanted me to take it, I could tell.

"Here you go," he said, pushing the joint in my face some more. "Take a hit. It's not the greatest weed but it's definitely not swag."

For some reason, I looked at the security monitor. I was feeling paranoid as hell. And I wasn't even high! What a pain in the ass. Marijuana will do that to you though. Even if you're not high, it makes you all paranoid and shit. You think you'll get busted any minute, like a cop will pop out of thin air and read you your rights. But I was so goddamn paranoid that my skin was crawling and I had goosebumps. I was cold *and* paranoid. I rubbed my arms as I looked at the security monitor.

"Look at them," I said, pointing to the monitor. "All of them are pretty pathetic, drowning their sorrows and cursing their existence. They should channel that energy into creating something, doing something, being somebody, instead of sitting at this bar wasted."

The bartender recoiled after I made that comment, a little offended. He pulled the joint back and gave me a look, a look of bewilderment. For a quick second, I feared for my safety. I didn't know why. I just did. Wouldn't you, trapped in a refrigerator with a bartender you didn't know? That's what I thought.

"Hey, you're talking about MY bar here. Those are MY customers. They put food on MY table, pay MY rent. You have no right to judge them. Who the fuck do you think *you* are?"

Noticing the rage building behind his eyes, I took a step back, a little more fearful now. I put my arms out to contain him if he moved but he didn't move. He just stood there, fuming about that comment. I didn't know what to do. He kept staring at me. I was used to the staring because of the crazy cabbie and all. But he wasn't giving me the I'm-a-little-crazy kind of stare, he was giving me the I-can't-believe-you-said-that-and-I-want-to-knock-your-fucking-face-in kind of stare. I didn't know what to do. I had been in a few fights in my time but they were more of the getting-kicked-in-the-balls kind of fights, not the kind where you're stuck in a refrigerator with a strange, wasted bartender. He sucked on the joint once again, inhaling deeply, coughing some more. He coughed like his other goddamn lung was going to fly out. I thought for a second that he might actually choke to death. I wished he would die. I never would have wished anything like that upon anyone but, for that moment, I wished he would die. But when he finished coughing his goddamn lung out, his anger subsided as his high settled into his brain. His eyes sagged as the last of the smoke exited his mouth. He looked pretty dopey then. People always look so fucking dopey when they are high. If I wasn't so scared, I would have laughed at how dopey he looked.

"I'm sorry," I whispered, softly like a little girl. But like I said, I was pretty scared. And nobody was around so I didn't feel too stupid about sounding like a little girl. "I didn't mean anything by it. I was just giving my social critique, my opinion. My opinion means *nothing*, really. I was just making conversation. You know, small talk and all."

A bigger smile crept across his face. He was so goddamn high that I was waiting for some reggae music to start playing and a fucking lava lamp to pop out somewhere. He looked really dopey and high and content.

"You're right. No harm, no foul. And look at Ernie," he said, pointing to the monitor. "He is a sad-looking bastard, isn't he?"

We both chuckled like we were best buddies again. Well, I kind of faked my chuckle but I faked it pretty good. I didn't want to piss him off anymore and get that look again, that *look* like he wanted to knock my face in. He grabbed an ashtray from behind a case of Budweiser and snuffed the joint out. It snapped and fizzed as he smashed it. He put a droplet of spit on the tip of his index finger and drowned the last bit of fire out. Then he slapped his goddamn hand on my shoulder and squeezed it. It was like we were old chums, old college buddies, you know? But I decided I was *not* going to leave him a tip now. He was fucking crazy if he thought I was going to leave him a tip after all this.

"How about another beer for the road?" he asked.

"You mean for my flight?"

"Whatever. The road, the flight, it's all the same."

He put his arm around my shoulder and led me out of the refrigerator. I was really glad to be out of there. I really was. It was like I escaped off a deserted island or something. That's how I felt, really free. Well, almost free. He locked the cooler shut with that big Master Lock and he led me out of the storage room.

Back at the bar, I gathered all my things together. I decided right then and there that my time in the bar was *over*. Just like that, I can make a decision at the drop of a hat. And I decided that I would rather be anywhere, I mean *anywhere*, than in that fucking bar with that crazy bartender and all the goddamn nose-pickers. All those nose-pickers could go straight to hell.

"I really need to get going. What do I owe you?" I asked.

"But you have thirty more minutes. That's time for another drink. We're just getting to know each other." He was really getting pushy about it. I bet he was trying to save face for a tip. I bet that sneaky bastard was doing that. All bartenders are sneaky bastards, didn't I tell you? It's true. It's absolutely true.

"I really must go."

"OK, OK. But before you go, let me give you something that will help you *relax* and enjoy your flight."

He was really trying to save face then. He sank his hand into his pant pocket and pulled out, amongst small wads of lint and food crumbs, a tiny white pill. He extended his hand to me like I should be grateful for what he had. He insisted that I take the small pill. I was reluctant to take anything from that crazy fucker.

"Here, this is for you. But don't take it *here*. Take it as soon as you find your seat on the plane. It will take a short while to kick in. But once it does, your flight will be relaxing and enjoyable. A famous celebrity told me about these once, sitting here at this very bar. They really do work."

I quickly took the pill and dropped it in my shirt pocket. I didn't want him saying another word or insisting that I accept anymore favors or drugs or anything. I just wanted the fuck out. I just wanted to be on my flight to Montgomery, sleeping nicely, thinking about my writing and New York and being famous and all the admiration I would receive from my fans. That's all I ever really wanted, to be a known writer. Was that too much to ask? At that moment, it seemed like it was too much to ask.

"Thanks. I really won't forget this. You are much too kind. How much do I owe you?" I was laying it on pretty thick. I wanted to get the fuck out incident-free.

"It's on the house. And I hope you enjoy your flight."

"I will. Thanks again."

"And please forgive me for what happened back there. I wasn't *right* in the head for a moment."

I gave him a fuck-you smile and left that fucking hole in the wall bar with the nose-pickers and the crazy, whacked-out bartender. I left the bar dragging all my luggage behind me. And after all that, I *did* leave him a tip. But it was the ultimate fuck-you gratuity. I left him one cent, one goddamn penny. That's worse than not leaving a tip at all. You know why? Because you know and they know that they gave shitty service. They know it because you left them the smallest amount possible. And they can't come chasing after you yelling about how you didn't tip them, because you did tip them, it was just one penny. And they can't go yelling that you gave them one cent because the other patrons would know that you fucked him because of bad service. That was the ultimate fuck-you. And he knew it.

"Have a nice flight, writer-man. Come back and see me, you bastard." I knew right then and there that he found the penny. But by that time, I was already boarding my flight to Montgomery, thank God.

5.

I found my seat on the plane, seat 8A by the window. Janet had really pulled it off. She was really sweet to do it for me too. I felt awful for what I said to her about looking like *Janet from Three's Company* but I quickly got over it. I wouldn't be seeing her for a while so I figured there was no reason to mull over it like a sad bastard. There was definitely no *time* for feeling like a sad bastard. I lifted one of my bags to the overhead compartment and lo and behold, it didn't fit into the space. I'm sure you know what I mean, right? Your carry-on luggage never fits into those goddamn compartments; they're always too small for any *normal*-size carry-on bag. They're big enough for a shoebox but that's about it. But who carries a bag the size of a fucking shoebox? Nobody, that's who. I made my bags fit though. I crumpled the corners of the bags and pressed and shoved them in there. I was sure my pens and business cards were ruined but I didn't care. I got my bags in those small fucking compartments. Watching the other passengers struggle with their bags brought a smile to my face. At least I got *mine* in there. I could sit and relax and write Janet a poem, watching the other sad bastards struggle with their bags, too concerned with the contents of their luggage to shove them in the small compartments like they should. I didn't care about my stuff, it could be ruined to hell for all I cared. I *really* didn't care. I got my trusty pen and paper and shoved my backpack under my seat. I was done holding onto it like my life depended on it. I was on the plane now and there was nothing more I could do about it. Fear of flying be damned!

I had my pen and paper ready because great writers are always *prepared* to write down their thoughts, no matter where they are or where they are going. It's true. A great writer has to be ready to write ideas at the drop of a fucking hat. An idea could come at any minute, like an idea for my next novel or something. I had to be ready. But to tell you the truth, not many great ideas would just pop in my head from nowhere. I usually get bits and pieces of ideas first before I get the *whole* great idea. I'm pretty prepared for it by the time it comes. I had bits and pieces come through today so I knew it was coming. So I decided to keep my pen and paper on my lap, ready for that moment.

The flight attendant came by and tried to help the other sad bastards who couldn't get their bags in their overhead compartments. She'd smile at them while she helped, even though I was pretty sure she thought they were *all* fucking idiots except for me, of course. I could deal with my luggage on my own. I tried to get her attention because I needed a glass of water so I could take this relaxation pill. I wanted nothing more than to *relax* and enjoy this flight. This would probably be the only down-time I would have for the next couple of weeks. I thought maybe the secret bar hand signal would work. But it didn't. I was waving my finger around like a fucking idiot. I probably looked like I had Tourette Syndrome and that's why she ignored me. Nothing I did got her attention. So I just decided to speak up.

"Miss? Can you bring me a glass of water? I have some medication I must take before the plane takes off and it's imperative that I do so." I couldn't believe I said the word *imperative*. I'm such a blabbing idiot. That's not a word you say, that's a word you *write* down. I must have been in my writer's frame of mind, for Janet's poem, of course.

"Sure. Give me a moment, please. I'm helping the other passengers," she replied with a sugary yet robotic response. The airline company must have trained her to talk that way, kind of nice, kind of business-like, kind of ambiguous. It wasn't very *appealing*. She was kind of sexy in a Barbie doll kind of way but her voice ruined it for me. She was really beautiful but that voice, that voice made her ugly to me. Has that ever happened to you? Have you ever seen someone who was empirically attractive but there was something about them that made them ugly to you? That's how she was, empirically pretty but ugly.

No matter, she returned shortly with a paper cup of water. She flashed me a fake, sugary smile when she gave it to me.

"Thank you, miss," I said, giving her a fake smile in return. But she couldn't tell it was *fake*. I can make pretty good fake smiles.

She started staring at me instead of walking away to help the other sad bastards with their carry-on bags. She tilted her head and got a good look too. She was staring up a storm and I didn't know what to say. When a woman stares at you, it's not like when a man stares at you. With a man, you can stare back with a what-the-fuck-you-looking-at kind of stare. You can't do that with a woman; it's not polite. Besides, if she wasn't so ugly to me, I might have been turned on a bit. It's kind of nice when a woman stares at you, at least when an attractive one does. It's true.

"I recognize your face from somewhere. Should I know who you are?" she asked. I was completely flabbergasted. She absolutely floored me. All of a sudden, she wasn't so ugly anymore.

"Yes, you should. My novel, THE RISE AND FALL OF A TITAN, will be in book stores in a few weeks. You must have seen my preview in Time Magazine."

"No, I don't think that's it. I'm not much of a reader. What was your name again?" Damn, the *name* business again. I was getting kind of tired of saying it.

"Simon Burchwood. My name is Simon Burchwood," I said. I was going to give her a business card but I decided to save it. I can't just hand them out to *anyone*.

"I'll think of it, where I saw your face that is. I'll let you know when I think of it."

"Please do that, miss."

She returned to the sad bastards as I popped the pill in my mouth and drained it down my throat with one large gulp of water. I reclined my seat and enjoyed the luxury and space of the first-class seating.

I closed my eyes and my mind drifted toward the future. I imagined the small auditorium above the Barnes & Noble flagship store in New York where I was going to read chapters from my new book. I imagined the adoring crowd of three hundred or so fans, maybe four hundred, listening intently to my every word. The cheers and applause they will give after I finish reading the samples from my new novel; the very book they surely will have read before I arrive. They will laugh in the right places, sigh at the poignant social commentary, and applaud at the satisfying conclusions. I will sign hundreds of autographs and shake hundreds of hands. I will surely be followed by dozens of fans after the reading to the bar across the street. They will buy me drinks and give kind words of support. They will ask about the next book, the one that is already stirring restlessly in my mind. They will ask what inspires me to write, where I find that inspiration, what makes me do it every day. They will ask me about Edward Norton, the movie star, and wonder how we ever became friends. They will place me on *that* pedestal that I cherish, the one that has been elusive for so long. Soon, I hope, my name will be in the headlines of every newspaper across the country. I don't know how that will happen but I can only hope. You have to have dreams to really *live*, you know. If you don't have any dreams, you might as well be dead. You might as well be a dead, sad, no-dreaming bastard.

This little fantasy made me really happy, for once. It was the one bright, shining moment of the day. But it wouldn't last long. My flight companion made his presence known as soon as he sat down. He started barking at the flight attendant, all rude and boisterous. He sounded like a real jerk.

"Hey sweet cheeks, get me a beer, will ya?" he commanded. And to my surprise, off she went, fast as hell too. She was ready to serve him.

I looked over to discover a punk rock kid, no older than twenty or twenty one, pierced in every orifice, tattooed all over his goddamn body, clad in black leather and denim, sitting in the seat next to me. He smelled of beer and cigarettes and arrogance and Aquanet and youth. His hair looked like it had been styled with a box of firecrackers. It was sticking up all over the goddamn place. He looked like a fucking peacock except with the tail on his head. Actually, he looked like a goddamn *idiot*. Once he saw me staring at him, he extended his hand to me like he wanted me to shake it. I knew if we greeted each other that he probably wouldn't leave me alone for the rest of the flight. I just wanted to relax, you know, not talk to some punk kid who looked like an exploding peacock ass-head. But he was so goddamn nice to me. He really wanted to meet me. It's true.

"Grant's the name. Rockstar's my game. Nice to meet you. Are you a computer programmer?"

"What's that?" I asked. He talked all fast and slurry like he was on speed or something. He must have been on drugs. You'd have to be on drugs to *look* like that, to be in the company of *normal* people looking like that. If my dad saw me dressed like that, he would have kicked my ass (no exaggeration there). He would have put his foot right in my ass. Literally. I had a hard time understanding him so I asked again. "Say that again?"

"You look like a computer programmer, with the Izod shirt and pressed khaki pants and the smelly Polo cologne. I'm from Austin and there are two kinds of people from Austin, weirdos like me and computer geeks like you."

"I'm from Austin too but I'm not a computer programmer. I'm a writer." I thought that would impress him. Man, was I wrong.

"Wow, even *worse*. I've never met a writer before. I always imagined writers to wear argyle sweaters and smoke honey tobacco in large wood pipes and smell like mothballs. You don't seem to fit that bill. You don't smell like mothballs. You're very uptight though, I can tell."

"For your information, I am not uptight. I was just relaxing for the trip. I will be reading from my new book at the Barnes & Noble flagship store in New York."

"Big deal! I'm playing in front of ten thousand people in Atlanta tomorrow night."

I knew the ante had been raised. We were getting ready to go fisticuffs over our cultural significance and I wasn't going to lose out to a punk rock kid with peacock hair. I was prepared to raise the ante as well.

"Well, I have an essay about my new book in Time Magazine."

"Well, I'm on the cover of The Rolling Stone!" Grant sing-songed like the chorus of the Dr. Hook song. He pulled a copy of the magazine from inside his coat and flaunted it like he just won the lottery or something. What a cocky bastard he was! And for sure, there he was, in vivid promotional colors, on the cover of Rolling Stone Magazine with his band *The Assholes* (how appropriate). The very magazine that promoted the genius of Hunter S. Thompson on its cover. The magazine that touched the pulse of American pop culture.

"This is the death of my career!" Grant screamed. He dropped the magazine on the floor like it was a stinking, hot turd. "Rolling Stone sucks! Waitress! Where's my beer?!"

The flight attendant arrived, beer and napkin in hand, with a big, bright smile on her face. It wasn't the fake, sugary smile she gave me earlier. It was a real, *genuine* smile. She knew who this asshole was and wanted to meet him. I was just some schmuck writer who was demanding water.

"I'm such a big fan," she gushed to the punk rock brat. "Can I have your autograph?"

"You want me to sign your tits?" he asked. And he was very *serious* about his answer too. He didn't laugh or chuckle after he said it, as if he was being sly or coy. He said it straight-faced as if he was requested to do that on a daily basis by *all* of his fans. No one asked *me* to sign their tits, not even my wife. Something would definitely have to be done about that, something very soon.

"No, I don't think my husband would like that. But you can sign this paper for me." She leaned over Grant and grabbed my pad of paper straight off my lap, without even asking. What the hell was that all about?! Doesn't she know that you never grab a writer's pad of paper without asking? What if I had an idea to write down at that very moment? She then extended her hand for my pen as well. And what was I to do? I just gave it to her. It's not like I had any paper to write on anyway. I was really beginning to hate Grant. He was getting on my goddamn nerves. She was gushing all over him too. It was pretty fucking pathetic. "Sign it to Susan. That's me," she whispered to Grant, her cleavage flashing from the top of her blouse like a goddamn neon sign or something. He couldn't keep his eyes off her breasts. They were the size of basketballs.

Grant scribbled on my pad of paper: *I'll fuck your brains out. Call my cell 512-555-5309... your idol - Grant, singer of the infamous Assholes!*

The flight attendant giggled after reading the note. She was so excited about it, she practically exploded. Her head turned all red and puffy with excitement. It was like he just gave her the secret to the fucking universe or something. She tore the piece of paper off and threw the pad and pen on my lap, just tossed it there like I wouldn't mind. I was beginning to fume inside. I really wanted to punch the both of them out, hit them both square in their noses. I stuck my tainted pen and paper in my backpack and picked up the copy of Rolling Stone. I examined the cover, the perfect photograph of Grant and his band, the bright typeface, the unusual but appealing layout, the eye-catching headline: *Would you buy a CD from an Asshole? You betcha!* Grant kept smiling like a goddamn bastard. I really *did* want to punch him in the face. It would have made me feel so much better.

"You think this is cool, huh?" Grant asked, jabbing at the magazine in my hand. I slowly pulled the magazine out of reach of his sarcastic finger. Grant continued blabbing. He was pretty good at blabbing, I could tell. "This is shit! It's just like Kurt Cobain said when they interviewed him, *Corporate magazines suck!*"

I was completely flabbergasted, almost at a loss for words. Well almost. He had stumbled upon one of the greatest marketing tools of pop culture and he wanted to wipe his ass with it. I was astounded. I really was.

"This is like finding the Holy Grail. This is like landing on the moon. You've made it. The world knows you've made it. Millions of people would do anything to be in your position right now, including me. You're *famous*. And there is nothing more important to the career of an artist than being famous. You are known. You are *somebody*."

"And you're getting on my nerves. All I care about are two things, getting laid and getting drunk. That's it! To a punk rocker, this is death. I've lost all my credibility back home. My core fans think I've sold out. I didn't ask for this. We didn't seek it out. It found us. And I wish it would just go away!"

Holy shit! This kid was lost, completely lost. And a fucking idiot too. He had absolutely no idea how good he had it. He really didn't.

"No, no, you don't. You've made it. This guarantees that you will be paid to be creative, that you won't have to struggle, that you won't have to sacrifice your art by having to work a real job," I said. But I knew he wasn't listening to me, which was *obvious*.

"I think we're just going to ride this short wave and burn out. We'll get laid, get drunk, finish the tour, then go back to Austin and disappear. That's what we want. We don't want all of this bullshit. It's not real. It means nothing."

"You're crazy," I told him before turning to the window. He was making my stomach hurt, what, with all his talking and nonsense and bad hair and beer breath. I watched the other planes on the runway lineup to take off. "You're absolutely insane. I waited over ten years to get where you've gotten in, what, a few months?"

The pilot announced that all the sad bastards needed to fasten their seatbelts as the plane crept backwards toward the runway. I rechecked my belt, giving it a small tug to make sure it was fastened really good. One thing I knew for sure, no matter what, if this plane *did* go down in a fiery ball, at least my seatbelt would be securely fastened. That's the one thing I did have *control* over. I knew where the exits were too. I knew no one actually read those little cardboard manuals about getting off a wrecked plane and breathing through those goddamn oxygen masks if they popped down but I did. I had them *memorized*. Everyone else just pulled out the puke bag and laughed because it was a *puke* bag. Who cares about a fucking puke bag? If I had to hurl, I'd do it right on the floor (with no cares about it too).

I looked over to see if Grant had fastened his seatbelt but he didn't even have the goddamn thing secured. What a crazy, sad bastard he was. As the plane started to rev its engines, Grant raised his knees to his chest, placing his hands on his feet, rocking in his seat like a stupid chimpanzee. I tried to ignore him but he kept rocking back and forth, hitting my elbow with his tattooed elbow. I closed my eyes and wished he'd disappear but it didn't help. He was still *there*, rocking back and forth like a crazy bastard. For a moment, I wished that the staring cabbie or nice Janet or the crazy bartender were sitting next to me, *anyone* besides this punk kid and his arrogant smell. He was driving me up the wall.

"You want to see crazy?" Grant asked, rocking back and forth like a sad bastard chimpanzee.

As the plane picked up speed to take flight, a blunt pain from the pit of my stomach startled me. I placed my hand over my gut and felt it grumble. It was pretty strange for my stomach to be upset. Usually, it was as strong as a goddamn battleship. But it was pretty pissed off at me at that moment. The pain quickly grew in magnitude as the plane shot down the runway.

"You want to be a rockstar like me?" Grant screamed. He was screaming all over the goddamn place like a madman. All of a sudden, the scary bartender didn't seem so scary anymore. "You want to be on the cover of The Rolling Stone?!"

And in an instant, my head felt as if it had swollen to twice its size and a case of beer had been flushed into my veins. I dropped my heavy head to my knees and covered it with both of my arms. I felt drunk as a skunk and all I could think about was that *pill* the scary bartender gave me. It didn't relax me. It was doing the exact opposite. It was scaring *the shit* out of me. I knew, right then and there, that I should have given him a better tip. I knew *that* for sure.

The plane accelerated at full speed down the runway, no way of stopping it, like a rocket, tipping its nose toward the sky. Grant jumped to his feet, flailing his arms like a stupid, crazy chimpanzee.

"You want to be a rockstar, you have to act like a rockstar!" he screamed, grabbing the back of the seat of the passenger in front of him. He violently shook the headrest as he barked over and over, "We're going to die! We're going to die!"

The other passengers screamed as the plane ascended toward the clouds. Grant laughed at their sudden distress. He laughed like the fucking madman he was with his peacock hair and his leather pants and his tattoos and his goddamn arrogance. For a quick moment, I thought about how I'd always wanted a tattoo but never had the *guts* to go through with it. I could hear the flight attendant and her big tits screaming too. She was screaming for her life. I wondered if she had any tattoos hidden on her body as the pressure change from the plane's ascension enhanced the already swollen state of my consciousness. And all I could eventually think about and see was the *darkness*. My vision faded and it became cold and dark and quiet and still. It became as dark and still and cold as a winter night in the Texas Hill Country.

6.

Before I even begin to continue, I must inform you that this is a dream sequence. Now, I know a lot of authors use various techniques to communicate a dream sequence without actually *telling* you it is a dream sequence. But I think that's complete shit. Really, it is. For instance, an author may use italics *and start writing like this. And it would have to take a fucking genius to realize that something was different about the story, right?* Or they may start writing in a different tense, so Simon would have to relay how he feels in the third person instead of actually speaking for himself, which is complete crap too. I'm not going to try to fool you with a bunch of bullshit; we've come too far for that. I know you are much smarter than that. It's true. So I'm just going to come out and say it. This is a dream sequence! And it will remain a dream sequence until I tell you otherwise. OK? All right.

Now, I don't remember much around the time I blacked out except that Grant was screaming like a complete idiot. I mean, what was he thinking? I'm sure the other passengers thought he was some kind of terrorist or something and pulled a Todd Beamer and kicked the shit out of him. If that happened then Grant deserved it, what, with his arrogant attitude and his goddamn tattoos all over his arms and neck and his crazy jumping and screaming. He really did *deserve* it.

Anyway, I started to dream about the job I had before I got my publishing deal. I don't know about you but when I dream, I'm completely aware of the fact that I'm dreaming. I know some people say they don't remember their dreams much and shit like that. But I do. Not only do I remember them but I'm *aware* that I'm dreaming *when* I am dreaming. Pretty crazy, huh? It's true. And when I said earlier that you had to dream to be alive, I didn't mean this kind of dream, the sleeping-kind. When I said that, I meant dreaming about your future. You know, having a plan for yourself - *a dream*. These other kinds of dreams, the ones in your sleep, well, everybody has those. And if someone tells you they don't dream in their sleep, they're full of shit. And you tell them they are full of shit. Most people are anyway.

OK, so I started dreaming about the place I used to work at. It was a company called TechForce. They designed probes and processors and all kinds of technology nonsense. I was one of their network-administrator-slaves. I supported the local area network and would help the other idiots that called themselves employees. It drove me absolutely crazy, especially since all I wanted to do was write for a living. But I had to support the wife and the kids and writing wasn't putting food on the table at that time. The TechForce job was my bread and butter.

One of the duties I had was to read over these performance reports that the network servers would cough up. They were these huge fucking reports that seemed like a thousand pages long that went into bandwidth usage and packet collisions and all sorts of technological shit that I didn't give a goddamn flip about. But my boss made me read through them and look for (what did he call them?) anomalies. I didn't actually care about *anomalies*. If I could connect to the network, then as far as I was concerned it worked. Who cared about this other crap? Nobody, that's who.

So the dream started with these goddamn reports. Except instead of having to read one of them, I was getting hundreds of them delivered to me, all of them a thousand fucking pages long and big as a phone book. It was driving me mad and they kept coming. I could barely start reading one before another goddamn report showed up. I'd place them on my desk, trying to be neat and orderly about it, but they kept coming. This office clerk brought them to me. In the dream, I really *hated* this guy. I wanted to kick him in the nuts for piling all of those goddamn reports on my desk.

"Where do you want these new reports, Simon?" he'd ask me. He had a squeaky little voice, kind of like a mouse squeak. He had a small, button nose and long, skinny teeth. He looked like a rat without fur wearing a short-sleeved oxford with a sock tie. I hated that rat clerk.

I looked around my desk for some free space for the new report but there wasn't any free space. I mean, with all the reports he kept bringing me, I ran out of goddamn room on my desk. It was completely full of these bullshit reports. The only room left was where my radio and coffee cup were and I wasn't going to give up that valuable real estate. That just wouldn't do. The only free space was on the floor.

"Set them down here," I told him, pointing to the floor.

"Here?" he asked.

"That's fine."

The rat clerk set the report on the floor and was gone as quick as he arrived. He was a quick little rat bastard.

All I could think about was that my boss was trying to kill me, what, with all of these goddamn reports piling up all over the goddamn place and the anomalies and the packet collisions and all the shit I didn't care about. I mean, how did they expect me to finish reading one when another would show up before I could finish? I kept thinking that they didn't pay me enough to *kill* me like that. I really didn't have a very good salary. In fact, it was complete crap. I could barely feed and clothe my kids. And how did they expect me to give money to my wife so she could buy me all the preppy, department store bullshit that she was obsessed with? It was a constant struggle with my salary. It's true.

I was shuffling through the reports like a madman, trying to finish one before another would arrive. But they kept coming and coming. It was driving me completely fucking bonkers. As I shuffled through the papers, I sliced the tips of my fingers. You know, I was getting those tiny yet extremely painful paper cuts there on the tips of my fingers. The pain became almost more than I could bear. But I continued on because of my kids. Their little brown eyes watched me from a picture taped to my computer monitor. One of the perks about the job (besides the fact that they were trying to kill me) was the insurance benefits. There was a time when I didn't have insurance for my family and my Sammie got a fever and almost died. It was horrible. Sammie (if you didn't know) is my son. He's four now and he's a little genius. He really is. He's already reading books and helping me with balancing my checkbook. It's true. I also have a daughter. Her name is Jessica but we call her Jessie. She'll be two soon. She's a genius too but in an artistic kind of way. You can show her a painting by a master like Monet and give her a pile of crayons and a piece of paper and she'll copy it exactly like she sees it. It's really amazing. Both of my kids are geniuses. My wife and I are really lucky. But anyway, the job I had before this one didn't offer insurance so when Sammie got sick, I was in a real financial bind, not having insurance and all. So I was grateful for that, the insurance that is, not the bind.

So I was shuffling through the reports, getting paper cuts and trying to stay alive, when someone tapped my shoulder and interrupted me. It was my fucking boss, Mr. Folsom. God, I *hated* that man more than anything in the goddamn world. I really did. He was the one that made me read these stupid reports. I hated him for that, especially since they kept coming and coming. But you know what I hated about him the most? He had this *lazy* eye, this really loose, twitchy, lazy eye. As he thought of hellish things to say and do to me, his eye twitched independently from the rest of his face, bulging and turning toward the God that had maimed him. When his goddamn eye would start to twitch all over the place, I couldn't look at him. Just the thought of his twitching eye turned my stomach.

"Simon, it has been brought to my attention that you are lagging behind in your work," he said to me, with gobs of spittle raining down on my desk. And his eye, that twitchy thing, spinning all over the goddamn place. It drove me crazy. "Your efficient co-workers seem to complete twice as much work as you do, with little *complaint.*"

I couldn't look him in the face because of that twitchy eye of his. I had to look at the floor when I spoke to him. "Mr. Folsom, I'm working as fast as I can. But I truly believe that if you assigned me duties that utilized my mind..."

"Simon, we do not pay you to *think.* We pay you to complete your work," he proclaimed, stepping back and forth like a demented drill sergeant, spitting showers of pungent saliva. His spit smelled like coffee and halitosis and decay and donuts and death. It made me sick to my stomach. "If you cannot complete your work, then you have no place here at TechForce."

A stack of papers appeared in his goddamn hands and he set them on the floor next to the other stack. He didn't even ask me if he could set them down. He just did. He was such a jerk that way, always doing stuff without asking me first.

"As you may well know, there have been rumors that TechForce may be reducing its workforce in the near future. Well, unfortunately, that rumor has turned out to be true. And I have been asked by upper management to recommend employees that I deem appropriate to let go..."

"Mr. Folsom, I..."

"Did I give you permission to speak?" he asked, his bulging eye peering at me.

"No, sir."

The rat clerk appeared with another stack of papers and handed them to Mr. Folsom. He thanked the rat clerk and set them on the floor next to the other two stacks without asking me. The clerk vanished with a *POOF*. There was actually a little cloud that poofed when he disappeared, like in the cartoons. Mr. Folsom placed his hands on his hips as his demented mind churned. His lazy eye bulged and turned red, spinning inward as if looking straight into his goddamn brain.

"If you do not show visible signs of improvement today, I will find it necessary to recommend that you be let go with future workforce reductions."

I sat there silently. I didn't know what to say. And it wasn't like I could look him in the face or anything, not with that goddamn eye spinning all around and driving me insane and his stinking spit flying all over my desk. He was really driving me crazy. Plus, I was thinking about Jessie and Sammie and how they needed insurance. I love my kids, you know.

"Feel fortunate that I haven't let you go sooner," he said, rubbing his lazy eye with his index finger. A small droplet of blood trickled from the corner of his eye as he rubbed it, falling like a crimson tear. I didn't know at first that it was coming from his eye since I was staring at the floor like a goddamn little girl. But once I saw it hit the floor, I *had* to look up. I mean, wouldn't you look up if you saw a drop of blood hit the floor? That's some strange shit, you know? So I finally looked at him and the blood was shooting from his eye like it was a goddamn geyser. "And let that be a lesson to you."

"Yes, sir," I replied. The blood geyser mesmerized me. It was spraying all over. I examined my own eyes, making sure they weren't shooting blood all over the goddamn place too. They weren't. They were normal (of course). I closed them and rubbed them a final time, just to make sure they were really OK. And when I opened them again, Mr. Folsom was gone. But he left behind two more reports on the floor. He couldn't just leave me with what I already had, the bastard. He had to leave *two more*. I really hated him. It's true.

The rat clerk appeared again with a new stack of papers as well. I hated him too. I hated them both. I was wishing they would go fuck each other.

"Where do you want them?" he asked. I didn't know what to say. I was speechless, what, with the blood everywhere and the stinking spit and the rat clerk and the reports piled from here to fucking eternity. I really felt like I was going mad.

The rat clerk repeated, over and over, "Simon, are you OK? Simon? Simon? Are you all right? Can you hear me?"

And I kept thinking to myself, *of course I can hear you*. I'm sitting right in front of you, aren't I, you rat bastard?

7.

"Simon, are you OK? Simon? Simon? Are you all right? Can you hear me?"

I slowly opened my eyes. I couldn't believe it but I was looking up at the goddamn ceiling. I didn't know where I was but I definitely wasn't on the plane anymore. I didn't hear Grant screaming like an idiot. I didn't hear the passengers screaming. I didn't hear the flight attendant with the big tits screaming. All I could hear was this *voice*. It was familiar as hell but I felt groggy and woozy. For some reason, I didn't care to find out who it was. All I knew was that my head hurt. It felt like I had been slugged with a sledgehammer. And the ceiling was really filthy. I mean, the panels were really dingy and dusty and gray. Someone should have gotten up there to clean that shit.

"Where am I? Did the plane crash?" I asked. Sometimes, I can act really stupid, you know? This time was no exception.

"Nope. The plane landed safe and sound," the voice replied.

"Am I dead? Is this heaven?" I didn't know if I was dreaming anymore or not. I was a real mess. It's true

"I sure hope not. Being trapped in an airport for eternity seems more like *hell* than heaven to me."

I found the strength to turn my head to see who was talking to me. A chubby and kind face, familiar yet not *too* familiar, stared right back at me. Just what I needed, someone else *staring* at me. I examined the face for a bit, the lines, the contours, and knew I had seen that face before. It was right on the tip of my tongue, you know. But I also had this sledgehammer headache. It was effecting my mental abilities.

"I know I haven't changed that much since we were kids. Just a few life-reaffirming weight shifts and a bit of hair loss from stress," he said.

"Jason?" I asked. I felted relieved. For a second, I really did think that I was in heaven. What a bummer that would have been, especially since I hadn't seen the fruits of my labor yet. You know, my book and publishing deal and all. I was glad to see his face. "For a minute, I thought I was done for."

There was another man there with him but I didn't know who he was. He didn't look familiar. Jason told him something like it was OK now and that he'd take care of it. The guy left really fast like he had been kept there against his will for an extremely long time. I hate impatient people, especially when you really need help from them. They're a real pain in the ass. It's true.

"When I saw the police rush onto the tarmac, I feared the worst. You know, terrorists and all."

"Grant, you insane bastard," I whispered to myself.

"What was that?" Jason asked.

"Oh, nothing."

"Anyway, they must have looked through your wallet and gotten your name because when they were carrying you off the plane, they saw my sign with your name on it. They carried you right to me. For a split second, I thought you were dead."

"Carrying me?" I asked.

"They said some kid went insane, screaming or something, and the flight attendants had to subdue him. They wanted to lock him in the restroom but the door was locked. That's where they found you, locked inside and passed right out on the floor. You must have blacked out or something."

"I don't remember," I said. I attempted to sit up. The sledgehammer ache swelled inside my head. I dropped my aching head in my hands. "The last thing I remember was the singer signing an autograph and this crazy dream about my boss ..."

"I guess this is what famous writers do, huh? Get drunk and pass out on airplanes, like famous actors and all."

"I wasn't drunk. I took a pill that this bartender gave me."

"Popping pills? Even better," Jason said, helping me to my feet. "Come on, let's get out of here. They wanted a doctor to look at you but I told them I'd take care of you. I had to sign a waiver and all so I wouldn't sue them if something was wrong with you."

I stood on my wobbly legs and patted myself down, checking personal inventory, you know. I had my wallet - check. I had my watch - check. My nuts were still hanging - check. I looked around for my carry-on bags and backpack and I didn't see them. For a quick moment, I felt an insane amount of *panic*. My chest felt like it was going to collapse and my heart started to race out of control. I was having a goddamn anxiety attack.

"Jason, where's my backpack?!" I asked, frustrated and worried. "My manuscript is in there! I can't lose it! It's my everything!"

"Calm down, Simon. It's right over here."

Jason led me over to the outer row of chairs that delineated the waiting area from the main walkway of the airport terminal. My carry-on bags were there in a small pile, obviously thrown there carelessly by someone who did not realize who I was. I shuffled through my bags to find my backpack, which I quickly slipped on over my shoulders, secure and safe. I would have gone ballistic if something had happened to my backpack. I don't know exactly what I would have done but it would have been pretty fucking crazy. It's true. Jason leaned down for my other bags.

"Don't worry, I'll get these. But please tell me you're not epileptic or something. I mean, this isn't going to happen again, the passing out and all. You'll freak my kids out if they find you in the bathroom passed out or something."

"No, Jason. I'll be OK. I promise."

"All right. Then let's go get the rest of your luggage."

We left the waiting area and walked down the terminal hallway toward the luggage pick-up. We walked side by side, quietly and awkwardly, recovering from a bizarre introduction after several years apart. It was strange seeing Jason again. I mean, we kept in touch and all but I hadn't actually *seen* him in a very long time. My mental image of him was stuck in the early part of my teenage years. That was a long, long time ago. Like I said, he looked familiar to me when I first saw him. But at the same time, he didn't. It's kind of hard to describe.

As we walked toward the luggage pickup area, I noticed stares from passersby, some I recognized from the flight. Their judging eyes tried to burn through me, tried to look in me, to see what I was all about. When my eyes met theirs, they would look away. I recognized this one guy from the plane. He sat across the aisle from where Grant and I were sitting. He watched us the entire time Grant and I were talking. I noticed him *staring* at us. I didn't mention anything about it at the time because it wasn't a big deal. But now that I think about it, he was staring his ass off. Don't people's mothers teach them that staring is impolite? I mean, for Christ's sakes, what are you looking at, you fat bastard? What?! Jason noticed the stares I was getting from everybody.

"It must be strange for you, the attention and all. It must be hard being a famous writer. I guess people recognize you, even in Montgomery, Alabama, the illiteracy capital of the United States."

"Surely, they do. It's the price you have to pay and I was willing before this all began and I'm willing now. Generally, my fans are pretty polite and discreet." I didn't want to mention that I recognized the staring fat bastard from the flight. It was irrelevant.

"Have you ever had a fan bother you? You know, stalker-like?" he asked.

"Once, at a writers' convention, a fan followed me in the bathroom and asked for my autograph while I was in the stall. You know, while I was going to the bathroom. He handed me the piece of paper and pen under the door while I was sitting down on the toilet."

"While you were taking a shit? I don't believe it." He was floored. I mean, he really didn't believe it. He had this look on his face like that was the most appalling thing that he'd ever heard.

"Yes, it's true. But that was a rare case."

We arrived at the luggage pick-up as the carousel began to spin. The luggage excreted from the hole in the wall, spilling down the inclined conveyor belt like limp garbage. The other passengers treated the strange luggage like it *was* garbage until they spotted their own goddamn suitcase or bag. Then the luggage became the valued thing that it really was, containing their conveniences and possessions and trinkets and reminders of home. I looked out for my own suitcase, ignoring the blue vinyl one, then the green cloth one and the black leather one. My suitcase eventually made its way out the hole, sliding down the metal conveyor, slamming into the retainer near my knees. I picked up the dingy, old suitcase and set it on the ground. Jason stared at my old bag. He really gave it good look. It was this nasty shade of milk-of-magnesia blue. I was kind of embarrassed to lug it around. I mean, I should buy some new bags after I get my check from the publisher. There's really no need for me to be lugging around a shitty, milk-of-magnesia blue suitcase, right? But Jason kept staring at it like he wanted it or something. After I buy some new ones, maybe I'll just give it to him. Jason was always a cheap bastard. His whole family were cheap bastards.

"Simon, this may sound a little ridiculous but that kind of looks like the bag you had when you moved away from Montgomery. I remember it like it was yesterday."

"Could be. I don't remember." I really didn't remember. My memory wasn't too good, what, with having a sledgehammer headache and all. Plus, that was a long time ago. It's true.

"Oh, I do. I remember going over to your house to help you pack your things for the move and help your family load the moving truck. I remember everyone in your whole family had one of these bags, like it was from a set or something. But I remember that they all looked old even back then, that the color looked old fashioned and all."

I picked the suitcase up. It was heavy as hell. It didn't have one of those handles. You know, one of those suitcase leashes (is it a leash?) so you could drag it around like it was some kind of disobedient dog. The suitcase was old as dirt, I think.

"Could be," I said. "Which way to your car?"

"Over here. Anyway, I'm pretty sure of it. You know, you should get a new bag, one with wheels and all, that you can pull around like a dog on a leash," he said. What was I just talking about? Jason and I were always on the same wavelength when we were kids. We thought exactly alike. It was nice to know that some things don't change. "I always get a kick out of seeing people pulling their luggage around. You know, like they're walking their dogs or something. You should get one of those bags and travel in style since you're a famous writer and all."

"This one does me just fine," I told him. I didn't want him thinking I would get a new suitcase and give him this one. He really kept staring at it. I bet he liked it or something. I followed him out the exit to the parking garage. "This one does the job."

"I remember the day you moved away. I remember it like it was yesterday. It was one of those defining moments for me. I was really sad that you left. My feelings really were *hurt* that your father had to get a new job in Texas. I resented him for a long time about that. But I got over it."

Man, he was really making me feel like shit and I had only been in Montgomery for a few minutes. Jason could blab too, just like me. He could talk your fucking head off if you let him. Sometimes, he needed a good slap so he would just shut up.

We took the elevator to the second floor in the garage. When the door opened, there was his car: a beat-up, shit-brown Chevy Chevette. It stuck out from the rest of the cars like a big turd served on fine china. Really, it was ugly as hell, a real piece of crap. Jason popped the trunk and loaded my carry-on bags and then my suitcase. He motioned for me to hand over my backpack. But I wasn't going to put it back *there*.

"I'll keep this one with me," I told him.

"OK."

Suddenly, my backpack started beeping all over the place. It kind of sounded like a bomb getting ready to go off. Wouldn't that have been killer? The garage exploding and all from a bomb in my backpack? Actually, that was a stupid thought, real childish and shit. Jason was curious about the beeping though.

"Sounds like your pager's going off in your bag."

"Oh, yes." He was right. He was a real fucking genius. It was my pager and not a bomb. "That's probably my accountant. We had an argument earlier about the per diem they gave me. I thought it was too low. He thought it was too high. We never came to an understanding. He probably wants me to call him back. I'll call him from your house."

"Sounds good to me," Jason said.

He unlocked both doors to his car and we got in. As he cranked the ignition, the car howled and screamed, like it wanted to keel over and just die already. It launched a cloud of black smoke from the tailpipe with a ferocious bang. Jason chuckled to hide his embarrassment.

"My Porsche is in the shop," he said, joking his ass off, of course.

"I understand." I didn't care but I grabbed the oh-shit handle above the passenger window and held on tight. I had a feeling he was a shitty driver and I was going to find out in the worst way. "Is this the car your mother used to drive us around in?"

"The very same one. Only it's in better shape now."

Jason pulled out of the garage, followed by the black exhaust cloud, and headed for the highway. He drove like a bat out of hell.

8.

The pine trees surrounding the old neighborhood were taller and more majestic than I even remembered them to be. I rolled the window down and let the fresh Alabama air rush in the car. The air smelled noticeably different than the Texas air, mainly because of the pine trees. But also, for some reason, my allergies didn't exist here like they did in Austin. My clear nasal passages took in the air freely and deeply. My nostrils were so clear that I felt like a different person. It's true. I hated having allergies. They made me fucking miserable, what, with my nose running all over the place and the headaches and the coughing and sneezing. The headaches were the worst part. But I didn't have them here. And the sun was getting ready to set soon. It made for a mesmerizing ride in Jason's crap mobile.

"It smells so good outside," I said.

"Wait till we pass that old, swampy lake behind the neighborhood. You'll change your tune then. Still smells like a toilet back there."

Jason downshifted the car into third and pulled into the turning lane for the entrance to our old neighborhood. Another black cloud rose from the back of the Chevette and the cars that were behind us honked and swerved. It was fucking hilarious. It really was. I thought Jason's car was about to kill itself, hari-kari style. It knocked and screamed as much as it possibly could. As the Chevette slowly approached the entrance, the neighborhood sign came into view, a small wood and brick job that appeared to have stood the test of time and the pranks from my childhood buddies. It was an unfortunate target of rotten eggs, stink bombs, spray paint, and toilet paper. There wasn't one weekend that that sign didn't have some kind of shit on it. The kids loved to muck it all up, don't ask me why. They just did. I was guilty too, of course. It's true.

"And here we are... Country Down Estates," Jason said, cranking the steering wheel to the right and pulling into the neighborhood. The street stretched a ways up an incline, just like I remembered, before actually entering the community. It seemed to me that I remembered the street to be a lot longer than it actually was. As a kid, it seemed like it took forever to go up that street. But in reality, it really wasn't long at all. Jason's Chevette screamed up the hill, chugging and clunking as he downshifted to second gear. That car was really on its last leg. I thought the transmission was going to fall out, the way it grinded and clunked and all.

"Come on, baby!" Jason screamed. "You can do it!"

As he pushed the Chevette harder, memories from my childhood came rushing into my head. I remembered riding my bicycle on this street, my ultra cool Diamondback BMX bike. I saved months and months worth of allowances and yard-cutting money to buy that bike. We'd pop wheelies off the curbs and make skid marks on the driveways of all the old men who hated skid marks on their driveways. Those old bastards, they just hated it when we came whizzing down the street. They'd run and get their water hoses and try to act like they were watering their yards. I think maybe they thought we'd leave them alone if they had the hoses but we'd zoom in and skid on their driveways anyway, just because they hated it. They'd scream and yell and squirt the skid marks so they wouldn't set on the hot cement. I always got a kick out of that. We left skid marks *everywhere*.

We also passed Beth Myers' old house, the first girl I ever kissed. I took a good look at the house as we went by, remembering sitting in her backyard behind the tool shed. We were dared by our so-called friends to kiss each other and we lived up to their dare, clumsily kissing, our eyes closed and our little hands clinched. We were so *scared* to do it. The sloppy, wet kiss repulsed the two of us, yet it brought us closer together in a rare moment of maturity and adolescent clarity. I kept that moment in a special place within my heart; this was the first time that moment had surfaced in a really long time. I wondered what good ol' Beth was doing these days.

"Isn't that Beth Myers' old house?" I asked, even though I already knew the answer.

"Yep, sure is. She's still around here somewhere. I'm not quite sure where but I know she stayed in Montgomery and went to college and all. I'm sure you could find her if you tried."

"I'm not sure I want to do that."

"Remember when you guys sucked face in her backyard? You guys sure didn't kiss right, not like normal people anyway. That's for sure. You two looked like a couple of catfish attached at the face and all." Jason started laughing like a goddamn hyena. He had this *laugh* that was a combination of wheezing and coughing and snorting, except that he'd do all those things really fast like he was choking on a hunk of beef jerky. It was annoying and funny to hear at the same time. He hadn't changed one bit. "That dare sure brings a smile to my face whenever I drive by that house. I bet that was the inspiration for a lot of stories you've written, huh?"

"Sure was. This old neighborhood has inspired countless poems and stories and even my new novel, in a way. I've sucked the marrow out of many memories and recollections and created some great literature."

"Did you ever imagine back when you lived here that you would finally get out of Montgomery and become a famous writer and all?"

"I always knew I would be a writer, even when I lived here."

This part of Country Down Estates was like the more upscale part, housing some of the higher ranked officers from Gunter, the nearby Air Force base. The well-manicured lawns were as green and neat as I remembered. My father was a newly promoted major back then and my family fit snuggly in the middle of the other majors and colonels' families and their near-identical houses. It was all a bunch of shit though. It all seemed nice and suburban and perfect but Montgomery was a really fucked up place. I mean, racism was still pretty rampant in this part of the country and Montgomery was no different. They tried to cover the racism with monkey grass and iced tea but it was still there, ugly as ever. But I'll get to that later. The part of the neighborhood where Jason lived was a few notches down the social ladder, houses that were a little older and a little bit rundown compared to the houses my family lived around. It was kind of like the middle class ghetto of the area. The strange thing about Jason's family though was that even though they lived in the rundown part of the neighborhood and their house was rundown and their cars were rundown, they had a *lot* of rundown things. I mean, they had four cars and a swimming pool and a lake house and a ski boat and they always seemed to have money. Everything they had just *looked* rundown. I never could figure it out. I never could figure out if they were just messy pigs or something like that. Maybe they just didn't care about all that *class* stuff. Who cares about that stuff anyway?

Jason put the car in neutral then stopped. We sat in front of another house full of memories for us.

"Remember that house?" he asked, pointing to the brown, one-story home.

"That's Darren Reedy's old house, isn't it?"

"Sure is," he said. He sighed and leaned back in his seat with his arms behind his head. He had this stupid look on his face, this content and happy look. I knew what he was thinking about.

"Whatever happened to that sick little freak?" I asked. Darren was a *sick* little bastard. It's true. But he was our friend too. Everyone has one of those sick bastard friends in their childhood. Darren was our sick bastard friend. "Remember how he used to torture his pets?"

"Darren's dead."

He couldn't have been any more blunt or direct about it. What a shocker! He just blurted it out, like it was nothing, like it was old news. I didn't know what to say. In a way, it wasn't like it was really surprising or anything like that. Darren was a sick little bastard that did sick things to defenseless animals. But it was just so definite and blunt and direct, the way he said it. Jason was like that, though. He was direct as hell. He got that from his mother. She was direct as hell too. His whole family was direct as hell. It drove me crazy sometimes.

"I just wanted to let you know in case you wanted to stop by or something. His mother is still quite upset about it and if you stopped by and asked her about him, she would probably break down. You know, cry and all. He died a kind of bizarre death."

"What happened?" I asked.

"I'll tell you about it later. No need to put a damper on your visit so early in. You have plenty of time to hear about it. Remind me tonight and I'll tell you."

Jason revved the Chevette into first gear and drove a few houses down. He stopped again and put the car in park. I was still in shock about Darren. I was too shocked to notice anything.

"And here it is. Does it look exactly like you remember?" he asked.

He climbed out and stood there on the curb by my side of the car. We were parked in front of my childhood home. Man, you want to talk about memories? This place was *full* of them. Still painted white and brown, it looked just like I remembered. Yet it was a little different too. The grass was shaggier and unkempt. The roof looked worn and in need of repair. One of the windows in the front was cracked. But I could picture myself playing in the front yard when I was kid, playing lawn darts or touch football. We'd play late into the evenings, well after dark. The house didn't seem as big as I remembered though. Isn't it funny how things are always not as big as you remember?

"It looks pretty close to what I remember. Pretty close," I said. "Who lives there now?"

"Nobody. It's vacant. It was up for sale but it didn't sell. I think the owners are going to do some work on it before trying to sell it again."

"Interesting."

"That's why it looks kind of crappy now. Not like when your dad was here. This lawn looked like a golf course putting green back then. Remember?"

"Of course I remember. I was the one who had to cut it every five days." My dad was a fucking slavedriver when it came to the lawn. It seemed like I was *always* cutting and trimming it. Raking, watering, weedeating, fertilizing, a huge chunk of my childhood consisted of taking care of this goddamn yard. And for what? Look at it now. Any signs of the hard work I did was gone. Completely gone. Jason noticed that I was still a little sore about the subject. To be honest, I was pretty goddamn sore about it.

"Come on. Get over it. That was a long time ago," he said, walking back to his side of the Chevette. "Betty's waiting for us at the house. She probably made us some cookies or something."

We hopped back in the turd-on-wheels and ventured toward Jason's house. More memories rushed into my mind: the bike races down Smithson Street, trick or treating and the poop-bag pranks, hikes through the woods behind the neighborhood, finding Playboys in the ditch behind the school. As the wind and the pine-tree smell rushed in the window, I felt like I was thirteen again. It's funny what your mind will file away if it's not using it. I hadn't thought about all of these things for a long time and they were coming to life by the dozens.

"Hey, there's Patty Green's house. Right there, the yellow one." Jason pointed to the little yellow house as we drove by. Patty had the unfortunate status of being the seventh grade whore. She quickly turned from prissy little Patty to Patty the hooker one night when a small group of boys and girls convened at her house for her thirteenth birthday party. The party started innocently enough with chocolate cake and vanilla ice cream and party games and presents and pin-the-tail-on-the-donkey. But once the uninterested parents moved inside to the bar for scotch on the rocks and cold beers, we kids moved to the garage for a quick game of Spin the Bottle. Patty received two spins since it was her birthday and she kissed *two* boys. She kissed Jason, who for the rest of his junior high days was in *love* with Patty, and Justin Moss. The other kids affectionately called him Mossy on account of his dingy teeth, rotten gums, and stinky breath. The combination of kissing two boys and the excitement brought on by all the goddamn sugar the kids ate generated the incessant, hateful chatter. Patty clearly enjoyed being the center of attention, which to our young eyes, meant she enjoyed acting morally irreprehensible, of course. She was labeled a whore that night and was scarred for the rest of junior high.

"I never got to spin the bottle because Patty took my turn," I said.

"She might not have been called a whore if you had gone instead. *Think* about it."

"Unless she kissed me, of course. I think her fate was set already."

I thought fondly of little blonde Patty. She was a beautiful little girl. And though I didn't have the courage to tell her back then because of the stupid talk from the other kids, I liked her very much, even when the other goddamn kids called her a whore. One thing I knew for sure back then was that Patty *wasn't* a whore and I sympathized with her unfortunate circumstance. The day before I moved away to Texas, I rode my bike all the way to Patty's house. I rode fast and determined, the adrenaline pumping through my veins, and leapt from my bike while it was still moving when I reached her house. Leaving it on its side in the street, I ran to the front door and rang the bell. I remembered hoping that her father wouldn't answer the door and fortunately, he didn't. When she answered, I took her by the hand without saying a word and led her to the side of the house. Next to the air conditioner, she looked to me to say something, anything, about why I was there. But I didn't say a word. I didn't know what to say anyway. All I knew was that I *liked* her. I leaned over and kissed her, a long lingering soft kiss. We slowly embraced each other, my hands on her hips, her arms draped across my shoulders. As my lips pressed against hers, I could feel the emotion overcoming her. Her lips quivered as we kissed. She knew, without me saying anything, that I liked her and didn't think of her in the hateful way the other goddamn kids did. And after five minutes, I pulled away from her and smiled. I didn't know what to say. I turned and ran for my bike. Picking it up, I mounted my trusty BMX bicycle and headed for home. I never saw or heard from her again after I moved away.

"Her fate, huh? That was unfortunate," Jason said.

"It sure was," I replied. I still didn't know what to say.

9.

Jason's house was exactly as I remembered, all sorts of run down and kind of smelly inside, like an old gym sock or a moldy bathroom towel. He inherited the house from his parents who died in a traffic accident a few years ago. They were hit by a guy on a severe alcoholic bender; apparently he had been drinking heavily for two weeks and slammed head-on into Jason's parents one night after drinking a six-pack and climbing behind the wheel of a Ford F150. Jason's folks were coming home from a late movie, celebrating their thirtieth wedding anniversary with popcorn and sodas and Sylvester Stallone. Jason's mom loved Sylvester Stallone. She never had a problem with expressing her innermost sexual desires about Rocky; she was very honest about her feelings for the Italian Stallion. I liked that about her. I liked a lot of things about her. Jason's father didn't mind that she liked Sylvester Stallone so much. He took her to that movie to make her happy. She was a cool lady, really cool. It's a shame that his parents are gone and too bad his mom didn't live long enough to see my success. She treated me like one of her own.

"Hey Jason, can I use your phone? I gotta call the wife and then my accountant," I asked. I had to check in with my two bosses; the boss of my life and the boss of my money.

"Sure. The phone is in the den." He pointed to the next room and I made my way in there. I mean, I tried to make my way in there; it was a complete *mess*. Boxes and crap stacked everywhere, just like it was when we were kids. He was the messiest of all my friends, a real pig. He used to throw his clothes everywhere and he had this hamster named Waldo that stunk up the whole room. He never cleaned out that goddamn hamster's cage. That hamster was a real sneaky bastard too. You wouldn't think a hamster would be such a sneaky bastard but he bit me all the time, even when I was being real *nice* to him. I hated that fucking hamster. He mysteriously disappeared one day though. I think their cat got him but I'll never know for sure. No one really *knows* for sure. And I think it will stay that way (unfortunately).

I sat on the couch and picked up the phone. It was one of those old rotary phones. You know, the kind with the big, round dial on the front. If you have never used one, it makes it hard as hell to dial. You have to wait for it to spin around, all slow and shit. It reminded me of the time I tried to write some stories using an old Royal typewriter, one of those manual typers. What a fucking pain in the ass! I like to write using a computer and a word processor. That's the way to go, with a Spell Checker and a Thesaurus and Grammar Checker. I like to use a modern phone with buttons too. But this old phone brought back crazy memories from when we were kids. I started to dial my home number (the dial spinning in slow circles and shit) when Jason started screaming at me from the kitchen.

"You want a Coke? I can make vanilla Cokes, remember?" Jason asked. He loved to make vanilla Cokes when we were kids. He'd make three or four of them every time I'd come over. Maybe that was why he was such a fat fucker when we were kids. I guess he still liked to make them. "Come on, you know you want one."

"OK." I did want one. Man, did that bring back memories too. I dialed my home number and listened to the line ring. It seemed to ring forever. I guess the wife was out shopping. My wife's name is Jessica, just like my daughter, in case I didn't tell you before. My daughter's a *junior*, as in Jessica Jr. My wife's Mexican and in Mexico, they do that shit. Mexicans are pretty crazy. They make the best food and beer, though. And women too, that's for sure. My wife loves to shop, almost too much. If we were dead broke and I found twenty dollars in my pocket and it was the last twenty dollars we had and I made her a proposition between giving it to her to buy some food for the family or to buy herself a new pair of shoes, she'd go for the shoes. Every single time. I know her so well, I'd bet millions on it. Anyway, the answering machine picked up. The stupid message came on.

"You've reached 512-555-6681. We are not in right now ..." We sure had a boring message on our answering machine. No imagination whatsoever. Although, I hate messages with imagination too. You know, the ones where some dumbass records a song or some clip from a movie, making the message ten times longer than it really needs to be. Then you have to wait ten minutes just to leave a five second message. I hate that shit too. "... but if you leave a short message, we'll make sure and call you back. Thanks!" We're going to have to change that message when I get back, really. Or just not use an answering machine at all. That's the way to go. The machine beeped so I left my message.

"Hey sweetie. Just calling to see how you are doing. I made it to Montgomery in one piece and I will call you back in the morning. Don't bother calling because I will probably be going to sleep soon. I didn't sleep one bit on the plane. The flight was really rocky. But I hope to get a good night's rest and I will call you first thing in the morning. Give the babies a big kiss for me. Bye." My message was almost as boring as the machine's message. I hate leaving messages on machines. It's true.

Jason brought me a vanilla coke and he plopped down on the couch next to me. He was really fat when we were kids but he was pretty slender now (more slender, that is). He must have lost over 100 pounds, at least. Maybe 150. He was looking pretty fit and trim. I wished I looked fit and trim. I'm kind of pudgy, you know? I should ask him how he does it, drinking 100 goddamn vanilla cokes and still looking kind of slim. He had all of his hair too, that bastard.

"You look really good, Jason. You've lost a lot of weight since we were kids. What does your wife think of you losing all this weight?" I wish you could have tried that vanilla Coke. It was fucking delicious!

"I lost the weight before we met. She didn't know me as fat Jason, just the skinny one and all. She laughs when she sees pictures of me when I was a kid. I looked like a different person."

"You sure did." I wasn't kidding either. He must have lost 200 pounds. He really was a fat fuck when we were kids. That didn't keep us from being friends though. I didn't hold it against him. It didn't matter to me even though I sure did notice that he was *fat* back then. Everyone noticed. "You look great though. Where is your wife, by the way? She out shopping?" I bet his wife liked to shop too. All women like to shop. It's in their genes.

"No, she's not a big shopper. She probably went to the store to get some groceries." Man, he sure was a lucky bastard if that was true. But I doubt it.

"That's kind of like shopping, I guess."

"I guess so," he said, sipping on his vanilla Coke. He really liked them a lot. He was sipping it like it was the *last* vanilla Coke on the goddamn planet, what, the way he was licking his lips and making all kinds of gratification noises. "So, tell me, what really happened on that plane, you passing out and all? You can tell me now that we're not at the airport anymore."

"I told you, I took a pill that this bartender gave me. He said it would *relax* me for the trip. He must have slipped me something illegal. I think he was mad that I didn't tip him. It's a long story."

"You want to tell it? We got all night."

"No, not really." There was a small picture frame on the table next to the couch and I picked it up. It was a picture of Jason and his kids. Man, they looked just like him. What a shame. It's pretty weird seeing your childhood friends as parents. I mean, I remembered him as the kid who the other kids dared to stick his finger in his butt and then put it in his mouth. And he did it. Now he's somebody's *father.* I guess, on the other hand, he probably thinks of me in the same way, except that I never put my finger in *my* butt. Looking at the picture really made me miss my own kids. I wondered what they were doing besides terrorizing our cat. His name is Mr. Bonkers and he's still mad at me for having kids in the first place. He's never gotten over it, that goddamn cat. It's not my fault he got dropped down the priority ladder. "These your kids, right?" I asked.

"Yep. They're my *seed.* Look just like me, huh?"

"That's for sure. Poor kids."

"Hey!" Jason yelled and then he slugged me in the arm. My goddamn vanilla Coke spilled everywhere. Actually, he frogged me. Frogging is like punching except that when you make a fist, you stick the middle-finger knuckle out. It really hurts. I decided to retaliate. I jumped him and gave him a good frogging on his left arm. I could feel his tricep knot up after I slugged it. He cried Uncle and I climbed off. He was such a wimp, just like when we were kids.

"You owe me another vanilla Coke. You spilled mine," I said. It spilled all over my goddamn shirt. I was soaking wet and sticky.

"Whatever you say." He was kind of sore that I frogged him, especially since I was the one that made fun of how his kids looked in the first place. I kind of felt bad about that. I mean, if anyone says anything about my kids, even looks at them sideways, I go crazy. I go completely nuts. He got up and went into the kitchen to make me another vanilla Coke. I could hear him rattling around for all the things he needed. He was really quiet and shit, talking-wise. He wasn't saying a goddamn word, the wimp bastard. I started to feel really bad then. I always feel bad when someone's not talking to me.

"Hey, Jason?"

"Yeah?" He waited a few seconds before he said that, like he had to catch his breath or something. He was really playing it up.

"I'm sorry. You forgive me?"

"Yeah." He started to make my drink. He was making all kinds of noise in the kitchen, banging things around. I didn't feel so bad anymore.

"Hey, now you can tell me about what happened to Darren Reedy. You said he had a kind of bizarre death. What did you mean by that?" It got really quiet in the kitchen; all the clanging stopped for a bit.

"Do you still smoke?" he asked.

"You mean pot?"

"No, *cigarettes*, you dummy. I don't smoke pot anymore. I want to smoke a cigarette out back on the patio."

"I'm still on the wagon but I'll go out with you." I felt really stupid. That goddamn bartender had me all screwed up and paranoid. I told you pot makes you paranoid, even when you're not high. I used to be a regular smoker, though. I maintained a two-pack-a-day habit after college. I was a real fucking professional. I didn't smoke anymore because of my kids but I told him I'd join him out back anyway so I could sniff his second-hand smoke. That was the most I got out of cigarettes these days, *second*-hand smoke.

"I have to call my accountant first," I told him.

"Isn't it kind of late for that?" he asked. He was right. What a fucking genius. I decided I would call my accountant tomorrow. He brought me my fresh vanilla Coke and we stepped out back.

The backyard looked just like it did when we were kids. The grass was kind of tall and shaggy and I could see an old, rusty tricycle and a dilapidated swingset in the distance. It was a little hard to get a good view of the yard since it was kind of dark outside. I could see the pool, though, and it was bone dry. Not a *drop* of water was in it. We used to have some crazy volleyball tournaments in that goddamn pool. We sat down on some rundown lawn chairs and set our feet on his rundown lawn table. Everything about his house was *rundown*. It was exactly like I remembered. Everything was rundown but there was plenty of rundown things to sit on. He lit a cigarette and blew a cloud of the delicious smoke in my direction. He knew I quit smoking three months ago. I wrote him long, agonizing letters about it. I had so much nervous energy to burn that I was writing all the time instead of smoking. In a two week period, I wrote my entire novel, four short stories, a dozen poems, and ten letters to Jason. I was fucking crazy. Those goddamn cigarettes. They were sapping the life right out of me. I took the smell of the smoke in anyway and sighed. It *still* smelled good to me.

"Camel Lights, right?" I asked.

"That's right."

"That was my brand too." The smell was starting to make me a little crazy. If you have ever been addicted to something, you know what I mean. If you haven't been addicted to something, then forget about it. You have no idea what I'm talking about. "Anyway, tell me about Darren Reedy. What happened to him?"

"Right, right, Darren Reedy." Jason was smoking up a storm. He was already almost done with that cigarette. He sucked it down like he did that vanilla Coke; like it was the last cigarette on Earth, except that he had a whole pack, smoking wimp bastard. Right then, the phone rang inside and Jason hopped up to get it. "Hold on. I'll be right back. I have to get that."

"No problem."

He disappeared into the house and left me with his pack of Camel Lights, a book of matches, and a lit cigarette in the ashtray on the rundown lawn table. One thing about smokers, they don't give a shit about you or your effort to quit smoking. They really don't, the selfish cocksuckers. I would know because I was one of those selfish cocksuckers. Smokers are real touchy about their right to smoke, even though they are slowly killing themselves faster than what is *natural*. Do you know why they are real touchy about it? They are touchy about it because they truly think it is *their choice* to smoke. And yes, at one point it was their choice. I mean, they chose to actually *start* smoking. They put the cigarette to their mouths and inhaled for the first time, even though it hurt like hell to inhale that smoke. And they chose to put the second one to their mouths and smoke that one too, trying to look cool about it. But once they got that nicotine in their bodies, their right to choose was gone. Absolutely gone. Because the day I decided to stop, I couldn't. *I chose to stop and I couldn't.* So I don't know what kind of *choice* that is. And even though I haven't had a cigarette in three months, I still thought about them every day. Can you believe that shit? Every day. Every hour. I was thinking about it right then. I thought about finishing that cigarette in the ashtray. I thought about putting it to my mouth and finishing it off. It's true. And I almost did when Jason came back out. And I guarantee he knew I was thinking about it too. He sat down and finished that smoke.

"Betty and the kids won't be home tonight. They're staying at her sister's house."

"That's too bad. I wanted to meet them."

"You'll meet them tomorrow. Want a smoke?" I knew he was going to ask me that. It's all about the choice, I'm telling you. "I know you quit and all but I still have to offer, you know."

"I know. No thanks." That fucking wimpy ass, hamster loving, fat fuck, rat bastard! "I promised Jessica that I wouldn't. Just tell me about Darren before I break that promise and start smoking again."

"All right. Anyway, well ..." He paused like it was going to be a really heavy story and all. I really wanted to hear about Darren Reedy, especially since he was such a twisted bastard when we were kids. But I wasn't sure if I wanted it to be a really *heavy* story, you know. I don't like really heavy stories. "... you remember how he used to torture his pets, right?"

"Of course." How could I not remember? I know I've been telling you that Darren was a twisted kid even though he was our friend but I haven't told you just *how* twisted he was. One time, I think I was in the sixth grade, I was hanging out at Darren's house after school. He had just discovered that aerosol spray was flammable and he was spraying hairspray on the wall in his room and igniting the spray with a lighter. He was getting the biggest kick out of turning that goddamn can of hairspray into a miniature flamethrower. His mom barged into his room and started yelling at him for trying to burn the house down. He was so mad that she stuck her head in his room that he turned red and started screaming back at her, which I thought was *crazy* because I never talked back to my mother. I would have gotten my ass kicked. But he screamed at her and told her to get out. And when she didn't, he blowtorched the family cat. They had this old cat that loved to sleep in Darren's room (don't ask me why). The cat burst into *flames* and ran out of the room. It ran outside and ran in circles, screaming and hissing. The poor cat died a few hours later. That's how *twisted* Darren was. He was a twisted little cocksucker. He didn't care one bit about anything or anybody. I'll never forget the smell of that poor cat's fur burning. "How could I not remember?"

"Well, believe it or not, after Darren graduated from high school, he got a job with City Animal Services as a dog catcher. He'd drive around town in this van, picking up stray dogs and other animals that people called them about. You know, people would call about stray cats and strange birds and barking dogs and all. When they would call, Darren was the one Animal Services would send out to check it out."

"I guess Animal Services didn't check any of Darren's *references*, huh?" They sure as hell didn't call any of his childhood friends, probably because he knew we would tell them what a twisted cocksucker he was. Darren was really sneaky like that. He was a lying cocksucker. Jason was really *smoking* it up, too. As soon as he'd finish a cigarette, he'd light up another one. It was driving me crazy. I really wanted to smoke one.

"I guess not. He works for the city, you know. They don't *check* references. Anyway, someone down at Animal Services started to put two and two together and they realized that Darren was bringing back only half of the animals that they were getting calls for. It just wasn't adding up for them. So they had someone tail him to see what he was doing."

"They hired a private eye to watch him?"

"Something like that. It was in the newspaper and all. Anyway, they sent someone to tail him and he actually was at least going out to the locations and checking out the calls. But, in fact, he really was only bringing *some* of the animals back to Animal Services. The guy tailing him observed Darren taking the other animals to a different location."

"Where was he taking them?" I had to ask this question to keep Jason focused. I could tell that his story could turn into a real heavy story and all. I didn't want to wait all night to hear what really happened to Darren. I was pretty tired from the flight, you know? Plus, Jason could blab and blab if you let him.

"I'll get to that in a second." Jason lit another cigarette. Man, he was like a fucking chimney with those cigarettes. He was making it really difficult for me to *resist* them. "The guy tailing him followed him to an old abandoned warehouse where he watched Darren unload the dogs and cats that he wasn't taking back to Animal Services. He'd take them in the warehouse and lock them up in these cages that he brought from the shelter. He literally had *hundreds* of dogs and cats. The guy who tailed him just couldn't believe how many animals he had in there."

"Didn't anyone notice all the barking and meowing from all those animals?" I asked. I really wanted a cigarette. They were calling to me like a goddamn Siren.

"That's the thing, Darren would duct tape their mouths shut and muzzle them. No one could hear them at all. Plus, the warehouse was in the middle of nowhere. Anyway, the guy tailing him watched Darren feed this Pit Bull some dog food, only it wasn't just dog food. He was mixing *gun powder* with the dog food." I really wanted to smoke now. Jason was smoking like a madman. "And after the dog devoured his food, I guess the gun powder did something when it hit that poor dog's stomach. The dog started to go crazy. And Darren sat there laughing as the dog went crazy, barking and whining from the gun powder in his stomach. Well, I guess Darren didn't expect that dog to bust out of his cage but he did. The dog was so pissed off from the gun powder in his stomach that he busted that cage wide open and lunged for Darren's throat. He grabbed on with those Pit Bull lockjaws and wouldn't let go. Darren fell to the ground and that dog whipped him around by his neck.

Pit Bulls are really strong, you know? They're not really big dogs and all but they are really *strong*."

"So, what happened to Darren?" Jason was starting to get sidetracked. If I hadn't asked the question, he would have diverged and blabbed and blabbed about the goddamn lockjaws and how strong Pit Bulls were and all.

"I'm getting there. Well, that dog whipped him around by his neck and kind of snapped it. And when Darren stopped struggling and all, that dog let go and just sat there. It sat there looking at Darren. Well, Darren couldn't move because his neck was kind of snapped and all. He just laid there on the ground."

"Oh man, that's *awful*." I wanted to smoke a cigarette so fucking bad. It was really hard to resist.

"Tell me about it."

"So, then what happened?" I asked. I had to keep Jason on target, otherwise, he'd get sidetracked or something again. He could be really scatterbrained sometimes.

"Well, this is where it gets really bizarre. The guy tailing him ran back to his car to make a call to Animal Services about what he just saw Darren doing and to request an ambulance, except that his cell phone wasn't charged. So he drove to a nearby convenience store to make the call. By the time he got back, most of the animals had gotten out of their cages somehow. And they were all around Darren, biting at him, peeing on him, yapping and hissing at him, taking turns getting back at him, I guess. They scattered when the detective guy came up. Darren died on the way to the hospital from internal bleeding and all. His mother was really torn up when she heard about it. She almost died from the shock. It was sad."

"That's awful," I said.

"Tell me about it. I told you it was bizarre. But I guess he got what was coming to him, being that he *tortured* all those animals and all. I just felt bad for his mother. She read about it in the paper. She hasn't been right since. She's kind of gone *crazy*, you know. When I saw her at the funeral, she said she had no idea just how troubled her son was. She knew a little, because of their pets and all, but she figured she just ignored how troubled he actually was and that he'd eventually grow out of it. I guess he never did." He crushed his cigarette into the ashtray. His pack was halfway empty. He was a smoking fool.

We sat there for a while in silence under the clear Alabama sky. What do you say after hearing a story like that about someone you used to know? Not much, I tell you. Even though he was a sick bastard, he was my friend at one point in my life. It was weird knowing how he turned out and that he was gone. He really was a twisted bastard but he deserved what he got, I guess.

"Tell you what, Simon," he said, getting up from his seat. "I'd like to stay out here and catch up but I have to get up for work early in the morning. I really don't have *all* night and I need to get to sleep. I'll leave you some blankets out so you can sleep on the couch. When I get up, we'll catch up some more over breakfast. How's that?"

"No problem," I said. It really wasn't. I was feeling kind of tired anyway from the flight. And that story about Darren about wiped me out. I told you it would be a really heavy story. It's true. I followed Jason inside and he got some blankets and a pillow for me. I sat on the couch and took my shoes off. The couch was kind of smelly but I was too tired to care. Jason turned off most of the lights and sat on the couch with me.

"In case you're interested, I'll leave some car keys on the kitchen counter, if you want to go for a drive or something. I don't want to *spoil* your trip and all just because I have to go to sleep."

"I think I'll go to sleep too. I'm tired from the flight."

"Well, the offer stands. And you don't have to drive the Chevette. You can drive my other car in the garage. It's OK with me." He got up and went to his room. He turned off the last light and shut the door.

I laid down on the couch and thought about Darren. I thought about this time he and I camped in my backyard. I had this little pop-up tent and we camped out there under the stars. We ate smores and told ghost stories and laughed and laughed. It was a real *shame* how it all turned out with him. It was a real fucking shame.

10.

I was really curious by what Jason meant when he said *my other car* so I put my pants back on and went into the garage to check it out. When we were kids, Jason's dad had this beat-up 1967 Mustang in the garage and he used to always tell us about how he was going to restore it but he never had the time to do it. It was rundown like everything else and even though he used to always talk about it, he never did *work* on it like he said he wanted to, even when it seemed like he did have the time to do it. It just sat there in their garage, all beat-up and shit. But when I stepped in the garage, I discovered that he finally did find the time to do it after all. For the first time since I had seen it back then, it looked like fucking brand new. It was the only thing in the house (as far as I could tell) that wasn't rundown.

And his dad did a real job on it too. It was this bright, pearl turquoise color with white leather seats and shiny chrome *everywhere*. I walked around it and looked it over and it didn't have one dent or scratch on it. It looked like it had just rolled out of the goddamn factory or something. I mean, it was *beautiful*. And I was (for the first time since I walked in Jason's house) really amazed. It was like a little pristine oasis out there in the garage in the middle of all this crap in the rest of the house. The driver-side window was down so I popped my head in. Again, the interior was in immaculate shape. And just as I had remembered, it had a *three* on the floor. The only thing not original (again, as far as I could tell) was the stereo. A completely modern stereo was installed with new speakers mounted in the doors. That was OK considering that automobile makers in the sixties didn't appreciate the importance of a high quality sound system in their vehicles. I could hear the car keys calling to me inside and I knew that I had to *drive* it. So I ran back inside.

I put a fresh, clean shirt on since Jason spilled my goddamn vanilla Coke on my other shirt, hopped in that beast of a car, and backed out of the garage. There was no need trying to be quiet about it since the Mustang rumbled like a goddamn monster. Jason had to have heard me, it was so *loud*. It's true. Plus, the garage door rattled and shook as the garage-door opener strained to pull it up the rails. I thought it was going to fall off the goddamn rails, it shook so much. I backed out of the garage past the turd-on-wheels Chevette and took off.

The Mustang handled like a *dream*. It really did. The clutch was nice and tight and responsive and the engine roared like a monster. I was afraid I was going to wake up the whole goddamn neighborhood the way it roared. It even had air conditioning. You know, one of those big air conditioning units that look like small refrigerators. It was mounted on the floor behind the stick shift. It rumbled and gurgled like a rusty window unit at a cheap motel and spit water all over the place when I turned it on but it worked. That's all that mattered. I decided at that moment that I was going to check out some places I never had a chance to go to when I was a kid, being that I was a minor and all. Since it was late, that limited it to bars and clubs but I was OK with that. It must have been close to eleven o'clock. I kept the beast in second and hauled some serious ass past my old house and Darren Reedy's old house and Beth Myers' old house. I turned on the main boulevard outside the neighborhood and took a left towards town. Everything was within twelve to fifteen miles of Country Down Estates. Montgomery was a sprawling goddamn *metropolis*. It's true.

I couldn't think of any reason why Jason would drive that turd-on-wheels Chevette over this beauty. I really couldn't. I wanted to give him the benefit of the doubt and thought that maybe driving the beast would stir up recent memories of his parents' death; maybe driving it would remind him of his father and how much he loved this car and all. But that didn't seem (to me, at least) to be a valid reason to subject the entire town to the sight and sound of the turd mobile. I mean, it was a goddamn eye sore. And the smell that poor-excuse-for-a-car emitted was horrendous. It smelled like the farts I get after I drink milk. I'm lactose-intolerant, if I didn't tell you before, and drinking milk gives me the worst gas. It's true. That's what that Chevette's exhaust smelled like, my milk-gas. And who would want to drive around with that? But Jason's family was never into looks and class and all. They liked everything rundown. Maybe driving something that wasn't rundown made him feel uncomfortable. And if that was the case, that would be a real goddamn shame. It really would.

Being that I had been away from Montgomery for so long, nothing looked the same to me. I mean, I recognized the main street and some of the businesses and buildings but it also looked quite different too. That happens, you know, when you move away from a place; it changes without your knowing, whether you want it to or not. Montgomery was trying really hard to be a goddamn modern mega-metropolis. It allowed the Home Depots and McDonald's and Starbucks and strip malls and fast food restaurants and convenience stores to invade its city limits. And in a way, that was comforting because there was now a level of familiarity to it that made things simple for a visitor like myself. I mean, the level of unexpected disappointment was lowered because of these conveniences. A goddamn cappuccino at Starbucks here would probably taste pretty close to a goddamn cappuccino from a Starbucks in Austin. But I didn't want that really. If I wanted a cappuccino that tasted like the ones in Austin, then I would have stayed in Austin. It's true. Why travel all that distance to get the same thing you would get at home? It cracks me up when I hear friends of mine say that when they went to Paris, they ate at McDonald's. Why the fuck would you want to do that?

Is a French McDonald's better than a plain old American one? I don't think so.

Anyway, I was looking for a place called Dan's Watering Hole. When I was a kid, I was fascinated by the *sign* this place had in front. The place looked like an old saloon, what, with the wood façade and the post for tying up your horse and the old barrels and the swinging door. But the thing I remembered most was the sign. The sign had a picture of a cowboy standing next to his horse in front of a barrel filled with some brown water. The goddamn horse looked drunk off his ass with his criss-crossed eyes with the x's in the middle and his sagging, drooling tongue hanging from his mouth. I was completely fascinated with that goddamn sign. Whenever my parents would drive by, I would always ask them why the cowboy would take his horse to a barrel that was *obviously* filled with alcohol. They never answered my question and I think that fed my curious imagination with plenty of bizarre scenarios. Maybe the cowboy thought it was funny to see his horse sitting there drunk and drooling. Or maybe that was all they had to drink being that they lived in a desert and water was scarce and all (duh). Or maybe the horse was my Uncle Sherman reincarnated as the drunk horse, being that he was a pretty mean alcoholic. My twelve year old mind just couldn't figure it out. Now that I'm older, I think it's funny that I thought any of those things were reasonable explanations for the horse being the way he was in that sign. I had a fervent imagination. It's true. But now that I was older, I wanted to check it out for what it really was: a hole-in-the-wall, serving cheap beer to the locals with a stupid cartoon for a sign. I really needed a drink anyway after that story Jason told me about what happened to Darren Reedy. It was a heavy story like I knew it would be and it really brought me down.

But unfortunately, Dan's Watering Hole was nowhere to be found. No evidence of that old saloon or the sign with the drunk horse on it was *anywhere* on the main boulevard. And I drove up and down a few times. I pulled the beast over to an old convenience store that I remembered from my childhood: *Tyrone's BGP Convenient Store.* The BGP apparently stood for Beer, Gas, and Peanuts, or at least that's what old Tyrone used to tell me when Jason and I would ride our bikes down to his store for ice cream sandwiches and sodas after school. And I always got a kick out of the fact that he used *convenient* instead of *convenience* on the store sign. That's what it said, it's true. Old Tyrone was really nice to us, especially considering that we were just two *white* kids from the nice, white neighborhood up the street. He didn't have to be nice to us but he was. I'll always remember his kind smile. I remembered thinking that I would hit the ceiling if he was still there. He would have to be *old* as hell to still be there. He was old as hell when I was kid. I parked the car and went inside.

It smelled just like I remembered, what, with that sweet candy smell and, of course, the smell of fresh, buttered popcorn. No matter what time of the day you went in, it always smelled like fresh popcorn inside. And even though it was rundown inside and out, it never smelled musty or mildewy like you would expect. It just *looked* kind of musty and mildewy, like the rest of Montgomery. But the store was laid out the same. The two middle aisles were filled with all kinds of candy from front to back. And the comic book rack was still there on the side by the window. I spent long hours there reading issues of Spiderman while I ate my candy and ice cream. Man, did that bring back memories. And there it was, past eleven o'clock and it still smelled like fresh popcorn inside. I grabbed a beer from the cooler and went to the counter. I wanted a small bag of popcorn and directions to Dan's Watering Hole. But old Tyrone was nowhere to be found. In fact, there wasn't anybody in there except for me. The counter was unmanned and the store was unpopulated. There was a small sign with a bell on the counter. The sign said: R*ing the bell for service.* So I did.

Pretty quick, old Tyrone came from a back door and hopped behind the counter. He didn't look as old as I thought he would. In fact, he looked pretty goddamn good. Well, you know what they say? Black people always *age* better than white people, at least in the looks department. He looked pretty goddamn good for his age, what with the pitch black hair and no wrinkles and all his white teeth. I was pretty sure he wouldn't remember who I was. I mean, it's not like we were friends and all. He was probably more a fixture of *my* memories than I was of his. But he plopped on his stool just like he used to and gave me a look of indifference and kindness simultaneously. He was chomping on a smashed up cigar, just like he used to. And he was wearing the same kind of Dickies overalls. Back then, he'd chew those cigars until they disintegrated.

"What can I do ya for, sir?" He used to call me *sir* when I was a kid. It's true. He looked really good for his age too. He didn't look a day over forty except for his tired, yellow eyes. That's what gave his age away. And he still chewed that cigar like he was a cow chewing cud or something.

"I used to live in Montgomery when I was a kid ..."

"Oh really?" Old Tyrone, he never used to let you finish a sentence. He would always butt in with some kind of question about your day or where you were from or where you were going. That's just the way he was. He hadn't changed a bit. And he chewed that cigar like a madman. "When'd you move away?"

"Oh, about sixteen years ago."

"It's been a long time, huh?" he asked. "Things have changed quite a bit 'round here, I'd say. Where'd you live? Country Down Estates?"

"That's right. That was my old neighborhood."

"That's where all you *white folks* like to live," he said. He was a real fucking genius. I thought he was going to choke on that cigar, the way he was chomping on it. "That might as well be a country club or some shit, huh? Sixteen years ago, huh? You remember the Browns? They tried living in old Country Down Estates about that time. You remember what happened to them?"

I remembered the Browns, all right. Who wouldn't? Dr. James Brown and his family moved into Country Down Estates right after we did. They moved into a big house right on the main thoroughfare of the neighborhood. As far as I remembered, they were the only black family in the neighborhood. Dr. Brown was a successful cardiologist and his wife was a family practitioner and they had two kids that were a little younger than I was. But I remembered being relieved that a *black* family was moving into the neighborhood. There was just too many *white* families around. But not everyone else felt the way I did about the Browns. Apparently, the Browns were not very welcomed in our neighborhood. Their neighbors didn't welcome them in like they did the other white neighbors. Eventually, I started to hear things like the garbage men wouldn't pick their trash up and the utility men wouldn't come out and turn their utilities on. A big stink ensued and even though I was a little too young to understand the situation, my parents would talk about it at the dinner table. My parents were really upset by it, especially since my dad was a Jew and he said he even caught some flack and stares from some of the neighbors. I don't remember exactly what happened to the Browns but they did eventually move away and there was some articles about their lawsuit in the paper. It was a really big deal back then.

"Yeah, I remember the Browns," I told him, kind of embarrassed that I was still a white guy. Sounds stupid but it's true.

"Well, anyway, what can I do you for? Need gas for your fancy car?"

There was something about old Tyrone I couldn't quite put my finger on. There was something different about him. I mean, he looked the same, what, with the overalls and the cigar and all. I caught myself staring at him. I stopped that pretty quick though. There's one thing you don't do, as a white guy, and that's *stare* at an old black guy. It's true. They take offense to it. But I didn't want to offend him. I wanted to ask him a question.

"Is your name Tyrone?" I asked. It was a long shot, I was sure, but I had to ask him if he remembered me. He kind of eyeballed me back, chewing on his goddamn cigar and scratching his head. I could tell he was trying to figure out who I was but he wasn't trying *too* hard.

"Sure is. Who are you? Barnaby Jones?" he asked. That was pretty goddamn funny, if you ask me. It really was. I liked it when black men used those kind of racial slurs, just like good old George Jefferson did. It really made me laugh. It's true. I thought it was hilarious.

"This may sound really stupid but do you remember me? I used to come in this store a lot when I was a kid and I read the comics and ate my ice cream over there by the window. You know, those days of reading Spiderman in your store really inspired me to do what I do today. I can pretty much say that I wouldn't be a published writer today if it wasn't for your store." I thought it might be pretty goddamn neat if he did remember me, especially since I was a writer now and obviously had moved away from this town to actually do something really *important* with myself. Man, was I wrong.

"You know, to me, all you white kids look the same. But to be honest, you must be looking for my pops. I'm Tyrone Jr. My pops don't work here no more."

I *knew* there was something strange about him. Something just wasn't quite right about old Tyrone but I couldn't put my finger on it. Now I knew why. He wasn't the same old Tyrone at all. He was a cruel imposter. I was really disappointed.

"Oh really? What's your dad doing these days? Is he retired?"

"He's dead."

There it was again, that blunt Montgomery attitude about death. He just blurted it out like it was nothing. It kind of got to me. It's true. And he wasn't affected by it at all.

"Oh," I said, kind of speechless for a second. I really wanted to change the subject but for some reason, I didn't. "Your dad used to tell me that BGP stood for Beer, Gas, and Peanuts. Is that true?"

"Nah, it stands for *Be Getting Profits*. He just used to tell other people that because it didn't sound so greedy. He was real smart like that. He was a smart businessman. And I'm sure he wouldn't remember no white kids reading his comics in no window. It used to piss him off when kids would read his merchandise without paying for it."

I was kind of getting the feeling that old Tyrone Jr. wasn't as fond of our common past as I was. I decided to really change the subject this time. Young Tyrone was starting to get on my nerves.

"I was looking for Dan's Watering Hole. Is that place still around here?"

"I haven't heard about that place in a long time. It's gone now. The owner sold it a while ago. But you can go to the new club now. It's called Cinnamon's. It's in the same building down the street. It just looks different now but it's the same building."

"Back that way?" I asked, pointing in the direction I came from, back toward my old neighborhood. He was really sucking on that cigar now. It was about to disappear down his throat.

"Yeah, just turn back and go that way. You'll see it on the left. You can't miss it. It has the real big *boobies* on the neon sign."

I got a small bag of popcorn and paid Tyrone for it and my beer. I didn't bother telling him it was nice to meet him and how his store brought back a bunch of memories and all that shit because it was obvious he didn't care about who I was. And I'm OK with that. It's true. I just left and got back in the Mustang. I took a swig from my beer and placed the popcorn between the seats. I backed out of the parking lot to old Tyrone's BGP Convenient Store and dropped the beast into first gear. I peeled out of the parking lot and didn't look back. I decided to leave old Tyrone, young Tyrone, his stinking cigar, the candy, the comic book rack, all the other white kids who didn't pay for their comics, and that goddamn store in my past, where it should be. Sometimes, reliving the past will do you no good. It's best to just leave things the way they were. It's true.

11.

I was really starting to miss my son, good ol' Sammie boy. I couldn't stop thinking about him for some reason. I was trying to find Dan's goddamn Watering Hole but Sammie boy popped into my thoughts with his cute smile and infectious laugh. He had this laugh that could make *anyone* smile (and I mean anyone). It's true. If you got to tickling him or making funny faces or raising your voice a couple of octaves and acting like your leg was broken while you limped around the house, he'd start laughing and giggling all over the place. His face would turn bright red and he'd laugh until he couldn't breathe anymore. Then after a deep breath, he'd laugh some more until his head was about to burst. He was really funny that way, Sammie boy. He was really happy *all* the time. I don't know where he got it from (probably my wife). He didn't get it from me. I can be a real sad bastard sometimes, especially when I start thinking about how I miss my wife and kids. I was *really* feeling like a sad bastard and the beer wasn't helping at all.

Old Tyrone's bastard son was right. Just a ways up the road was a bright neon sign with a couple of big *boobies* on it. The place wasn't called Dan's Watering Hole anymore; it was now called: *Cinammon's Big Boobie Bonanza*. And on the sign were the biggest boobies I'd ever seen. It was a really funny goddamn sign too. It had a picture of a girl bending over and her breasts were so big that they hung pretty close to the ground. They sagged down like a couple of watermelons stuffed in a pair of gym socks. But the funniest part was that the nipples flashed on and off like a beacon. They were pretty mesmerizing the way they flashed on and off. Whoever thought of making them flash on and off like that was a fucking genius. It's true.

I pulled into the parking lot to figure out my options for the rest of the evening. On one hand, I really wanted a strong drink to calm my nerves from the really *heavy* story Jason laid on me earlier, the story about what happened to Darren Reedy. There weren't any other places around close that were open besides Cinammon's Big Boobie Bonanza unless I wanted to drive closer to downtown. And I didn't want to do that because it was getting late and, besides, I didn't feel like getting mugged downtown by some bum. Downtown Montgomery was full of goddamn bums. They were all over the place. On the other hand, I didn't necessarily want to go into a bar called Cinammon's Big Boobie Bonanza either. It wasn't my style to hang out in one of those kind of places. You know, a strip club and all. I never was one to hang out in strip clubs like a dirty old man or something. But as I looked around, and since I didn't want to go downtown, I realized that my options were pretty limited. So, on the strength of the funny sign alone, I decided to go inside. For some reason, I thought it wouldn't do any harm to get one drink in there. Besides, I thought the booze would help me sleep. So I turned off the beast, finished my beer, put the popcorn in my pocket, and went in for a drink.

Once inside, I realized why the nipples on the sign flashed on and off. It was *really cold* in there. They must've had the thermostat set to fifty degrees because even *my* nipples seemed to flash on and off too. It's true. I paid the hostess ten dollars (ouch!) for admission and was led to my table by my cordial waitress. She said her name was Ginger and she asked me what I wanted to drink. Her nipples were flashing too, I could tell. It must have been hard for her to work in those conditions, what, with the thermostat set to fifty degrees and her nipples sticking out because it was cold and all. I bet she could file some kind of complaint with the local workforce board or something. She definitely had legitimate grounds for a *complaint.* I know if TechForce made us work in those kind of conditions, I would have filed a complaint. Who can work with their nipples hard all the time? A real idiot who puts up with that, that's who.

I told Ginger that I wanted a whiskey and coke and she flashed me one of those fake, sugary smiles like the flight attendant on the plane gave me earlier. It must be a mandatory part of the service industry or something, those kind of *fake* smiles. I would make a great waiter because I had those fake goddamn smiles down like nobody's business. I flashed her *my* fake smile and she took off for my drink. She was fast as hell too, the way she took off. And before I could bat an eye, she was back with my drink. She sat down next to me like I had invited her for a drink, crossing her legs and giving me that fake goddamn smile. She was really putting it on too, like she had a thing for me or something. I looked around and noticed that I was one of only a few patrons there. She must have been desperate for a tip. Since she was so fast, I gave her a buck. I always tip based on the *quality* of service and since she was so fast, I felt she deserved it. She seemed grateful. She put the buck on her tray and set the tray on my table. Then she leaned over and started talking to me, all loud and shit because it was too loud in there, what, with the heavy metal music blaring and bells and whistles all.

"What kind of girls do you prefer?" she asked, practically screaming in my ear. It was pretty goddamn unattractive, if you ask me, all her screaming and sitting at my table uninvited. "Do you prefer blondes or brunettes?"

I thought that was a pretty bizarre question to be asking a married man. I mean, my wedding ring was big as hell and since it had a few diamonds on it, it flashed like a band of stars on my hand in that dark lounge. But for some reason, the question got me *thinking.* I really started to wonder about it, the question and all. What kind of girl *did* I prefer, blondes or brunettes? My wife was a brunette so I thought it must be brunettes, considering that I married one. But it also seemed like most of the women I had dated before my wife were brunettes too. So that *must* have been the answer: *I preferred brunettes*.

"I guess it would be brunettes," I told her. I had to really scream it too because it was so loud in there. She kind of backed away because of all my screaming.

"Why did it take you so long to answer?" she asked. I thought that was kind of a stupid question. She was a real fucking genius, I could tell.

"Because I'm married to a brunette," I answered.

"But that doesn't necessarily mean that you *prefer* brunettes because you are *married* to one. Don't you ever have fantasies?"

Now *that* was a really stupid question too. Ginger was really starting to get on my nerves with her stupid questions and fake, sugary smile. I really wanted her to just leave me *alone*.

"Sure, I guess I have fantasies about blondes. Can you come back later? I just want to drink my whiskey in peace."

"Is something bothering you? You seem kind of stressed out. How can you be stressed out in a *place* like this?" Ginger was really getting to me now with all her prying questions. But you can't just ask a woman to get the hell away from you. That would be rude and not gentleman-like. It's true. I had to be cordial about it, even if I did just want her to fuck off.

"Look, Ginger. I have a really important reading coming up in New York in a few days and I just want to rest and reflect and drink my whiskey and be left alone right now. My new novel will be out in a couple of weeks but an old friend of mine has *died* unexpectedly and it's really thrown a wrench into matters." I was really letting the lies fly. I mean, she didn't know that Darren died a few *years* ago. How would she know? I wasn't really one to lie but this was an exception. I had to get her away from me. "It's been hard."

"You're a writer?" she asked. "What was your name again?"

"My name is Simon. Simon Burchwood. Do you like to read?" I asked. I thought *that* was a funny question to be asking a waitress that worked in a place called Cinammon's Big Boobie Bonanza. But as soon as I asked it, she started to lean in really close again. She was making me nervous and shit, what, with all her leaning in and her fake interest in me. I didn't know what to do. I was sorry I asked her if she liked to read.

"Oh, yes. I *love* to read. In my free time, that's all I do is read. I belong to several book clubs and I read at least a few novels a month. What kind of novels do you write? Mysteries? Romances?"

"Well, to be quite honest, I write in the literary tradition of Vonnegut or Bukowski. I don't like to classify my work in terms of genres. For example ..."

"I understand. You know, I always wanted to write when I was a little girl." Man, it was starting to happen again, what, with the interruptions and the dreams of being a writer and all that shit. But like always, I was prepared for it just like before. You always have to be prepared for someone who is about to tell you about their goddamn lost dreams. I pulled my wallet out and started looking for one of my business cards. "But that was just one of my little-girl dreams, like being a princess or a ballerina or something like that. It was never something I *actually* thought would come true. Hey, do you know what my favorite book is?"

"No, what is it?" I asked, pulling out a few business cards and setting them on the table.

"*To Kill a Mockingbird*. I absolutely loved that book, especially since it took place in Alabama. I really could relate to Scout. She's the main character, you know."

"That's really great and all. But to be honest, Ginger, I don't prefer blondes or brunettes or any genre of books or whatever. I just want to be left alone and grieve for my friend and get ready for my reading in New York. Is that OK? Would you mind? If you're curious, here's my business card. You can read some of my work on my website and leave me a gratuity if you like it. How's that?"

And in an instant, that fake, sugary smile was gone. She took my card and looked at it like I handed her a rock-hard turd. That was the first time the card didn't *impress* someone. I was in shock. It's true. It really caught me off guard. She sort of scowled after she looked at the card.

"Why would I want to leave *you* a gratuity? Why would I want to do something like *that*?" And then she walked off. I felt really bad for being short with her but I had to do it. I mean, she wasn't going to give me any privacy, what, with her blabbing mouth and her favorite book and her hard nipples and her dreams of being a writer or a ballerina or some shit like that. She was really getting on my goddamn nerves. What did she think? That I wanted to be catered to like a goddamn invalid or some dirty old man that doesn't know any better? I was really starting to regret going into Cinammon's Big Boobie Bonanza, even if the drinks were strong and the service was good. That's what the sign said outside, right under the big, sagging boobies: *Cinammon's Big Boobie Bonanza, where the drinks are strong and the service is great!* What a farce. What the sign should have said was: *Cinammon's Big Boobie Bonanza, where the drinks are strong but the waitresses bug the shit out of you about how they want to be goddamn ballerinas!* I decided to move to another section and finish my drink. I figured that if I was bothered by a different waitress that, at least, my odds were pretty good that she wouldn't be an avid reader and that her dreams as a little girl mainly consisted of working in Cinammon's Big Boobie Bonanza as a waitress. I found an empty table in the back and sat down.

There were two young ladies dancing to the song *You Shook Me All Night Long* by AC/DC on the stage at the other side of the club. One thing was for sure, no one could claim false advertising against

Cinammon's Big Boobie Bonanza because the two girls' boobs drooped just like the woman pictured on the sign out front. The only difference was that they didn't have the ecstatic look on their faces that the woman on the sign had. The two dancers looked pretty *bored* and kind of annoyed actually. They only had two old guys sitting up front watching them and they were two cheap bastards too. They weren't giving them dollar bills for tips; they were giving them coins for tips. But they weren't handing them the coins. They were flicking the coins at them (kind of hard too). I felt kind of sorry for the two young ladies. I mean, what kind of career was that? Having two dirty old men fling coins at them while they danced and gyrated and all? I was feeling pretty down about everything, the Darren Reedy story, my Sammie boy, old Tyrone's death, Ginger and her goddamn ballerina dream; it was all depressing the shit out of me. I decided to change seats and face the bar instead of the two sad dancers. So I moved to the chair across from where I was sitting and faced the back of the club. I was almost finished with my drink by that time. I decided, that once I was finished, I would go back to Jason's house and get some rest. Tomorrow was going to be my only day in Montgomery and I was going to take advantage of the day to the fullest before leaving for New York. My schedule in New York was going to be hectic, what, with the reading and the book signing and the publicity spots and all. I was getting tired just thinking about it. And then I was interrupted by another waitress.

"Can I get you another drink?" she asked. She was very polite, kind of demure, and blonde. It was a big change from Ginger, the wannabe ballerina who loved to read.

"No, I'm about ready to leave ..."

"What were you drinking? Whiskey? Scotch?" she interrupted, before I could finish. Everybody was interrupting me that day. It was getting to be pretty fucking annoying. She sure was nice about it though. I guess you just had to hear the *tone* of her voice. She sounded really sweet and considerate.

"I was drinking whiskey and coke but I have to get ..."

"I'll bring you out a fresh one," she said and then she was off before I could say another word. She was quick as lightning. All the waitresses there were quick as goddamn lightning. I'll give them that. And before I could bat an eye, she was back with my drink. But she didn't sit down, all uninvited, like Ginger did. She just stood there with an angelic smile on her face. She was very polite that way. "Anything else I can get for you?" she asked.

"No," I replied. I didn't want to be rude. She was giving excellent service *and* she was really nice.

"Why did you move from Ginger's section? Do you mind telling me?" she asked, really curious and shit.

"No, not at all." I really didn't mind. It's true.

"I've heard that she can be pretty *pushy* with her customers."

"If you want to know the truth, yes, she *was* being kind of pushy and all."

"I knew it," she said, and she was pretty excited about it too. She jumped up and down like she won the lottery or something. "I'm always hearing *that* from customers, that she's really pushy. I try not to be pushy. I believe your tip suffers when you're overly pushy. Customers don't want that, you know? Customers just want to be left alone unless they invite you to sit down and join them. I never sit down unless I'm invited to sit down. You just don't want to ruin someone's evening by inviting yourself to the party."

"You know, I haven't heard truer words today." I wasn't trying to be rude. Maybe it sounded rude but I wasn't trying to be. She was really nice. I was just being honest. It's true. "What was your name?"

"My name is Felicity. And yours?"

"Simon. Felicity, that's an interesting name. Would you care to join me? I wasn't looking for company but you seem like a really nice young lady." I was feeling pretty hospitable and all. She seemed pretty happy that I asked her to join me.

"Thanks." She sat down and set her tray on the table. The waitresses all seemed to like setting their goddamn trays on your table. She didn't lean on me, though, like Ginger did. I was grateful for that, especially since I was married. I didn't want some strange girl leaning on me. It just wasn't right.

"Would you like something to drink?" I asked.

"No, not while I'm on duty. I'll get all goofy if I start drinking alcohol while I'm working. People will take advantage, you know."

"I understand."

"So, what do you do for a living?"

"I'm a writer. I just recently received a big publishing deal. I'll be reading from my new novel, THE RISE AND FALL OF A TITAN, in New York in a few days. I'm pretty excited about it." I was hoping that she wouldn't start blabbing about her dreams like everybody else. I was getting pretty tired of hearing about everyone else's goddamn dreams.

"That's wonderful," she said. And that was all she said. She didn't say anything about wanting to be a writer or an astronaut or a ballerina or a fireman. She just smiled.

"You know, I was waiting for you to say how you have always wanted to do something, like write or paint. People are always telling me how they haven't fulfilled their dreams."

"Well, I haven't really figured that part out yet. I guess there really isn't anything I have decided on doing with my life. I'm still looking, I guess. Right now, I'm just content with working. The only thing I know I want is to be a mother. But I haven't found the right guy yet."

"You know, being a parent is a truly wonderful thing. It really is. I have two kids myself."

"Really? That's wonderful. I'm jealous. I want to have kids too." For some reason, she seemed a little sad when she told me that. I thought of showing her some Christmas pictures I had of Sammie and Jessie. But then I thought that probably wouldn't be such a good idea. I didn't want to seem like I was gloating and all. "You know, you're really nice. There aren't too many nice guys that come into this place. We usually have a bunch of lowlifes that try to pinch my butt or take me home. It can be kind of depressing." I actually knew what she meant. Then she kind of leaned over toward me. "Can I tell you something?"

"Sure." She was wearing a mesmerizing perfume. I didn't know what it was but it really smelled sweet, like a rose or something. And it smelled kind of familiar too. You ever walked passed someone who was wearing the same perfume as someone you used to know (like an ex-girlfriend)? It reminded me of a perfume that an old flame used to wear.

"My name really isn't Felicity."

"It's not?" I asked. Man, it was getting too good. This had *excitement* written all over it.

"No, Felicity is just my *stage* name. Everyone here has a stage name, in case of perverts, you know?"

"I see. So Ginger isn't really Ginger's name."

"No. Her real name is Bertha May. She was named after her grandmother, I think."

"I can see why she changed her name to Ginger." We both started to laugh. Bertha May was a pretty goddamn ugly name to start with but it matched her personality better than Ginger did. "So what's your name? If you don't mind me asking, that is."

She paused for a second as if she was debating the consequences of telling me her real name. But she didn't think about it for too long. I guess she thought I wasn't a pervert or something.

"My real name is Patty. I'd tell you my last name but that would be going too far. So Patty's all I'll tell you. I shouldn't even be telling you my name because it's against the rules."

I was surprised to hear that name, especially since Jason and I had been talking about pretty blonde Patty Green from school when we were kids earlier today. I kind of gave Patty the waitress a little stare. I tried to be really nonchalant about it too but she noticed I was staring at her. She got kind of embarrassed. I realized I was probably acting like an idiot, staring and all. It's rude to stare, you know.

"What?" she asked, a little self-conscious now.

"Oh... nothing," I said.

"No, what is it? You were looking at me like you were trying to remember something." And I *was* trying to remember something. She was a real genius. I was trying to remember exactly what little Patty Green looked like. But my memories of her were foggy now. It was a long time ago.

"Have you always lived in Montgomery?" I asked.

"Why, yes."

"And did you go to Jefferson Elementary?"

"Yeah. How did you know?"

And that was the last question I had to ask. I didn't want to go any further. A small part of me thought it would be nice if *this* Patty was the same Patty Green I knew from back in school. But for some reason, I didn't want to find out. I guess after Tyrone's bastard son ruined my recollections of old Tyrone and the BGP Convenient Store, and after I decided that some things were better left in the past, I think I just didn't want to ruin anything else that night. In a way, it would have been great to see little Patty but not in *this way*, not in Cinammon's Big Boobie Bonanza. I just didn't want to pursue it. I decided, right then and there, that it was time to go.

"Thanks for the drink, Patty ... I mean, *Felicity*. But I have to get going."

I dropped some money on the table, grabbed my things, and was out the door before she could say a word. I knew she was lightning fast so I didn't give her a chance to change my mind. She was really nice and all but that didn't matter. One thing was for sure, I didn't want anything to taint my childhood feelings for little blonde Patty Green. It was too sacred. So I went straight for the beast in the parking lot, except, with all my goddamn luck, I tripped and fell hands-down on the asphalt. I cut a gash in the palm of my right hand and it hurt like all hell. But I ignored the pain and embarrassment, hopped in the beast, and took off. I took off and never looked back.

12.

After my chaotic flight and first day back in Montgomery, Alabama, I really expected to have some kind of crazy dream that night. I really did. But you know what? I didn't dream about one goddamn thing. It's true. I just slept so soundly that I didn't even remember *going* to sleep. Maybe it was the beer and whiskey that knocked me out. But sometimes, I'm conscious when I'm sleeping. It's usually towards the end of my sleep that I become conscious. I usually can see the cold darkness of my deep sleep and I imagine that that's how I probably would feel if I was floating in outer space. Pretty crazy, huh? Anyway, I was enjoying the cold darkness of my sleep when I was violently awakened by a jab to my crotch. I can't think of any other way for someone to wake you up that could be *worse* than a jab to the crotch. I opened my eyes and discovered a little demon that was the spitting image of Jason when he was a kid. It's true. He looked just like Jason did and was a fat little bastard too. And he had that same cackling, hyena laugh. I sat up and clinched my fist like I was going to take a swing at him. But I think he knew that I knew that I was *not* going to punch a kid, especially Jason's kid. He just sat there cackling at my sore crotch.

"You must be Jason Jr." I said, fighting the urge to really let him have it. I wanted to knock his goddamn head off.

"That's right, *fucker*. How are your balls, *fucker*?" He started dancing a maniacal little jig, laughing at the thought of how my crotch must have felt. He kept cackling and cackling. It was one of the worst ways to wake up. It's true. I really wanted to slug him. "Do they hurt, *fucker*? Huh? You want some more? Huh?"

"Is that how you talk to your elders? That's not very respectful, you know. You shouldn't use that kind of *language*." It was obvious that he didn't care anything about what I thought. He kept dancing and cackling and I knew if he had the chance, he'd jab me in the nuts again.

"Is this yours?" he asked, whipping my red backpack around from behind his back. Man, I really wanted to slug him then.

"Yes, it is. And it's very important to me. Now, will you please give it back?" I asked. There really was no point in trying to talk some sense into him. I just had to be direct and to the point. He was a crazy little bastard.

"Come and get it," he said, taunting me by keeping the backpack just out of my reach.

"Please, don't make me get up and get it from you. I'm asking you nicely. Please give me the *backpack*."

Then a woman started yelling from the kitchen. It must have been Jason's wife, Betty. She didn't sound too happy about having to call her little demon in for breakfast. She had a sweet voice but it was obvious she was at the end of her very short rope.

"Jason, Jr.? You better get in here in FIVE, FOUR, THREE..."

And just like that, he dropped the backpack like it was a hot coal from hell and ran for the kitchen. The countdown always seemed to work with kids. I didn't know what it was about counting down that made them lose their lunch like it does. It just seemed to work every time like you were counting down to Armageddon or something. Even when I was a kid, the sound of the countdown sent me into a frenzied panic. What would my dad do? Break my neck? Kill me? Who actually knew. He never really finished the countdown though. I guess it was the impending doom of what *might* occur that scared me the most.

And what language Jason Jr. used. I'm telling you, if my parents heard me calling one of their friends a *fucker*, they would have snapped my neck. It's true. I would have been grounded for months and fed oatmeal and water for every meal. I didn't curse around my kids. It's disrespectful and I didn't want them picking up the habit. My father cursed like a sailor. It always bothered me. Jason's dad cursed too and so does Jason. Now his son was afflicted. Cursing was a goddamn curse.

With my backpack safe and sound, I went into the bathroom for a quick face wash and to brush my teeth. I don't worry about putting on clean clothes until *after* I take a shower, so I put my dirty shirt back on and ran my fingers through my hair to make myself presentable. I noticed, while raking through my greasy mane, the fresh gash in my hand from the night before. I must have taken at least a hundred layers of skin off my palm when I fell on the goddamn asphalt. It looked and hurt like hell. I thoroughly washed the wound and rummaged through the bathroom for some antiseptic and a bandage. I covered the embarrassing sore and headed for the kitchen for some breakfast and to meet the rest of Jason's family. I hoped that they would be a little more civilized than the crotch-jabbing demon.

The kitchen was setup just like I remembered. It was a moderately sized kitchen that had a breakfast nook and a huge window overlooking the pool in the backyard. The morning sunlight seemed to drench the room with warmth and hope for a good day. It's true. That kitchen always gave off a very positive feeling when I was a kid. Maybe because it was always filled with family and friends and laughter and good food. Jason's two boys were at the table eating cold cereal and Betty was at the counter toasting some bread. It was very much as it should be in there.

"Too bad there isn't any water in the pool, huh? It would be a good day to go swimming," I said. Betty turned around with a big smile and open arms.

"Simon, it is so nice to *finally* meet you." She threw her arms around me and gave me a big hug. She was a good hugger. She really put herself into it. It was genuine, I could tell. She held onto me for quite some time. "I've heard so much about you."

"It's nice to finally meet you too," I said.

Betty was a rather attractive woman with natural-looking beauty and straight, shoulder-length blonde hair. She didn't wear a lick of make-up and her enthusiasm for her family was apparent. She didn't look a day over twenty one though I'm sure she was close to my age. She reminded me a lot of Jason's mother, not how she looked, but how she carried herself. She seemed confident and natural and full of energy. I stood back and took the whole room in.

"Yes, it is too bad about the pool," she said, going back to her motherly duties. "Jason keeps telling me that he'll be fixing it and he never does. There's just not enough time in the day, you know?"

"That's for sure," I said. It was true. There was only so much time in the day, especially for goddamn housework. Jessica got on me too about not doing housework but when I finally did have a free minute in my otherwise hectic day, why the hell would I want to do housework? I'd rather be writing or watching a movie starring Edward Norton or Robert De Niro or some other Hollywood tough guy.

"Have you met our boys?" she asked. I gave Jason Jr. a little glare and he glared back. He didn't say a word, though. He just sat there eating his goddamn Apple Jacks. Betty turned around and introduced me. "Boys, this is your *Uncle* Simon." That cracked me up that she called me that, you know, *uncle*. "This is Jason Jr., our oldest boy."

Jason Jr. extended his hand to me in a young gentleman-like fashion and shook my hand politely. I was waiting for his evil cackling and his maniacal dancing and his crotch poking but he just sat there. He didn't say one goddamn dirty word. But he noticed the bandage on my palm and squeezed really hard before he let go. It hurt like hell.

"Nice to meet you, sir," he said, with the biggest bullshit-eating grin he could muster. I knew it was a bullshit-eating grin because I was the master of bullshit-eating grins. But one thing I knew for sure, he wasn't going to call me a *fucker* in front of his mom. I bet she would slap the taste out of his mouth if he did that in front of her. I could tell she would. She seemed like the disciplinarian of the house. I bet she wore the pants in the family. Jason was too lazy to wear the goddamn pants in the family.

"And this is our youngest boy, Ryan," she said, pointing to the tiny boy sitting next to Jason Jr. They both were the spitting image of Jason, the poor bastards.

"It's nice to meet you, sir," little Ryan said. He sounded like a little bird.

"And it's nice to meet *you*, Ryan." I carefully shook his hand and he continued eating his cereal as well.

"Can I get you some breakfast, Simon?" I hadn't heard sweeter words in the last twenty four hours. My stomach agreed with my brain.

"Yes, please. That would be fantastic," I said. And just like that, she started whipping up some eggs and bacon and biscuits and orange juice and the works. It was great. The school bus honked its horn out front and the boys hit the floor running. I heard them in the other side of the house gathering their goddamn school supplies and running for the door. They both yelled their goodbyes to their mother and slammed the front door as they left. Betty continued cooking my breakfast, unfazed by the ruckus. It was probably a typical morning for her, except for me being there.

"They can be such a handful, especially Jason Jr. He's such a little sparkplug." Man, was she telling the fucking truth. "I hear you have kids too, Simon. Tell me about them."

"I have two kids, a girl and a boy. Their names are Jessie and Sammie. I miss them dearly." It was true. I did miss them. I missed them and my wife more than anything.

"I bet you do," she said.

Just then, Jason made his entrance and plopped down at the table. He was ready for work, all clean and closely shaven and freshly dressed. He smelled like Old Spice, just like his dad did. Jason worked for the Civil Service down at the Air Force base. I wasn't quite sure what it was that he did but I did know that he enjoyed his work. He never, ever complained to *me* about it.

"How's it going partner? Sleep well?" he asked, slapping me on the back. He was ready to chow down. I could tell.

"Yes, sure did."

"And I see you met the wife and the kids ..."

"Yes, dear. We introduced ourselves," Betty said, placing two full plates of eggs and the works in front of us. Jason immediately started shoveling his breakfast down his throat. He must've been in a goddamn hurry, the way he was eating. I wasn't in a hurry so I ate my breakfast like a civilized human being. I told you Jason was a goddamn pig. It's true. Betty was a sweet young lady. Jason was pretty lucky to have someone who would put up with *his* shit. He was a goddamn lucky bastard.

"What do you think of the Mustang? I heard you take it out last night." He was talking with his mouth full of food. He was acting like a real pig, spitting and chewing and swallowing and picking his teeth. He was a sight to behold.

"It's an amazing car," I said.

"Sure is. What did you do last night? Go to Cinammon's Big Boobie Bonanza?" he asked, laughing all over the place like a goddamn idiot.

"No," I replied. I told you we thought alike. It was pretty fucking *scary* how we thought alike. He got a real kick out of asking me that, too, in front of his wife and all. He kept cackling all over the place, just like his demon kid. "I just went for a drive," I said.

"Right. Here's the deal, Simon. I couldn't get the day off but we have plans for tonight. You can hang around here and do what you like, relax and all. Tonight, we're going down to Mitchell's to hook up with Stanford. Do you remember Stanford?"

"Of course I remember Stanford. What's he doing these days?" Man, did that name bring back memories. Stanford was this black kid who hung out with us after school. His family lived downtown in the projects but he would stay with us after school and play. We used to hike all up and down the woods out behind the school and our neighborhood. We used to find Playboys and shit in the ditch and stashed them in our makeshift fort. We found all kinds of crazy stuff. He also witnessed my first kiss with Beth Myers, the bastard. He was one of the kids egging me on to do it. He'd take the bus home every day before it got dark so his parents wouldn't get mad. Our neighborhood was pretty far from the projects.

"He's a professor down at the community college. He teaches literature."

"Stanford? A professor?" I couldn't believe it. He was a great kid but he was dumb as a rock back then. He must have gotten his act together. His parents were both drug addicts and criminals and repeat offenders. I was certain that he would go down that same path as well. I guess he didn't, the lucky bastard.

"Yep. After you moved away, he got really smart all of a sudden. He made straight A's, aced the S.A.T., and got accepted to Harvard with an NAACP scholarship. He came back here after he graduated. He wanted to do something for the community. He's really sharp, you know."

"Sounds like it." I was really amazed. It's true. It's almost impossible to turn a kid who was dumb as a rock into a professor, especially with all the cards he had stacked against him.

"Anyway, we're meeting him at six o'clock. I'll pick you up after I get off work."

"Sounds good to me."

"Betty will keep you company. She usually does housework during the day. You know, cleaning and all. But I'm sure she'll find some time to keep you company."

"I'll probably do some writing today. I haven't had a chance to get some ideas out of my head."

"Oh, right. You're the *famous writer.* I forgot." He was kind of sarcastic about it. I could tell. But I didn't let it get to me. I was fortunate and I knew it. I didn't take my career for granted at all. Jason shoveled the last of his breakfast down his throat and jumped up to kiss Betty goodbye. "I will see you *two* later."

"Bye honey," Betty said, blowing Jason a kiss goodbye. And soon after, he was gone, slamming the door behind him. I could hear the turd-on-wheels screaming and wailing out front. It screeched off into the distance, disturbing the entire neighborhood no doubt, what, with its clanging and cloud of black smoke. Betty set the last of the dishes in the kitchen sink and wiped her hands.

"Well, I'm going to shower and get ready for my day," she said. "Make yourself at home."

"Thanks." I finished my breakfast in peace, looking out at the empty pool, soaking in the morning rays of light. It definitely felt like it was going to be a good day. It's true. With the exception of getting jabbed in the crotch by Jason's demon seed, it really did start off to be a good day. It really did.

13.

Just like Ernie the nose-picker from the airport bar back in Austin, Jason was missing the stink-covering gene in his DNA. It's true. Jason was a goddamn pig. And staying at his pig sty was kind of a no-brainer for me, as far as trying to stay clean and respectable. I mean, I kind of figured I would be in the shower *constantly* if the house was as messy as it was when he was a kid. And he didn't let me down in that department. He hadn't changed a goddamn bit. And I was positive that Betty was about fed up with his goddamn messiness by now. I mean, you usually gravitate towards people that are similar in *nature* to yourself. Take me and my wife Jessica, for example. We are both neat freaks to the point of *obsessive* behavior. We're perfect for each other. And I'm sure that Betty was prepared to deal with Jason's lifestyle being that they dated for a while before they got married. But you can only do so much to try to change someone like Jason. Being a pig is in his genes. I'm sure she got to a point where she stopped trying to fight it and just said fuck it, I'm married to a pig. I bet it's true.

After I finished my breakfast, I could just smell the stench from the goddamn couch on my arms and hands and knew I was covered with a film of filthiness. I just had to get in the shower to get it off. So I took a nice, long, hot shower and scorched the filth right off my skin. And I could hear Betty getting ready to do the female, hour-long primp session that every woman does. Every woman takes at least an hour to take a leak, take a bath, condition their hair, exfoliate their skin, wash their face, scrub their calluses, shave their legs and their pits, pluck their eyebrows, blow-dry their hair, and put on their make-up. And that's if it's a quick day. If a woman is in the throes of depression or deep contemplation, it could take up to two goddamn hours (what else could they be doing?). With this in mind, I didn't want the hot water to run out so I showered as fast as I could under the scalding water. When I was finished, I dried my hair, put on deodorant, splashed on my favorite cologne, plucked a few nose hairs and a few stray hairs on my right shoulder, popped a zit on my forehead, brushed my teeth and gargled with Listerine, trimmed my sideburns, and dashed on some talcum powder. I saved my wounded palm for last. It seemed like it wasn't healing at all and the scrape looked more like a shallow hole than a surface wound. It hurt like hell and was oozy and tender and pink. I sprayed the sore with some antiseptic and covered it with the largest band-aid I could find. Then I wrapped my towel around my waist and gathered my toiletries. I was ready to get dressed.

I figured Betty was still in her bath because I didn't hear a sound when I came out of the bathroom. I went into the living room as quick as I could and opened my suitcase on the couch. I didn't have to do too much *thinking* for the outfit because my wife packed my bag. And you know how that was. I pulled out a fresh pair of khakis and an Izod shirt, similar to the outfit I wore yesterday, and laid them neatly on the couch next to my suitcase. I found a pair of boxers and an undershirt at the bottom of my bag and when I dropped my wet towel on the floor so I could put them on, Betty came barging into the living room, dressed and primped and all. There I was, butt-naked and wet with a pair of boxer shorts in my hand, wearing nothing but my humility. And she just *stood* there, motionless except for her eyes, which (of course), beamed down right at my goddamn bare crotch. It was as if all time had stood still for an eternity and I was standing outside of myself, watching the two of us awkwardly look at each other. I was so goddamn embarrassed (it was cold, you know). As soon as I snapped out of my trance, I covered myself and my shame with my boxers.

"Oh, Simon, I'm so sorry. I had no idea that you were in here getting ready. I thought you were still in the bathroom." She seemed genuinely embarrassed, at least as far as I could tell. But she wasn't in a hurry to leave either. She just stood there, almost like she had never seen a naked man before. Her eyes continued to look in the direction of my crotch. I made sure that the boxers were at least covering all the vital parts that I didn't want her to see anymore. I didn't want my nuts and bolts hanging out all over the goddamn place.

"It's OK," I said. "I thought *you* were still in the bathroom too." She finally headed to the kitchen, without saying another word, which was my queue to get dressed as fast as possible. Man, was I embarrassed. It's not every day that a strange woman sees you naked, at least not me anyway. It's not like I'm proud of my body and want to show it to the whole goddamn world. I'm kind of pudgy, you know. I need to work on that. I put my khakis and Izod on and closed my bag and went into the kitchen to save face. I really had to. It was imperative.

Betty was standing at the counter making coffee. She didn't turn around to look at me. I guess she was embarrassed too. Probably wasn't too often that she saw a pudgy, naked guy in her living room, except for maybe Jason. I mean, he was leaner now than when I knew him as a kid but he was still kind of pudgy. I must have really caught her off guard. I had to make it right, though. I didn't want to spend the entire day in that messy house in awkward silence. That would have just driven me crazy.

"Do you feel as stupid as I do?" I asked.

"Probably more so," she said. She was putting the coffee grounds in the filter. She didn't turn her head at all.

"That was the first time someone has seen me naked besides my wife since before I got married. I hope it wasn't too *traumatizing* for you." I kind of chuckled after I said that and she giggled a bit too. The day wasn't a complete disaster yet. It's true. At least we could laugh about the whole goddamn thing.

"To be honest, I wasn't traumatized at all. Not one bit, *not at all*," she said, kind of flirtatious. And I wondered what she meant by that. I mean, I'm her husband's friend and all, not a goddamn stripper. "I'm sorry that I *unexpectedly* walked in on you. I'll announce myself next time."

"I'm sorry too. Let's start over. How's that?"

"OK."

I sat at the kitchen table and she brought me some fresh coffee. She made herself a cup and joined me at the table. We sat there for a bit, basking in the morning light, without saying a word. I felt kind of weird and all that my friend's wife had just witnessed me in all my naked glory. And she didn't seem at all *embarrassed* about it. In fact, it seemed like it brightened her morning or something. She sat there with a big, mischievous grin on her face. Anyway, it seemed like thirty minutes went silently by but I was OK with that. It's true. And it was a goddamn good cup of coffee. Jason was a lucky bastard, I tell you. Then she broke the silence.

"Do you have any plans for today?" she asked.

"Oh, I have to call my accountant about my per diem and then I was hoping to do a little writing. It's been a few days since I've put any thoughts to paper."

"That must be interesting work. Being a writer, that is. I bet you've met some pretty interesting people," she said. It was apparent that she was impressed with me. I could tell. People always seem to be impressed with my career choice. It's true. People are always envious of what other people are doing, especially if what they're doing sucks compared to what other people are doing. And I have to admit, being a writer *does not* suck. My job at TechForce, now that job sucked.

"Oh yes, I've met all kinds of interesting and famous people. Singers, actors, politicians, reporters, disc jockeys, athletes, you name it. I'm pretty fortunate."

"Name someone famous you've met recently," she asked, leaning in towards me. She was really looking at me too, what, with her big, green eyes and all. They were a pretty shade of green too.

"Hmmm, let me think." That was a tough question. My life had been so hectic up to that point that no one came to mind. Really, I was drawing a blank. "To be honest, my life has been so crazy the last six months that a name doesn't come to mind right now. I'll tell you as soon as I think of someone."

"That's OK. I'm sure you're really busy writing and signing books and doing interviews and going to movie premieres and all that. It must be so *glamorous*. I bet you travel quite a bit," she said. Her eyes kind of glazed over and I could see that she was looking into another world, one quite different than hers, one that was glamorous as hell. Then a look of disappointment appeared on her face. "Do you get to go to exotic places like Paris?"

"Paris is beautiful," I said. "It is especially beautiful in the fall, when the trees are turning and the lovers are strolling. You'd love it there."

"I imagine it *would* be beautiful. We don't travel much. We have a modest life." She truly looked disappointed like she was forced to be in the life that she chose. I started to feel kind of sorry for her and I wasn't sure why. I mean, she did live in a rundown house with rundown things. But I'm sure she knew that before marrying Jason. Besides, he was a great guy, no doubt about it. It's true. He may have been pudgy and kind of a pig but he was genuinely good. As long as I knew him, he never hurt a fly. And he never would. I knew that for sure. But her eyes began to water up and she looked away, putting her hands over her mouth as if to hold back something she shouldn't say.

"Are you all right?" I asked. She looked like she was about to start crying or something. I wasn't quite sure why but she did look that way. I wished I could blame it on my naked, pudgy body but I was sure that wasn't it. I felt like something was really wrong. I can sense that in people. It's true. Even in people that I don't know very well. I'm very perceptive that way.

"Me? Oh yes, I'm... fine."

"Are you and Jason fine? You know? Your marriage and all?" She hesitated for quite a bit, not saying a thing. I could see that she was trying to think of a diplomatic and selective way of saying the things that were rolling around in her mind. I'm also pretty sure that she knew that I might tell Jason anything that she might tell me. That was probably a big concern for her, I'm sure. That's always a concern when people are about to complain about their spouses. It's true. "Whenever Jason would write me, he always made it sound like things were great between you guys. I'm pretty sure he wouldn't try to fool me about something like that. He's pretty straightforward and all. But I guess you know that."

"Oh yes, he's quite the *straightforward* type. There's no doubt about that."

"OK then. I'm glad to hear that you two are OK. For a minute, I thought you were going to tell me something pretty personal. I mean, you looked like you *needed* to tell me something. But I guess it was nothing." She placed her hands on the table and started twiddling her thumbs around. And that goddamn disappointed look reappeared on her face. It was right there, like a mask. Or even better, it was like a fucking neon sign (that's it). Have you ever seen anybody look like that? You know, like they *really* want to tell you something but they just sit there not saying a goddamn word. That's how she looked, verbally *constipated*. It was driving me crazy. I wanted to reach across the table and strangle her, she was making me so nuts. But I didn't do a thing. I just sipped my coffee. I tried to change the subject. "This is good coffee. Is it *fresh ground*?"

And then the levee broke.

"I don't know how to say this because I don't really have anyone to talk to anymore. I mean, all my best girlfriends moved away a long time ago and I haven't made any new friends. What I'm trying to say is, I'm having a hard time finding the words to say ..." That was for goddamn sure. She was talking in circles. But I knew she really wanted to tell me something and since Jason was an old friend, I figured I'd try to help her along.

"Is everything OK?"

"Are *you* happily married?" she asked. The question hit me like a sledgehammer in the face. It really stunned me. I don't know why. It just did.

"Oh yes, I am happily married. I love my wife more than anything."

"Because, I'm not. I'm not happily married. Jason always promised me that our financial situation would get better and it never has. I think he's content to live this way. But I'm not," she said, covering her face with her hands. She was really crying up a storm too. I didn't know what to do. I placed my hand on her shoulder to try to console her.

"Jason has always told me everything was OK. He has never said a negative word about you or your marriage. I believe he truly loves you."

"I believe that too. I never said he didn't love me. I said that I'm not *happily married.*" She wiped the tears from her face and started twiddling her thumbs again. She twiddled them faster and faster the more she talked to me. I thought they were going to spin right off her hands, she was twiddling them so goddamn fast. It was distracting me. "Jason is a good person. But I've realized over the last year that we weren't meant for each other. We haven't had sex in over two years and ..."

"Have you talked to him about it?"

"No, because I know it won't do any good. I know all the answers to my questions. I know what I have to do. I just haven't done it yet."

"And what is it that you want to do?" I asked. I was really afraid to ask that question. It's true. But I asked it anyway because we had already gotten that far. I had to know even though something in me also wanted her to stop telling me these things. She was getting on a level that I didn't need to be involved with. But there I was, sipping good coffee and listening to my old friend's wife tell me that she wasn't fucking happily married. On one hand, I felt privileged that she wanted to talk to me about these things, these very *personal* things. But on the other hand, I felt like I was in the wrong place at the wrong time. I felt conflicted about giving any advice to her because I will always have loyalty towards my friend. I felt really torn and trapped.

"I want out of this marriage but I don't know how to do it," she said, lowering her voice as if someone else was around and listening. She was being really quiet and careful and all. "I don't know how to proceed. I don't just want to ask him for a divorce. I want him to *hate* me. I want him to have a *reason* to divorce me." And right then and there, I felt something on my leg. It was *that* feeling, you know, that feeling of someone's fingertips on you, on a part of you. It's an unmistakable feeling. I closed my eyes and wished that she'd disappear. It's true. I wished she'd fucking disappear. "You could help me," she said.

"Why would I want to do that?" I asked. My eyes were closed as tight as could be. I couldn't see a goddamn thing. But her hand kept moving up my leg. I could feel her nails through my khakis. They felt long and manicured and smooth. I hate to admit it but I started to get a little excited. I mean, she was an attractive lady with blonde hair and green eyes and natural beauty and all. It was hard not to feel that way, even though I didn't *want* to feel that way. But she had me in an awkward position. "Jason's my friend," I said.

"I know he is," she said. She was whispering now in a goddamn sexy voice. She was whispering really quiet like she didn't want anyone to hear her, like Jason was in the next room or something. Then her fingers reached the crotch of my khakis. She was running her finger up my zipper and I could feel her breath on my face. She must have been close. I couldn't tell. My goddamn eyes were shut tight as hell. "And I know you wouldn't want him to be in a *loveless* marriage, would you?"

"I guess not," I said. I was kind of frightened. She was making me so goddamn nervous now. I kept thinking of Jason coming home to make a vanilla Coke or to smoke a cigarette or to take a crap or something. He would do that, you know, come all the way home to do one of those things. He's a goddamn pig like that.

"We could go back in the living room. You could undress again, like you just got out of the shower." I was shaking all over the goddamn place. I was *really* that nervous. "We could act like this conversation never happened. We could do something that could get me *out* of this marriage," she said.

"And what's that?" I asked, like a goddamn idiot. I was pretty sure that I knew what she wanted. It's true.

"You know ..." And then she slipped her tongue in my ear. But right then, like a goddamn *revelation*, the doorbell rang. It rang frantically and repeatedly and loud as all hell. She pulled away and I opened my eyes. She was already out of the kitchen, answering the front door. I heard a conversation between her and a repairman, or maybe a cable man or something. I wasn't sure and I didn't care. I just wanted out of the house. I just wanted out of that goddamn place. I decided right then and there that it was time to leave.

I grabbed my wallet and my backpack off the couch and headed for the front door. Betty was talking up a storm with the cable man. She was leaning in all close to him too like a goddamn whore, what, with the way she was smiling at him and leaning on him with her hand on his waist and batting her eyes and all. But I could see that he didn't mind. I knew that this wasn't a random house call. And I knew that he wasn't a random goddamn cable man. I excused myself and walked out the door, almost shoving the cable guy to the ground. Betty called to me as I walked away, a little embarrassed at how I shoved the cable man aside. I could hear her calling my name as I walked down the street. But I didn't look back. I just walked straight ahead, like I knew where I was going, even though I had no idea where I would go.

It was kind of an unexpected goddamn thing to do, I admit. But sometimes, unexpected things lead to more unexpected things. It's true.

14.

I probably walked two or three miles before my heart finally stopped racing. Betty the whore got me pretty riled up. I mean, I was excited and nervous and confused and all sorts of disappointed. Betty was a very attractive young lady. There's no doubt about that. But I knew there must have been a *reason* why she married Jason. Don't get me wrong. Jason is a hell of a nice guy. We go way back, what, to like the second grade or something. But he is a goddamn pig and his house is full of rundown crap and he drives around in the turd-on-wheels and he's not the best looking guy in the world. There must have been something screwed up about Betty that would make her *want* to live like that. You know, because it's rare that an attractive woman would want to marry such a goddamn pig. And now I knew what it was. Betty had issues, *serious issues*. It was pretty apparent to me that she had some mental problems or something. I mean, she was fucking crazy. Did she think that I would actually go through with it? Or that I wouldn't tell Jason about her proposition? I don't know. I was pretty confused about it. Initially, I was really happy for Jason, especially when I first got to his house. I thought he was happy. And when he wrote me those letters, he sounded really happy. It was all bullshit though. I started to feel really sorry for him. I would be devastated if I found out that my Jessica was acting that way behind my back. Seriously, I think I would kill myself. She's my everything. It's true. All of my success is because of her and the kids. They inspired me to follow my dreams. I even dedicated my new novel to them. The dedication reads: *To my wife and kids - my inspiration, my everything.*

But like I said, after I walked for a while, my heart stopped racing and I was glad I was outside. It was a beautiful day, what, with the sun out and the birds singing and all that crap. The smell of pine came in on the wind from the woods surrounding the neighborhood. I decided to take a shortcut and walk through the woods. I knew a path that would take me pretty close to Gunter Air Force Base. Maybe (I thought) I could find Jason and get our evening started early. I'll have to get him pretty drunk before I tell him what a whore his wife is. It's going to break his heart. I know it. It's true.

I cut through the yard of the first house I could find, jumped the backyard fence, and took the grassy hill down to the woods. Man, talk about memories. These woods were the central location to many of my childhood adventures. I had my first fight back here. It was with Kenny Jones, that little bastard. Thinking back, he wasn't a bully or anything like that. He was actually a scrawny little fuck who annoyed people more than anything. He'd taunt you with his whining and his buckteeth and his tongue-wagging and his red hair and freckles. He was really *annoy*ing. I remember riding my bike through the woods to get home after school one day. And he and a small group of his friends were standing out here making little bonfires with Kenny's dad's Zippo lighter and a can of lighter fluid. As I rode by, he started taunting me about little blonde Patty Green. He had his suspicions about me liking her since I never joined in on the taunting she received from the other kids at her birthday party. I never bought into the whore-teasing she got. I *really* did like her. But Kenny started taunting me about it in the woods (Simon and Patty sittin' in a tree, etc.). That scrawny fuck started wagging his tongue at me, yelling that I was in love with Patty and that she was a whore and all. And I just felt the rage build inside of my little heart. My little heart just couldn't take it, especially not from a scrawny fuck like Kenny Jones. So I hopped off my bike and let him have it. The fight didn't last too long. It was one of those kicked-in-the-balls kind of affairs. I gave him a swift kick in the nuts and he toppled over his bike and laid there on the ground. That was it. It was over in less than five seconds. But my dignity and Patty's honor was saved in that eternal five seconds. I was really quite happy about that. And his friends just stood there in awe. They didn't do a goddamn thing. Kenny showed up to school with the goofiest limp the next day. And he got a real lashing when the other kids found out what had happened in the woods. He didn't taunt me much after that. And Patty never found out what I did for her. It's a goddamn shame.

And it's memories like that that I don't want to ruin by finding out if that was little blonde Patty Green working at Cinammon's Big Boobie Bonanza. The fact that she might actually be as whorish as the kids said she was would just ruin these memories for me. And sometimes, especially when I'm by myself, these memories are all I have, even if I didn't dust them off and let them out too often. I walked past the spot where I kicked Kenny in the nuts. There wasn't a single sign of our incident: no burn marks, no rumpled grass, no tire tracks from our bikes, nothing. There wasn't one goddamn sign of that incident, just my memory of it. That was a shame too. They should have built a memorial here for that fight. It changed my life.

Before I knew it, I was at the end of the woods and I could see Gunter Air Force Base in the distance. It wasn't too far away, maybe a mile or so. I continued to huff it. I was enjoying the weather so much that I didn't even notice how far I had walked, maybe ten miles or so. What was another goddamn mile after walking ten miles or so? I jaywalked across the main boulevard and headed into another neighborhood that surrounded the entrance to the air force base. It was called Montgomery Manors. I had another friend in the seventh grade who lived in this part of town, good old Tony Boland. We used to call him Tony the Loverboy. He was a really smooth cat, real good-looking and all. All the *girls* liked him. He was one of *those* guys. Everyone knew one of those guys when they were young. You know, the kind that all the girls liked. Well, Tony was the Loverboy in our group. He looked like a god next to the rest of us pudgy dip-shits.

Anyway, I walked past the street Loverboy Tony lived on. He had this girlfriend named Leslie and she lived next door to Tony's house. She was a cute little thing with brown hair and blue eyes and twenty-year-old tits on a twelve-year-old's body. She looked well beyond her years to us other twelve-year-olds. All the kids would say she looked *older*, like that was something special. She *did* look pretty mature for a twelve-year-old. And she was in love with our Loverboy Tony. Tony used to tell me how he'd sneak into her house late at night and they would do *it*. That's how he'd say it to me: *we did it last night.* And I would always ask him to tell me just exactly what they *did* in her room. I was so clueless back then. I had no idea what he was talking about. But the thing was, Tony was pretty clueless too; I just didn't know it at the time. So, one day he told me to spend the night over at his house and he'd tell me *exactly* what they did. So I packed my bags and my mom dropped me off at his house after school. And this is what we did.

Tony's room was upstairs so we'd stock up on a bunch of supplies like cream soda and Twinkies and make a camp in his room. He had this huge pop-up tent and we'd get inside and lay our sleeping bags out and pile up all our junk food in between us. Tony played the Prince album *1999* on his record player. He loved the song *Little Red Corvette*. That Prince guy seemed like a dirty little bastard and Tony said his music got him all riled up and excited. He then told me how he'd sneak into Leslie's room really late at night and they'd listen to Prince music and take off all their clothes and do it. When I asked him to tell me exactly what they were *doing*, he told me he was sticking his *thing* in her *thing*. Since I was pretty fucking clueless, I had no mental image to compare this information to. I mean, I knew what my *thing* was but I didn't know what a girl's thing was. And Tony wasn't much help in the description-department. He just kept telling me how it was nice and warm and comforting and that it was near her butt. But what *did* help with my mental image were all those Playboys we found in the ditch behind our school. Tony had a few of them stashed under his bed and he pulled them out and used them as a diagram for his story. He'd point to the grown women's parts and correlate them with Leslie's little girl parts. He tried to explain how Leslie's thing was exactly the same as the lady in the picture except Leslie's was smaller and *not as hairy*. That confused me even more, the not as hairy part. And that's all he told me about doing *it*. I didn't know anymore than I did before I spent the night. But I did have this respect for Tony that I didn't have before. He had gone where only grown men had gone and I thought he was the *cooler* for it. I really looked up to him. Leslie called him on the phone later that night and he slipped out the window and didn't come back until the next morning. I stayed in his room by myself, eating Twinkies and listening to Prince for the rest of the night.

A couple of weeks later, Tony's dad called my mom and asked her to bring me to his house. He said he needed to talk to the both of us. When we got there, he told us that Leslie was pregnant and that her and Tony had run away. He wanted to know if I knew *where* they were. And of course, I didn't. But he was really torn up about it and was sad that his son had gotten a girl pregnant while he was in the *seventh* grade. The police eventually found Tony and Leslie. They had broken into her uncle's house on the other side of town and were living there, pretending they were married. Tony's dad eventually sent him to a military school in Atlanta. And Leslie's parents made her get an abortion and sent her to a Catholic girls school in Birmingham. I never saw Tony again after that. My mother assumed that I was doing the same thing Tony was doing until I convinced her that I didn't even have a girlfriend to do that with. She knew that was true. I was into comic books and my BMX bicycle more than girls at the time. I was such a dork in the seventh grade. I didn't become interested in girls until the summer *after* the seventh grade when I met Valerie and discovered fondling. But I would remain a virgin until I was seventeen because of all of this. The thought of getting a girl pregnant at that age was horrifying to me. It's true.

I eventually found myself at the gate to the air force base (time flew by). I had no idea where Jason worked so I asked the guard at the gate if he knew him. He said he didn't. The guard was a real fucking genius, I tell you. He was this big oaf with a crew-cut and an M.P. uniform and chewing tobacco lodged in his teeth. I didn't want to piss him off, though. He was *armed*, you know.

"Are you sure you don't know him? You must see him every day when he drives through this gate?" I asked.

"What kind of car does he drive? I nice one or a clunker?"

"A real clunker. He drives a beat-up Chevette that kicks and screams all over the place." He must have notice that turd-on-wheels. You can't miss the piece of shit.

"Oh yes. I do know who you're talking about. Does he work for Civil Service?"

"That's right. He works for Civil Service."

"I'll get someone to give you a lift. Just sign this visitors sheet."

I signed the visitors sheet and another M.P. gave me a lift in one of those military Jeeps. He was a real fucking genius too. He looked just like Gomer Pyle and had that same way of talking, real slow and all. He kept asking me questions on the way over to Jason's building like he was interrogating me or something. It was getting on my nerves.

"What do you do for a living?" he asked, all loud and slow and annoying as hell. He had to talk loud because the Jeep was a convertible. He had to fight the sound of the wind and fighter planes flying all over the goddamn place.

"I'm a writer. My new novel, THE RISE AND FALL OF A TITAN, will be published in the next few weeks."

"Really? I always wanted to be a writer ..." Thankfully, before he could finish, we reached the building and I hopped out of the Jeep so fast that I forgot to ask Gomer for directions. I just shot in the building and asked the first guy I saw if he knew who Jason was. He did and he took me to his office. The building smelled like all the other government buildings I'd been in: stale and musty and old. Jason was sitting behind his desk not looking particularly busy or anything. He was pretty surprised to see me.

"What are you doing here? Is something wrong?" he asked. He was pretty smart, you know. We thought a lot alike.

"No, nothing's wrong. I just decided to go for a walk and I ended up here."

"You walked all the way down *here* from my house? Are you crazy?"

"I guess so."

I told him how I was walking down memory lane and he understood. He told me he did that a lot too, walk down memory lane that is. You can get pretty distracted walking down memory lane. I got so distracted that I walked fifteen goddamn miles. When you think about it, that's a pretty long ways. And my feet were sore as hell. They were throbbing like crazy. Walking that far was pretty stupid. It's true.

15.

After sitting in Jason's office for an hour, I still couldn't figure out what he did for a living. I mean, it didn't seem like he really did *anything* in particular. He focused *all* of his energy on a game of Solitaire on his computer. He was pretty goddamn good too; he'd win every other game or so. When actual work finally did come in for him to do, in the form of an e-mail request, he'd slam his fists on his desk and yell about goddamn this and that fucker that. He really hated when his boss would interrupt his game with *actual* work. Jason was such a lazy goddamn pig. It's true. But in a way, I understood. When I was employed by TechForce, I avoided actual work as much as possible. It's not hard to do, you know. I would just do the absolute minimum to get by. The rest of the time, I was writing my novel, THE RISE AND FALL OF A TITAN. In fact, the titan that I referred to in the title of my book was the former C.E.O. from TechForce: Mr. Hans Fitzsimmons. But I'll get to that later.

So actually, I understood why Jason liked his job so much since he could play Solitaire all day long. And I understood Jason's hatred towards his actual work. I hated to work too. That's why I followed my dreams and became a writer, because I hated to work eight to five for someone like Mr. Folsom and his goddamn lazy eye and Hans Fitzsimmons and his goddamn embezzling. It just made me sick. It's true. But watching Jason play Solitaire for hours made me sick too. I mean, you can watch someone else play video games for only so long. After a while, it gets pretty goddamn boring, especially if they are making plays you wouldn't make. Jason was pretty good at Solitaire; it was obvious he played it all the time. But he also made a lot of stupid moves. He must have had the game set to an easy level. The computer was pretty forgiving to his stupid moves. And his stupid moves were driving me crazy. But that was one thing we had in common: a love for video games. I've watched Jason make millions of stupid moves playing hundreds of stupid games.

"Hey Jason, remember that video game system you had when we were kids? The one we played Donkey Kong on?" I asked.

"The ColecoVision?"

"Yeah, that's it. The ColecoVision. That thing was great. Remember how we'd play Donkey Kong for hours on end?" I asked.

"Because we thought we could get to the end of the game, right? Even though there wasn't an end?"

"That's right. We must have wasted thousands of hours on that game trying to get to an end that was never there." It's true. We must have literally played thousands of hours of video games. We were both pretty lazy kids. When our other friends were outside playing soccer or little league baseball, we were inside playing goddamn video games. Maybe that's why we were so pudgy, drinking all of those vanilla Cokes and playing video games and exerting about one calorie every hour. I mean, we were at least moving our thumbs pressing the controller. But besides that, we were pretty sedentary. It's true. "Hey Jason?"

"Yeah?" He didn't even look at me. He was mesmerized by that goddamn computer game.

"Do you think there is any way you could leave early today?"

"Why? What's the rush?"

"I know you're really busy here at work but I kind of need to talk to you about something."

"What do you need to talk about? I thought you said nothing was wrong earlier?" he asked. I'm telling you, Jason was a goddamn genius. He knew me all too well.

"You're right. I did say nothing was wrong earlier. But I still need to talk to you about *something*."

"What is it?"

"I'd rather tell you somewhere else. You know, over drinks and all." Like I said, I was going to have to get him nice and drunk before I told him what a goddamn whore his wife was. I just knew that it would break his heart.

"All right. Let me go talk to my boss. He usually isn't so generous, though. I'm just warning you now. We may have to sit here until five."

"OK. But five is only a couple of hours away. Tell him you haven't seen me in *years*. Tell him we're trying to catch up. Ask him to be generous for once. Tell him you'll make it up by coming in early one day." Jason looked pretty nervous about talking to his boss but he went anyway. I was pretty proud of him for that especially since he was glued to his game of Solitaire. I'm telling you, video games are as addictive as crack. Once you're hooked, you're done for. Your normal life is done for. And if there is any way you can play video games at work, then your work is done for. It's true.

Jason came back shortly after with a big shit-eating grin. But it was a sincere shit-eating grin, I could tell. My pep talk must have worked.

"I can't *believe* it," he said, smiling from ear to ear. "He *is* being generous today. He never lets me off early. Even when Jason Jr. was sick and Betty had to take him to the hospital, my boss made me finish out my shift."

"But sometimes you never know if you're going to get something unless you ask for it."

"I guess so. I guess so." Jason shut down his computer, reluctantly exiting from his Solitaire game, and compiled a bunch of paper work orders. He reminded me to grab my backpack and I followed him into the office next door. He dropped the work orders on his coworker's desk. He dropped them like they were cancer-riddled. His coworker was entrenched in his own game of Solitaire and was pretty pissed off that Jason interrupted him.

"Hey man! Can't you see I'm working here?!" his coworker said. He was really pissed off. It was hilarious.

"The boss said I could take off early," Jason told him. I was really proud of him for being so strong.

"What? Let you off early? What the fuck?!"

"I guess he's being generous today." Jason smiled and walked out of the office. I followed right behind him. The coworker was livid. He was screaming about having to do Jason's work or some other bullshit about how he was *busy*. But I knew that he was mad because he had to actually work now. Everyone hated actually working. But Jason never looked back. It must have been some kind of defining moment for him. He walked out of that building as proud as a peacock. It's true. He was strutting like a goddamn peacock. It was great.

"I can't believe I have the day off early. It's going to be a great day after all," he said. Man, I was really feeling sorry for Jason now. Especially since I was going to be telling him about his whore wife. I felt bad for instigating the whole thing, leaving work early that is. I hate to be the one to ruin someone's day. I thought I was doing a good thing by having him leave early but I realized it was going to be all in vain. I didn't say anything though. I let him bask in his glory uninterrupted.

We hopped in the turd-on-wheels and Jason accelerated the poor car as fast as it could go. He was really excited about being off work. The car shook and screamed as he shifted gears, pushing the car to its limits. We left the guard at the security gate behind in a cloud of black, putrid smoke and carbon monoxide.

"It's so great to be off!" Jason said. He was happy as a fucking clam. "This calls for a celebration. The first round of drinks are on me."

"You're on," I said, smiling at what a fantastic idea that was.

"What did you want to talk to me about?"

"I'll tell you at Mitchell's." Mitchell's was this well-known hole-in-the-wall bar right outside of the air force base. Everyone in town knew about Mitchell's. Not only was it a hangout for the personnel of the base, it was the watering hole for this part of town. Even when I was a kid, I remember seeing the parking lot completely full every time we drove by. Everyone who drank booze in this part of town hung out at Mitchell's at one point or another. It was one of *those* kind places.

"OK. But don't forget to tell me. Stanford won't be there until five thirty so we'll just have to get started without him."

And that's where we left it. We headed for Mitchell's with a black cloud behind us and enthusiasm in our hearts. I felt bad about what I was going to tell him once we got to Mitchell's and got greased up a bit on some booze. But I also felt a little excited because Jason was excited to be off work. He kept going on and on about how his luck might be changing and all that kind of shit. It's hard not to feel excited when you are around someone else who is excited. It's pretty goddamn contagious, if you ask me. If you don't get excited around someone else who is excited, you must be a pretty sad bastard. It's true. You probably have a hard piece of coal for a heart.

Anyway, we promptly arrived at Mitchell's since it wasn't too far from the base. The parking lot was full just like it was when I was a kid. We had a hard time finding a spot, it was so goddamn full. Jason ended up driving over a curb and parking in some grass behind the building. When he went over the curb, the bottom of the car scraped on the cement. I thought the goddamn axle and muffler were going to fall off. But I don't think Jason cared much since he had a nicer ride at home. You know, the beast Mustang he had in the garage. The only reason he held onto the turd-on-wheels was, I think, because it had some sentimental value with his mother. I can't really say for sure, because I wouldn't drive a piece of shit like that no matter how much my mother would have liked it, but I think that had something to do with it. She drove us around everywhere in that car. It was hard not to think about her when we were in it. He put the turd-on-wheels to rest and we went for the entrance.

"This place hasn't changed at all in years," he said, fixing his hair with his hands. For such a goddamn pig, he sure was concerned about his hair looking nice.

"Really? I've never been here."

"After we get our drinks, go check out what's hanging above the bathroom doors. It'll depress the hell out of you. Trust me."

Once inside, it was obvious that Jason was right about the place. It seemed kind of frozen in time, what, being that it smelled damp and musty and everything was solid wood: the floors, the bar, the walls, the tables and chairs, the bar stools, everything. It seemed cavernous and quaint at the same time, probably because of the high ceilings. But the place was absolutely packed. And all types were there in the smoke-filled room: soldiers, locals, men, women, all ages, all drunk. Some of the patrons were playing pool while others watched or played darts. But no matter what the different patrons were doing, they were all drinking and smoking. It seemed like everyone was *smoking* except for me. And a part of me thought that was a goddamn shame.

Jason pointed to the only empty table and I went for it. Pretty soon, he arrived with a pitcher of beer and an ashtray. I knew he was going to start sucking down the cigarettes. And I was going to be right there with him sucking up all of his second-hand smoke. I was looking forward to it.

"Go check out the bathroom, like I told you. I'll start pouring the beers."

He pointed to the back corner of the building and I made my way there, carefully stepping between groups chit-chatting and drinking their cares away. I noticed the only modernization in the place was some video games over by the pool tables. But even those weren't as modern as they should be. They were all games from the early eighties, my childhood heyday. They had a couple of pinball machines, an Asteroids machine, a Pac-Man machine, and lo and behold, a goddamn Donkey Kong machine. I knew, before the end of the evening, that I would be spending some time getting reacquainted with that game. Man, did that game bring back memories. I even counted how many dollar bills I had for quarters, just to be ready.

The bathroom had a long line but I didn't care. I wasn't there to use the can. I got in line and waited to advance towards the doors. On the walls were literally hundreds of photos of this guy Mitchell standing next to various celebrities. I figured it was the same Mitchell that owned the bar. And he must have been pretty old now, if not dead, because all of the celebrities were pretty goddamn old themselves. There was a picture with him and Bob Hope, another with George Burns, another with some lady who kind of looked like Marilyn Monroe. It was all pretty creepy and old and antiquated. I started thinking about death and it was depressing the hell out of me. I decided I wasn't going to look at the pictures anymore. I looked straight ahead as I moved towards the bathroom doors. And then I noticed what Jason was talking about. Right above the doors, right below the Ladies and Gentlemen signs, were two small signs. They said: *Whites Only*. I couldn't believe it. Really, I couldn't fucking believe it. I found myself staring at the signs, locked onto the historical significance of it all. Until I was rudely interrupted by the guy standing behind me.

"Pretty crazy, huh?" the guy asked. He was tall and lanky and all sorts of drunk. His alcohol-soaked breath fell on me like a stinking dense fog.

"Yes, it sure is." I didn't want to go into it too much because I didn't want to start a conversation with the guy. I mean, his breath smelled of death and I didn't know how long I could take it.

"You know why they kept those signs there, right?" he asked. I shook my head, not saying a word, trying to hold my breath so his stench wouldn't float toward my nostrils. "The owners wanted to remind people about just how far we've come from the past. It's a pretty powerful statement, you know?" I didn't know what he meant. To me, it seemed like a blatant sign of disrespect towards African-Americans. The stinky guy didn't seem to think so. "It takes a lot of courage to stare at the *ugly* truths of our past, doesn't it?"

"I guess so." I walked away without saying another word. The guy was getting on my nerves, what, with his stinking breath and know-it-all attitude. I wanted to be in friendlier company. I didn't want to be standing in line for the can talking to some stinky-breathed freak and wasting all my time. I had to think of a way to give the news to Jason about his whore wife. I didn't want to think about segregation and white-only bathrooms and all of that shit. That was the topic of conversation for television talk shows and documentaries, not standing in line for the crapper. I quickly made my way back to the table.

"Pretty crazy, huh? You know, the signs and all?" Jason asked. He had poured two beers while I was gone and I was grateful.

"Yeah, yeah." I grabbed my beer and took a big swig. My heart was starting to feel really heavy, what, with all I was going to have to tell him about his whore wife. I wasn't sure I could go through with it. I mean, I didn't want to necessarily be the catalyst to the end of his marriage. I wasn't sure I wanted that kind of responsibility on my shoulders.

"Are you sure you're all right? You're acting kind of funny. Does this have anything to do with what you wanted to talk to me about?"

"Kind of," I said. My heart rose into my throat. I could feel a big lump there in my neck and I was having a pretty hard time breathing and all. I almost felt like I was gasping for air or something.

"OK. Well, just belt it out. Tell me."

I took another big gulp of my beer and went for it.

"Are you and Betty all right?" I asked. He just looked at me kind of puzzled and all. It felt like I was gasping for air all over the place like an idiot.

"What do you mean?"

"You know, are you guys *OK*?" Jason looked a little relieved after I asked a second time. It looked like a goddamn boulder had been lifted off his shoulders.

"You can tell, huh? You can tell that I've been feeling down?" That was an unexpected answer but I accepted it. Anything was better than *me* having to tell him what a whore his wife was. It's true. I wasn't sure I was up to it anymore.

"Sure Jason. I can tell." I was pretty fucking clueless actually. He seemed like the same old Jason to me with his vanilla Cokes and his rundown house and all. I didn't know what to say. "Why don't *you* tell me what's wrong then."

Jason lit a cigarette and topped off our pints of beer with the last of the pitcher. I could see that his thoughts were rattling around in his head. He took a long drag off his smoke and dropped his head to the table. I thought about how heavy his heart must have been feeling. It must have been feeling a lot heavier than mine. For a brief moment, I felt sorry that I had dragged him out of work early. I really thought that I was doing the right thing. I wasn't trying to break his heart. It just seemed like it might already be broken. And that just made my heart feel heavier. He and I were definitely two sad bastards. It's true. We had heavy hearts plus we were out of beer.

"Hey, before you tell me, I want you to try something. When the bartender looks over at us, wave your finger like this." Jason lifted his head and I showed him how Ernie the nose-picking barfly from the airport bar waved at the bartender for another drink. "I want to see if he'll bring us another pitcher without us having to *tell* him what we want."

And when the bartender looked over at us, Jason waved his finger at him like I showed him. And wouldn't you know it, the bartender turned around and poured another goddamn pitcher for us. And it was the right brand too. Maybe we weren't two sad bastards after all. Maybe our luck *was* getting better.

16.

The bartender promptly sent a waitress with the fresh pitcher of beer to our table. She delivered it with two chilled glasses and a sweet smile.

"Anything else I can get for you, gentlemen?" she asked. I was amazed. This was a professional goddamn establishment. I guess that's why it's been around for so long. But I wasn't going to make the same mistake I did last time. No matter what, I was going to leave a *tip*, at least fifteen percent, no fooling around this time. The last thing I needed was revenge from a disgruntled waitress or bartender, again.

"No ma'am. Thank you," I said. She flashed us another sweet smile and went to the next table with the same quality of fine service. "Man, this place is great. They really know how to treat their customers." I started to pour the next round when I realized that I was getting off track. Jason sat across from me, his heart heavier than before. His head laid on the table as if pinned under a boulder of sadness. "Jason? I'm sorry I got off the subject. Are you going to tell me now?"

"I guess so." Jason lifted his head and lit another cigarette. He had blazed his way through half a goddamn pack since we arrived. He was really smoking them up. He must have been sadder than I thought. "Let me collect my thoughts."

"OK. Take as much time as you need." Jason took a long drag off his cigarette and contemplated what he was going to say. So *I* contemplated what I was going to say at the reading in New York in the next few days. I was thinking about giving some background of my former employer and C.E.O. of TechForce, Mr. Hans Fitzsimmons, before I read passages from my book. I thought that a brief summary of his misdeeds might give a little more weight to the selected passage, especially considering that I wasn't going to be reading the entire goddamn book. You see, Mr. Fitzsimmons embezzled millions from TechForce by taking out personal loans and then rewriting the accounting books to show the loans as capital investments. Supposedly, he was giving the C.F.O., Mrs. Gretta Jackson, the wiener-schnitzel-express during his lunches at a nearby Motel 6, thus giving him unfettered access to the accounting books. But I'll go into more detail about that later.

"OK. I'm ready," Jason said, lighting another cigarette. I was getting the full-on secondhand smoke experience. I might as well have been blazing down the cigarettes too. We were sitting in a cloud of yellow nicotine smoke. It was great.

"OK. Shoot," I said.

"I think Betty is having an affair," he said. And just when I thought that Jason didn't get it, he turned around and exposed himself as the fucking genius that he was. I mean, he was a pig and all but he was very sharp. Nothing got by him. It's true.

"Are you sure?" I asked. I really played it up too. I acted surprised and hurt and shocked and all. He had no idea that I knew just how much of a whore his wife really was.

"I'm pretty sure. I'm not exactly sure *who* she's having an affair with, but I know something is going on. And I know it's going on in my house when I'm at work." Jason was a goddamn Sherlock Holmes, that's for sure. But I'll give him some credit when credit's due. He was smart enough to put two and two together. I mean, it was pretty goddamn obvious to *me* that she wasn't faithful to him. But most people in the world don't care enough to notice that kind of shit about their spouses. Most people don't *care* at all. It's true.

"Do you think it's someone that you know? Or do you think it's someone random, like the cable man or something?" Jason's mind went into overdrive mulling over new scenarios and culprits he never thought of before. Maybe I was giving away too much information. But as long as I didn't have to tell him anything and he could figure it out by himself, I was OK with it. I mean, how would you like to tell your best friend that his / her spouse wanted to sleep with you so their marriage would fall apart?

"You know, we do have some *new* cable services that I never authorized. Maybe that means something now that I think about it. What do you think?" he asked. Right then and there, I decided that I wasn't going to say a goddamn word about what Betty said to me. I wasn't going to say anything about how she saw me naked, how she touched my zipper and asked me to have sex with her, how she stuck her tongue in my ear, or how she wanted to destroy her own marriage. I realized that I didn't have to anymore, what, with the cable man being a new suspect and all. It was beautiful. A big burden was lifted off my shoulders. "I'll have to ask my neighbors if they've seen the cable truck around lately during the day. I'll ask Mrs. Burke. She's always home during the day, watering her flowers and all. Goddamn it! I can't believe this is happening."

"Good idea. I'd pursue it if I was you. If I had any suspicions that my Jessica was cheating on me, I'd pursue it. You have to. It's your obligation."

"Has your wife ever done anything like this?"

"No, never. We have a good, solid relationship built on trust and honesty." It's true. We did have a good relationship. It was everything I wanted it to be. Jessica was my best friend. I've never had any doubts about her commitment to me.

"Good for you, Simon." Jason looked pretty goddamn depressed. He was gulping down his beer and smoking his cigarettes like they were going to be illegal tomorrow and he wouldn't be able to have them, like tonight was it. So he was drinking and smoking like a madman. I really felt sorry for him. I really did. It was really awful being in a position like mine. I mean, I felt like such a goddamn liar. It's true.

"Do you know what you need? You need a vacation." I wasn't sure where I was going with that but I went with it. He was depressing the hell out of me with his drinking and smoking and moping all over the goddamn place.

"A vacation? Doesn't seem like a good time to do *that*."

"Why don't you come with me to New York," I said. And that was it, my solution. It was perfect. "Listen, I need someone to help me out and you need a vacation. Why don't you come with me? I'll make sure the publishing company pays for everything. I'll tell them it's a business need. They'll go for it." I'm telling you, I was a fucking genius.

"Really?" he asked.

"Yes, really. Please come. It would be great. Plus, you would be helping me out. I'm sure you could really use the time away to think about your situation without any interference."

"I don't know. I don't know what Betty would say ..." You really have to keep your eye on Jason. Otherwise, he can get off track so easily.

"It'll only be a few days. Be a man, tell her you *want* to go. Plus, she'll have some time to be with her cable man."

"Hey!" That really pissed him off but I was trying to be light about the situation. Nothing helps mend a broken heart more than a little humor. It's true.

"I'm just kidding. So, are you in?" I could see that he was really debating about the whole idea in his head. I imagined his head space to look like his living space: *cluttered and rundown and messy.* "Come on. You can tell her when we get home and we'll leave tomorrow. You don't have to work on Saturdays, do you? The plane leaves around noon. But you have to let me know soon so I can call the airline in the morning to get you a seat."

"I don't know ..." He was starting to drive me crazy with his indecision. I wanted to slap him across the face.

"You're going," I said. Someone had to be a man about it. I guess I was the one wearing the pants.

"All right. I'm going," he said and thank God. I was about to tell him to fucking forget it. I almost did. He was driving me crazy.

"Then it's settled. We'll pack tonight and leave in the morning. Don't worry about a thing. I'll take care of everything."

"Thanks Simon." He looked really happy, like the boulder of sadness had been lifted. It was the least I could do, especially considering how close I was to sleeping with Betty. Like I said, she got me pretty excited. And she was an attractive young lady. It's true. I know I didn't mention it before but the goddamn guilt was getting to me. I had to get it off my chest.

Anyway, about this time, good ol' Stanford walked into the place and Jason started whooping and hollering like a goddamn idiot. It was pretty embarrassing. Everyone in that place was looking at us like we had just taken a crap on the table and were dancing in it or something. Jason was the kind of person to do that, whooping and hollering all over the place. I was a little more subdued than that; it wasn't my style. But Jason didn't care what people thought. I mean, he was a goddamn pig, you know? He obviously didn't care. Plus, he was really getting tanked from the beer. We were going to have to order another pitcher soon.

"Hey Simon? Stanford's here."

"I noticed," I said, my sarcasm definitely coming through. To be quite honest, I didn't really care for Stanford all that much. I know I said we were friends when we were kids and all but I didn't like him anymore. As far as I was concerned, he was a goddamn thief. And when Jason first told me that we were going to see him, I wasn't all *that* excited. It's true.

"You still aren't holding a grudge, are you?" Jason asked.

Damn straight I was still holding a goddamn grudge. All right, I'll just come out and say it. One day after school, the three of us were hiking in the woods behind our school. We were playing like we were Green Berets or something, running through the woods, making camps and climbing trees, destroying enemy training grounds. It was great. We always had a good time together. It's true. But for the first time, Stanford asked if he could go back to my house and call his parents. For some reason, he wanted them to come get him instead of riding the goddamn bus home. So I decided, what the hell, that he was my friend and that he could come home with me. I thought it would also be nice for my parents to finally meet him since Jason and I had talked about him so much. So he walked home with me. We waved goodbye to Jason when he went to his house and Stanford followed me home. I introduced him to my parents and they asked him to stay for dinner (which he gladly did). He called his parents and gave them directions to my house. They told him they'd be there in an hour. While we waited to eat, I took him to my room and showed him my prized comic book collection. I had been collecting Spider-Man comics for years and had a pretty nice collection. Stanford loved Spider-Man too and was in awe of the immense collection I had put together. He couldn't keep his goddamn hands off my Amazing Spider-Man number six, the most valuable one in my collection. He kept looking at it and turning it over and over, checking out the front and the back. I told him that he couldn't open it because I was saving it for its collectible value. But he wouldn't put it down, even when I asked him to. He just kept saying how neat it was and how neat my collection was and how poor his goddamn family was and how he couldn't afford to collect comics. I really felt sorry for him. I really did. But I wasn't going to let him *read* that comic; it was too valuable to me.

So then my mom called us into the dining room and we ate dinner. Stanford stuffed his face like he hadn't eaten in seven days or something. He was shoveling everything into his goddamn mouth like he was a starving kid from Africa. It was unbelievable. My dad even noticed when his usual portion was a little smaller than usual. And while we were eating, Stanford's parents parked out front and honked their horn so he would come out. Stanford fed us some bullshit about how his parents were too embarrassed to meet my parents because they were poor and that he had to run to my room really quick because he forgot something. And after a quick thank you, he was gone. And so was my Amazing Spider-Man number six. I noticed it was gone later that night when I went to put my collection back in the closet. That thieving bastard had taken my most prized possession. And even though I didn't actually see him take it, I knew he took it. He couldn't keep his goddamn hands off it. I confronted him about it the next day but (of course) he denied it. And I didn't know how to get to his house so I could go look for it. That was the first time I had experienced heartbreak. It's true. Of course, our friendship dissolved soon after even though Jason tried to keep it alive. Jason didn't believe that Stanford would steal something of ours. That's always been a major disagreement between the two of us. So if you ask me if I still hold a grudge, then the answer is *hell yes*.

"Yes, I still hold a grudge."

"Over a stupid comic book?" he asked.

"Do you know what that comic would be worth today? I should probably ask Stanford. I bet he'll know."

Stanford greeted Jason with a handshake and a hug. He looked just like he did when he was a kid, except that he was taller and had a mustache. He was still skinny as hell and he wore these oversized glasses that looked too goddamn big for his head. But most importantly, he still wore a bowtie. He used to complain that his parents made him wear it but he obviously liked wearing one since he was *still* wearing one. What a goddamn liar, and a thief too. He then turned to greet me. He stuck out his hand as if nothing had ever happened when we were kids.

"Well, if it isn't Simon Burchwood. How have you been?" he asked, grinning from ear to ear. He was a good bullshitter, I could tell. He was giving me the biggest shit-eating grin he could muster.

"I'm fine, Stanford." I gave him the biggest shit-eating grin I could muster in return. He was such a sucker. He couldn't tell that I was still mad at him but I was. It's true.

Jason directed us to sit down and he waved the magic finger at the bartender for another pitcher of beer and three fresh glasses. When the waitress brought them over, she asked us if we wanted anything else and Jason asked her for a pack of smokes. He was smoking up a storm. It was really unbelievable. He must have been pretty drunk or something. He was acting all loopy and goofy and kind of drooling on himself. Jason gets that way when he gets drunk. It's pretty goddamn embarrassing. Stanford kept staring at me through his big goddamn glasses.

"It's really nice to see you, Simon. I hear you're a famous writer now."

"Yes, that's true. My new novel, THE RISE AND FALL OF A TITAN, will be published in the next few weeks. They say I'm going to be the next John Kennedy Toole, except that I'll live to see the day that my novel is published, of course."

"That's fantastic. You know, I teach literature down at the community college. You should come down and talk to my students. Maybe read some of your work and give them some advice on writing for a living." He kept grinning from ear to ear and beaming at me with his goddamn Coke-bottle glasses. He was looking at me like nothing ever happened when we were kids, like we never had a falling out. It was unbelievable.

"The only advice I can give is to not take any advice. They are going to write if they want to and fail if they want. Besides, I'm leaving for New York tomorrow. I won't have the time to stop by to give a lecture." I was really starting to boil under the collar. In fact, I was livid. And his staring made it worse, like he knew that I knew that he took my Amazing Spider-Man number six. I really wanted to grab him by his scrawny throat and give him a good choke.

"That's OK. Maybe next time. Say boys, what are we drinking?"

"We're drinking beer. What does it look like?" I said.

Jason noticed how quickly my tone had changed and he was giving me the crook-eye. But I didn't give him the pleasure of returning his crook-eye. Just the thought of what happened to the Spider-Man number six was making me boil. It's true. Eventually, Stanford got it in his thick head that I wasn't too pleased with his visit.

"Simon, I get the feeling that something's bothering you? Are you upset with me?" Stanford asked. Can you believe it? He had some goddamn nerve, I tell you.

"Yeah Simon, is something wrong?" Jason asked. And with the look of concern on his face, I didn't want to let him down. So I folded my cards. Even though I really didn't want to let go of my Spider-Man number six, I finally decided it was time to let it go.

"No, I'm all right. I just need a breath of fresh air or something. Maybe I should step outside."

"You want me to go with you?" Jason asked.

"No, I'll be OK." I got up and left the goddamn thief and Jason at the table. I stepped outside for a breath of fresh air and to cool off. It was a nice, chilly evening and there wasn't a cloud in the sky. I could see the moon, big like a glowing basketball, hanging low behind the tall pine trees that surrounded the parking lot. I took a few deep breaths of the cool air. It rejuvenated me. I clapped my hands together and started reciting my mantra: *It's over. It's over. It's over. It's over.* I decided to go back inside and join the others. I sat down like nothing had happened and took a swig of my beer.

"I'm glad you could join us again," Stanford said. He was really egging me on too, what, with that goddamn grin and his big glasses and his goddamn bowtie. Even though I had calmed down, I still wanted to punch him in the face. "I hope there are no hard feelings between us."

"Oh, you mean over *my* Amazing Spider-Man number six?" I'm telling the truth when I say that I really didn't mean to say that. It's true. But the goddamn thief looked at me like I spit in his face or something. He was shocked.

"You're still mad about that?" Stanford asked.

"Yes, I'm still *mad* about that!" I could feel myself losing control. Jason looked shocked that I let that slip. He really did. He wanted to intervene, I could tell. But he didn't say a word. He didn't have to.

"Well, I didn't take your stupid comic book! To tell you the truth, I was too *proud* to steal anything when I was a kid because I didn't want to ruin what small bit of *dignity* my family had left me after being so poor! So you can stick all your suspicions about me stealing your dumb comic book right up your ass!" He was pretty pissed at me, I could tell. His beady eyes were even beadier behind those thick lenses of his and his neck had swollen to twice its size behind that stupid bowtie. He was so mad, he actually turned bright red. He stood up and loosened his goddamn bowtie. "Jason, it was nice seeing you again but I must be going now. I'm not going to let my evening be ruined by such ridiculousness. Good evening." And then he was gone. Man, that was a great goddamn reunion if there ever was one. It's true. Jason looked like he was pretty sore at me.

"If you weren't taking me on this trip to New York, I'd be pretty upset with you right now," he said.

"But he *did* take it. He stole that comic book from me."

"Who cares! That was a long time ago and in the grand scheme of things, it really doesn't matter. What does it matter? It doesn't matter one bit."

Jason got up and headed for the crapper. I finished the last of my beer and refilled my glass. I decided, right then and there, that I was going to play some Donkey Kong and forget about Stanford the goddamn thief or Amazing Spider-Man number six or my stupid suspicions and all. I waved to our waitress and she promptly came over. I gave her five bucks and asked for some quarters in change. She obliged. She was a real professional. It's true.

"Anything else, sir?" she asked.

"Oh yeah, and a pack of Camel Lights." This was the last night of my vacation before my big premiere in New York. So I decided to live it up. I had inhaled so much goddamn secondhand smoke that I might as well have been blazing myself. So I did. And it was fucking great.

I made camp in front of the Donkey Kong machine with my glass of beer, my pile of quarters, my fresh pack of Camel Lights, my complimentary matches, and an ashtray. I lined up the spare quarters at the bottom of the screen, just like I did when I was a kid. That (in case you didn't know) was a sure-fire way to let people know just how serious you were at playing the game. And I was as serious as five dollars worth of quarters. I dropped the first quarter in and listened to the ridiculous cartoon-style theme song. And there was stupid Donkey Kong, scaling the girders and stomping them into their angled positions. In his arms was my Princess Pauline, just like I remembered. It was beautiful. I decided right then and there that once I got my big advance from the publisher that I would go by my *own* Donkey Kong machine. I bet my kids would love it, especially Sammie. That boy loves video games. He's crazy about them. He'll sit and play for hours and he won't even go to the bathroom until he's gotten to a certain stage in the game. That boy can act pretty stupid sometimes, just like his old man. I was really getting into the game too when I heard a young lady's voice.

"Can I bum a cigarette?" she asked. I was too busy playing the game to look. She sure had a sexy voice, though. It was nice and deep and confident. I wanted to look except that my game was just too important.

"Sure, go ahead. There are some matches right there too." I heard her take the pack and pull out a smoke. She lit it and placed the pack back down on the machine. But she didn't walk away. I could feel her presence right next to me. I could also smell her perfume too. The scent was really distracting my game.

"I didn't think it was really you last night until I saw you sitting with Jason over there. And then I knew it had to be you. It must be you, Simon Burchwood. Do you remember me?"

When I heard my name, Donkey Kong didn't seem so important to me anymore. When a strange woman asks you something like that, you have to look to see who she is. It's pretty goddamn imperative. So I turned to discover the kind waitress from Cinammon's Big Boobie Bonanza smoking one of my cigarettes. She gave me the same kind smile that she gave me the other night. She looked genuinely glad to see me, like we were old friends or something.

"It's me, Patty Green. Do you remember me?"

And in an instant, I experienced déjà vu, a daydream, a memory, and a flashback all at once. It was pretty crazy. It's true. I didn't know what to say. And before I could turn back to my game of Donkey Kong, it was over. Game Over.

17.

I was standing face to face with my childhood crush. This was the first time I had seen her since the night I kissed her goodbye over sixteen years ago. Well, I take that back. I did see her last night at Cinammon's Big Boobie Bonanza but, at the time, I didn't *actually know* that she was the same person I kissed when I was a boy. I only had my suspicions that she was the same little Patty Green that I had a crush on through all of my elementary school years and part of my junior high years. But now I knew for sure. She was the same little Patty Green, my crush, my Princess Pauline, my Guinevere. And she was smoking one of my cigarettes and standing in front of a goddamn Donkey Kong machine with me. It was picture perfect.

"Of course I remember you," I said. "How could I not?" For some reason, I was nervous as hell. I was shaking all over the goddamn place. I could barely keep my hand still to hold my cigarette. I nearly burned my nose when I took a drag, I was shaking so much. It's crazy how women can make you so goddamn nervous. It's true. "What a strange coincidence seeing you here."

"I guess it is kind of coincidental. But everyone in this part of town hangs out here. It's the place to be if you want to drink," she said. I didn't get a really good look at her last night because the lights in the Big Boobie Bonanza were pretty dim, probably to conceal how ugly the dancers really were. But in the brighter lights of Mitchell's lounge, I could see that little Patty Green had grown into a stunning woman. I mean, she was absolutely *gorgeous*. It's true. All signs of her adolescent-self were gone. She was no longer a skinny, flat-chested, little girl. She had grown into a curvaceous and stunningly beautiful young woman. The only characteristic that had carried on into her adult state was her hair. It was the same straight, golden blonde hair that I remembered. It was even about the same length and style that it was back then: straight, parted down the middle, and a tad longer than shoulder-length. "And I see that you need a drink. Your glass is about empty. What are you drinking?"

"Budweiser," I responded. The word shook off my tongue with a thud. I had a difficult time speaking. It's true. I was shaking all over the place. She must have noticed how nervous I was. You couldn't miss my shaking limbs, like I had Tourette's syndrome or something.

"I'll get the first pitcher. How's that?" she asked. Then she saw me glance in Jason's direction. He was sitting at our table like a sad bastard, what, with his head on the table and his lit cigarette dangling in his hand. He looked like he wanted to kill himself or something. "Is he all right? Should we go sit with him?"

"No, we shouldn't bother him. He's really depressed. He and his wife might be getting divorced."

"Really? He and Betty? That's terrible," she said. I forgot how small a town Montgomery was. Everyone knew each other and knew each others' business. It was pretty goddamn annoying. I realized I might have slipped a bit by saying that they were getting divorced. I decided to massage the story a bit.

"Well, not exactly divorced. But they are having problems. He's pretty down about it. We should leave him be for now."

"Are you sure?" she asked. Man, her perfume was mesmerizing me. It smelled so good and sweet. I imagined her rubbing it onto her neck and chest. That thought made me even *more* nervous.

"Yeah, I told him I'd take him to New York with me tomorrow for a little vacation. Hopefully, he'll have some time to think about what he wants to do about Betty." Patty noticed two empty stools at the bar and she took me by the elbow and led me there. The minute her fingers touched my skin, a bolt of lightning shot through my entire body. I was shaking all over the goddamn place. I was that nervous. I hate how women can do that to you. Women can make men act like such idiots. It's true. Men have no control over it. We sat on the stools and Patty ordered a pitcher of beer from the bartender. They must have known each other because she knew his name and he winked at her after she ordered. I bet she was making the bartender nervous too. How could he *not* be? She was gorgeous. He promptly brought us a pitcher and two fresh glasses.

"That's very sweet of you to do that for your friend, taking him to New York. You must really care about him."

"Well, he is *still* my best friend. Even after I moved away, we kept in touch through letters. We wrote so much that sometimes it felt like he was still my best friend." I looked over my shoulder to see how Jason was doing and he was still suicidal. There was a fresh pitcher of beer on his table and he was obviously getting drunk out of his goddamn gourd. I guess the realization that his wife was such a whore was really getting to him. "He followed my entire career through clippings I sent him in the mail and then in more detail through my web site. Undoubtedly, he is my biggest fan."

"That's great. So, how does it feel to be a famous writer?" she asked. Man, that was a loaded question. It really was. I had to really think about that one. I had been so busy up to that point that I really never thought about it. It's true. When you have publishing deadlines and agents calling and editors e-mailing you and writers' block and all, it's hard to think about anything else besides work. I didn't know what to say.

"It's my every dream come true," I said.

"So what do you like best about writing?"

"Where do I start? I like *everything* about writing. I like that I can express myself to my adoring fans. I like that I can paint a picture of how my thoughts work through words. I like that I can genuinely speak my mind about what I feel about this world, unencumbered by doubt and self-awareness. And I really like the idea that I might have a profound effect on someone and their outlook of our society. I feel very empowered by that. Plus, I like that I'm invited to all kinds of celebrity events and get to meet all kinds of famous people. That is definitely a major perk. I was able to introduce my wife to her idol, Selma Hayek, at a celebrity golf tournament in Dallas. It was amazing."

I was blabbing all over the place like a big dope. I was so nervous that I was running at the mouth. It was ridiculous. I looked over my shoulder to see how Jason was doing. He looked like he was dead, sitting there with his goddamn head on the table like someone had shot him. The only reason I knew he wasn't dead was because the pitcher was practically gone. He must have been drunk off his ass. The bartender saw that I was looking at him and he walked over to us.

"Hey, is your friend OK?" he asked. "He looks *wasted*. If he's drunk, you'll have to get him out of here."

"Don't worry about it, Steve," Patty said. They must have been friends, the *way* she was talking to him and all. "We'll make sure he gets home all right. No worries, I promise."

"I trust you, sweetheart." And then he winked at her like they had a *thing* going or something. It was pretty annoying, all of his goddamn winks and questions and good service. He was making me sick.

"So, what about you?" I asked. "You said last night that you still didn't know what you wanted to do with your life. How'd you end up at Cinammon's?"

"Oh, I don't know. I still live at home with my folks and I needed to make some decent money and Cinammon's is pretty close to the house. It just kind of worked out that way. It's not the greatest job in the world but the tips are pretty good. Besides, being close to home is nice because both of my parents are really sick and I have to take care of them." Her face exposed the sadness that she was hiding deep down inside. It seemed like she had to use all of her strength to keep from crying. It really started to depress the hell out of me. I mean, I was so fortunate that my family was pretty healthy. I guess I took it for granted sometimes. I felt sorry for poor little Patty Green. "They both have cancer."

"I'm so sorry, Patty. That's terrible." She looked so sad that she almost made me cry. Well, almost. I had to fight back those goddamn tears. I was choked up and all.

"It's OK. I've dealt with the pain and disappointment. But I'm spending as much time with them as I can and that's enough for me. At least they know how much I care about them. My dad always tells me that maybe after they are gone that I'll find my way. Maybe that's true. We'll see."

Normally, I would have had about enough of all this depressing stuff about death and shit like that. But I could see that Patty was genuinely grappling with her emotions and wasn't just blabbing up a storm like most people do about themselves. Most people are pretty selfish and arrogant, even when they say they are not. It's true. Most people just care about themselves and don't give two shits about anyone else, even when they say they are taking care of a loved one. Most people only care for their loved ones because they want to make goddamn certain that they are in the will somewhere, getting some piece of crap heirloom or something. But I had to give Patty some credit. She was the *genuine* article, that's for sure. She was a really good person. I could see that she wanted to cry so I put my arms around her and she did cry a bit on my shoulder. I could really smell her perfume then and it was driving me crazy, even with all of her crying and sniffling. I gave her a bar napkin and she wiped the tears from her eyes. She didn't wear a lick of makeup so her mascara didn't run like with most women. She was naturally beautiful that way. A lot of women in Montgomery were naturally beautiful.

"I'm sorry. It makes me cry thinking about it. I'm really sorry," she said.

"It's OK. Really, it is."

And then Steve the goddamn winking bartender came over and ruined everything. He was getting pretty good at that.

"Hey, I don't mean to break up your beautiful *moment* but you're going to have to get your friend out of here. He's wasted and I don't want to be responsible if he gets in a car and runs over someone's baby."

Steve was right. Jason was wasted and passed out. I could see the drool draining from his mouth onto the table. He looked pretty goddamn pathetic. I decided that it was time to get him home.

"I'll take him home," I told Steve the jackass bartender. He was really getting on my nerves. And wouldn't you know it? He winked at Patty again, the bastard. "I'm sorry, Patty, but I have to get Jason home. We're leaving pretty early tomorrow anyway so we should get some sleep. I hope you don't mind."

"I don't mind at all. Actually, can you give me a ride home? I took a cab here from work."

I hesitated for a second because I remembered that we came in the turd-on-wheels. But for once, I put aside my pride and said yes. I paid the winking bastard for both tabs and gave him a good tip, at least twenty percent. I wasn't going to take any chances with *this bartender.* I threw Jason's arm over my shoulder and pulled him up from his seat. But I almost broke my back because the bastard weighed a ton. It's true. I mean, he looked slim and all but he must have weighed a lot more than he looked. He was heavy as hell. Patty led the way, saying *excuse me* to the lazy cocksuckers who stood in our way of the exit. I dragged the heavy bastard to the turd-on-wheels and laid him on the ground next to the car. I was about out of breath. It took a lot out of me to drag that pudgy fucker that far.

"Are you OK?" Patty asked. I guess she saw that I was about to have a heart attack. I must have looked awful, panting all over the place.

"Yeah, he's just *really* heavy."

I opened the door and lifted and shoved and pushed my friend into the backseat. Actually, he was partially on the seat and partially on the floor. But at least he was in the car. And he was snoring like he was hibernating or something like a goddamn grizzly bear. Patty and I hopped in and we took off, the turd-on-wheels kicking and screaming all over the place because of the extra weight of three people. We left a cloud of black smoke that would have covered a football field.

"I appreciate you giving me a ride home, Simon. You didn't have to." She was being all sweet and sincere. She was making me nervous again.

"What are old friends for, right?" She agreed and we sat in silence through a few traffic lights. We didn't say one word to each other. But we *sure* could hear Jason. He was snoring like a real bastard from the backseat. He was passed out cold and drooling all over himself like he had rabies or something. He was driving me crazy with his snoring and snorting and gurgling.

We eventually made it to Country Down Estates, passing Cinammon's Big Boobie Bonanza on the way. The two of us smiled in acknowledgement as we passed it, kind of like we both knew it was now a place of some fateful significance. As I pulled into the neighborhood, Patty finally started to speak.

"Simon, I know what you did to Kenny Jones back when we were kids. His friends told me all about the fight and what Kenny said. They told me how you stood up for me." Her voice was really soft and quiet and sincere. I was really starting to get nervous now. My hand was shaking so much that I had a hard timing driving the turd-on-wheels. "And you never called me any of the names the other kids called me. Why was that?"

"Because I knew it wasn't true. I never understood why they called you that anyway. We were all too young to be hookers and gigolos and all that stuff."

"That's true. In fact, I didn't lose my virginity until I was eighteen. All I was guilty of was kissing a few boys and being myself. And you were the only one who understood that. You didn't think badly of me." My heart was racing and my hands were shaking. All this talk about her virginity and kissing boys was getting me riled up. I don't know why, it just was. "And this may sound funny, but to this day, when I think of you riding your bike all the way to my house and kissing me, I think that was probably one of the most romantic things anyone has ever done for me."

I couldn't speak because I was so goddamn nervous. She put her hand on mine and gave it an endearing squeeze. I almost drove off the goddamn road, what, with her touching me and saying nice things about me. Before I knew it, we were at her parents' house and I parked the car in front. She hopped out of the car and came over to my side. Before I could turn off the engine, she pulled me from the car, the doors still open, the engine still running, the headlights glaring. She led me through the front yard and to the side of the house by the air-conditioner. She turned to face me and held both of my hands. She smiled sweetly as the air-conditioner whirled and wheezed behind us. I was experiencing that condition again of having déjà vu, a daydream, a memory, and a flashback all at once, except it was more *intense* now. I felt like I was thirteen again, heartbroken over my impending move to another state and leaving behind my crush, my true love. And before I knew it, she leaned in and kissed me. But it wasn't the gentle peck of a naïve little girl. It was the kiss of an experienced, grown woman. She rolled her tongue into my mouth in search of my tongue. And when our two tongues met, the déjà vu, daydream, memory, and flashback all stopped instantly. I immediately thought of my wife and kids and how I *wasn't* thirteen anymore and that I was kissing Patty the whore who worked at a titty bar called Cinammon's Goddamn Big Boobie Bonanza and Whorehouse and I wanted to puke. I quickly put a little distance in between us, at least an arm's length. She looked confused and a little hurt. I didn't know what to say. But I did know that I was tainting my memories again. The innocent little kiss as a child had turned into an adulterous moment. And more than anything, I hated myself for letting it happen.

So I left her there again, just like I did when we were kids, standing by the air-conditioner next to the house of her sickly parents. I hopped in the turd-on-wheels and headed for Jason's house. I drove there as fast as I could get the turd-on-wheels to go. And I hoped, with all of my heart, that I would never see or hear or kiss her ever again.

18.

I woke up the next morning on Jason's filthy couch and I was drenched in a cold sweat. For the first time in what seemed like years I slept so soundly that when I came back to consciousness, I felt really disconnected from myself, as if I had left my body for the night. And also for the first time, I witnessed a dream as a passive *observer*, like I was an audience member in a movie theater. I was so completely engrossed in the visuals before me that *I was not aware* that I was dreaming. It's true. Have you ever watched a movie that touched you so much that you were emotionally kidnapped? That's how I felt. Usually when I dream, I am aware that I am dreaming and I have some influence over what happens. Not this time. I watched helplessly as the dream ... no, as the nightmare progressed before me. It was awful and violent and so unlike what I usually see while I sleep.

This is what I remember. I was driving my family in our Volvo, heading to some vacation destination down a long, deserted highway. I'm not exactly sure where we were going but it seemed like we were probably headed to the Texas coast. The terrain looked rural and flat and barren like south Texas does on the way to the beach. As a family, we loved going to the beach together and there were several places along the Gulf Coast where we would vacation: South Padre Island, North Padre Island, Galveston, Corpus Christi, Port Aransas. I was wearing my prized Hawaiian shirt, the shirt I christened as my driving-to-the-beach shirt. And the rest of my family dressed accordingly; my wife in a designer outfit looking gorgeous and ready for the sun, and my kids in shorts and t-shirts singing from the back seat. Jessie and Sammie loved taking turns singing their favorite pop songs and my wife and I, once we learned the chorus, would sing along with them. And that's where the dream began a continuous loop for what seemed like an eternity. You ever noticed *that* in your dreams, how sometimes it seems that your mind becomes fixated on some particular part or sequence? Well, that's what happened. It went on and on like that and I was repeatedly experiencing a continual state of familial bliss, singing pop songs and driving my family to the beach. And then, without warning, I found myself watching our car as a bystander from the side of the highway. I watched as a small cloud of white smoke burst from beneath the back of our car, propelling it up and over in the air. The car slammed top-down on the highway, blowing all the windows out like hot shrapnel. And the Volvo slid in a horizontal avalanche of sparks, smoke, gravel, glass, metal, plastic, and caustic liquid chemicals for hundreds of feet. I immediately ran toward the accident, frantic and scared that I wouldn't reach the wreckage soon enough to save my family. And as I approached to within a hundred feet or so from the edge of the highway, the car exploded into a fiery ball of charred, twisted metal. The blast knocked me on my back. I didn't let that impede my rescue so I quickly jumped to my feet and got as close as I could to the burning car. But I could only get so close. The car burned too hot for me to get near it. I looked around for any sign of water or liquid that I could douse the flames with but there was nothing. There was no sign of anything that could help me anywhere. There was nothing except the highway and the barren landscape of my dream. I watched in horror as my family burned inside the wreckage, still moving, still exerting every ounce of their will to survive. And I was helpless to do anything. I remember thinking that I couldn't live with myself without my family. So I jumped into the burning funeral pyre to be with the ones I loved most: my wife and children.

And that's when I woke up in a cold sweat, feeling like my life had been drained out of me. At first, I didn't know where I was. But I quickly noticed the rundown clutter that *was* Jason's house and realized just what had happened. I had been dreaming. But no matter how horrific the nightmare was, I knew it was *only a dream*. I never thought that I would thank God that I was sitting in the midst of a goddamn pig sty. But that's what I did. I assumed that the dream was trying to tell me just how much I loved my family and that I missed them, especially since I hadn't seen or spoken to them in a few days. And to me, that was almost like an eternity in itself. So I decided right then and there that I would call my wife and tell her how much I loved her and the kids. I looked around for any signs of Betty before I uncovered myself. I like to sleep in the nude (in case you didn't know). And the last thing I needed was Jason's whore wife jumping on my naked body so she could destroy her goddamn marriage. I didn't see her so I got up and put my shirt and pants on and went to the kitchen for a glass of juice.

Oddly enough, Jason was in the kitchen sitting at the breakfast table. He had a note in his hand and a look of dread on his face. He didn't look good at all.

"Good morning, sunshine," I said, going to the cabinet for a glass. He didn't look up from the note or greet me in return. Jason always was a grumpy bastard in the morning. "A little grouchy, I see. I bet you're really hung over. By the way, you got any orange juice?"

"Betty left me," he said, his eyes locked on the note with disbelief. "She took the kids over to her sister's house and she doesn't know when she'll be back. She might not come back at all."

"Really?" I went to the refrigerator for some juice but there were only cans of Coke. Jason's house was filled with all kinds crap with no nutritional *value* whatsoever. It's true. Everywhere you looked there was junk-food crap. I mean, how does he expect to live past fifty while he pumps his veins with all of this garbage? I grabbed an orange soda (since it was the closest thing to what I was looking for) and sat down at the table. "What are you going to do?" I asked, kind of disinterested.

"I don't know, Simon. I just don't know." His eyes welled up with tears as he tried to hold back his emotions. I could tell he was experiencing some strong emotions he probably hadn't felt in a while. He cleared his throat and wiped the tears from his eyes and shook off the pain. "Maybe I shouldn't go to New York. Maybe I should stay home and try to *fix* my marriage."

"Don't be ridiculous. You're coming with me. The best thing for you two right now is some space. Let her stay at her sister's house. Maybe she'll realize what she's missing while you're gone." I thought it strange that anyone would miss Jason's rundown house and all his rundown things and his junk food. But I knew, deep down inside, that Jason was a good person. I mean, he loved his wife even though she was a goddamn whore. And that is *really something*. It takes a lot of character to dig down past her obvious faults and find something good in her. And whatever that was that he found, he loved it dearly. "So go pack your bags. I'm going to call and reserve you a seat on the plane. Plus, I gotta call my wife and accountant. I haven't spoken to either of them since I got here."

"Do you really think I should go?" he asked. He was really starting to act like an idiot. Who questions going on a *free* vacation? A goddamn idiot like Jason, that's who.

"Yes, you're going and that's final. You'll be back in a couple of days and you two can talk about your problems then. You'll have a fresh head, I'm telling you. It'll be good for the both of you."

"OK then. I'll leave her a note and pack my bags. I'm going with you to New York and that's final." And that's all it took. Sometimes, it felt like I had to lead him through his own life, like he couldn't make his own goddamn decisions. It was really starting to drive me crazy. He stood up and grabbed his forehead like it was about to fall off, wincing his eyes and rubbing his brow. "And yes, for your information, I have a hangover. A *bad* one, too."

He left the kitchen and headed for his room, I suppose. I'm sure he had to think of what to write to his whore wife about suddenly leaving for New York. And I'm sure he didn't have much to pack besides a pair of underwear and a couple of clean t-shirts. He wasn't a goddamn fashion model and all. He was just good old Jason, a goddamn pig *and* my best friend.

I decided to call my wife so I went into the living room to use the phone. I really wanted to hear her and the kids' voices after that nightmare I had. I dialed my home number, using the goddamn rotary dial on Jason's ancient phone. The number-wheel turned slow as hell after I selected each number and it seemed like it took an hour just to dial. But I soon finished the sequence and listened to the phone ring. It seemed to ring forever. And then the answering machine came on, "You've reached 512-555-6681. We are not in right now but if you leave a short message ..." It was the same goddamn boring message. I decided right then and there that when I finally got home, I would change that stupid message for good. I was sure we could think of something a little more creative than that one, but not *too* creative. Then the machine beeped. "Hey sweetie. Just calling to let you guys know that I'll be leaving for New York later this morning. I guess you all are at Grandma's house, being that it's *Saturday* and all. I miss all of you terribly and every day apart is a day I miss. Jessie, be a good girl and help your mother around the house. Sammie, I can't wait to get home and beat you at Nintendo. And Jessica, my sweet angel, every minute I'm away is equal to the number of kisses you'll receive when I get home. I'll call you when I get to the hotel in New York. Bye." I really hate leaving messages on answering machines, especially when I have some endearing things to say. The messages never sound as good as I intended them to sound. They always sound muffled and forced because I know I only have thirty goddamn seconds to leave a message. Otherwise, the machine hangs up on you. And there is nothing worse than having to leave a second message after the machine hangs up on you the first time. I needed to call my accountant but Jason started yelling at me from his room. He loved to yell at me from the other side of the house.

"Hey? Simon?" he yelled, like a big dope.

"Yeah?"

"Do I need to pack any bathroom stuff?"

"What do you mean?"

"You know, like shampoo or toothpaste?" It was pretty fucking obvious to me that Jason hadn't left Montgomery on trips or vacations. For a second, I felt like I was taking a goddamn Beverly Hillbilly to New York and he was asking me if there was going to be any road-kill to eat or a cement pond in the BIG CITY.

"Jason, I'm sure they'll have that stuff there for us. It's a pretty nice hotel and all."

"OK. Just checking."

I started to dial the number of my accountant when I remembered that it was Saturday and that he probably was out playing golf or some shit like that. The bastard was *always* playing golf or hanging around his country club like some big shot or something. It always drove me crazy especially when I really *needed* to talk to him. I mean, he should be balancing books and verifying goddamn receipts and all. But it never seemed like he ever did any of that because he was always at the golf course. If I played golf as much as he did, I would never get any writing done and I'd be a goddamn professional golfer instead. It's true. I made an executive decision and decided that the weekend was going to be paid for on my credit card and that I would take care of everything with him when I got back. Plus, I would talk to him about his golfing. It was beginning to interfere with my business. Then Jason started yelling from his room again.

"Hey Simon?"

"Yeah?" I was getting tired of yelling back and forth. I mean, he could at least come into the room where I was so we could talk like decent human beings and not yell all over the place like a pair of idiots.

"Why don't you have a cell phone? Wouldn't it be easier calling your family and your accountant with one rather than having to look for a phone to use?" I'm telling you, Jason was a goddamn genius. It's true. He was always *thinking* and using his brain.

"Maybe it would be *easier* to contact them with a cell phone. But it would also be easier for people to find *me*. And sometimes, especially if I'm trying to write, I don't want to be bothered, you know. I don't feel comfortable knowing that people can call me whenever they want and try to find me whenever they want. Plus, we live in a civilized society, you know. I can find a phone anywhere if I need to call someone."

"That's true," he said. I could hear him rummaging around in his room, probably sifting through piles of dirty clothes and crap like that. "Betty and I got cell phones so we could keep in touch with each other. You know, in case of an emergency or something."

"Well, I would advise that you *not* bring your cell phone to New York."

The rummaging stopped immediately after I said that. Then Jason came into the living room, looking a bit confused and concerned.

"You don't think I should bring it to New York?" he asked, holding the phone in his hand. It was one of those older model cell phones, the kind that looks like the military combat phones you see in old war movies that were the size of a goddamn cowboy boot with an antennae sticking out of the top.

"No, I don't think you should bring it to New York. If you're going to assist me, then you are going to have to follow my rules. I will not want to be bothered or have you bothered by *anything* until I'm finished with my appearance. It's that simple."

"But what if there's an emergency with the kids?" He was really starting to drive me crazy with his indecisiveness. I mean, who was the *man* in the house anyway? It obviously wasn't him. It's true. He definitely didn't wear the *pants* around here.

"Look, Jason. We'll be staying at the ----- ----- Hotel in New York. In your note, tell Betty that if there is an emergency, to contact us there. The room is registered under my name. That's all she needs to know. My wife has the same information. If she really needs to find me, she knows where to find me as well."

Jason and his combat phone went back into his room to finish packing. I called the airline and reserved Jason a seat on the plane. I almost changed my mind about the whole thing, thinking that he would probably be a big distraction in New York, what, with his whining about his whore wife and his scrotum-poking kids. It was enough to really ruin the entire goddamn trip. But I also knew that the trip would be good for him and I really needed the help. I was going to have a lot to do in New York. So I booked the seat anyway and decided to just press on. Nothing was going to get in my way on the road to notoriety and fame: not the crazy taxi driver or the psycho bartender or Ernie the Nose-Picking Barfly or Grant the Asshole or Patty the Adulterer or Darren Reedy's death or Betty the Whore or Stanford the Thief or Jason the goddamn whining, pathetic pig and his scrotum-poking kids. Well, I take that back about Jason. It wasn't *all* his fault, I'll give him that. But the whining could be *controlled* and we were probably going to have to have a talk about that. It's true.

I finished packing and went to retrieve Jason. He was writing a note to Betty, sitting at her vanity table in the master bathroom. He looked like he was *really concentrating* like he was writing his last will and testament or something. It was all just too ridiculous. I stood there and waited for him, my bags on the floor and my backpack nestled on my back, standing right behind him. He finished the note by dotting his i's and crossing his t's.

"How does this sound?" he asked, propping the note in front of him like it was the goddamn Gettysburg Address or some shit like that. "To my dearest Betty - I've gone with Simon to New York to assist him with his publicity appearance. If there is an emergency, you can contact me under his name at the ----- ----- Hotel. Hopefully, when I get back, we can discuss the recurring problems we are having in our marriage. There is nothing more important to me than you and the kids. If you need money, I have left some in our hiding place (you know where that is?). I will be back in a couple of days. Your dearest husband, Jason." He set the note down on the vanity and looked at me in the mirror. He was obviously looking for some kind of encouragement from me or something, being that I was the famous writer and all. "How does that sound?"

"Pretty good. Let's go." I was ready to get the hell out of Montgomery. It's true.

"You don't think I left anything out?" he asked, worried that his note wasn't in the final-draft stage.

"Nope. It's perfect." I grabbed my bags and headed for the garage. Jason soon followed behind.

"Where are you going?" he asked. "The Chevette's out front."

"Jason, we're not going to the airport in *that*. Let's take the Mustang. Let's go in style."

"Well, OK. Let me lock up the house."

I don't know who Jason was locking his house up from but he did it anyway. I couldn't imagine any thief *wanting* to get into his place unless they were desperate. What were they going to find of value in there? Nothing, I tell you, except the largest stockpile of junk food and rundown things. I loaded up my bags in the Mustang and Jason soon came out to do the same. He looked sad as hell so I told him I'd drive.

As I pulled the beast out of the garage, he started to weep a little. He was depressing the hell out of me. Nothing is worse than seeing a grown man cry. I mean, it's like watching a mountain crumble or an old-growth forest burn to the ground. You don't know what to say. It's true.

"We'll only be gone a *couple* of days," I said, shifting the beast into second gear.

"I know. But I've never been out of Alabama. And I have this bad feeling that I'm never going to see my family again." He really started to cry then. He was crying like his mother died or something. It was depressing as hell. I decided right then and there that I wasn't going to say anything else until we got to the airport. That felt like a good strategy to me. And that's exactly what I did. I kept my mouth shut the entire goddamn way there.

Besides Jason crying up a storm, all I could think about was how happy I was to finally be getting the hell out of Montgomery. I mean, I was glad to come back and visit. But after seeing all the sad bastards that I had left behind when I was a kid, I was really glad to be moving on. Sometimes, it's just best to leave things that are in the past *in the past*. It's true. I mean, I had really fond memories of friends and places in Montgomery but you can't relive everything *exactly* like it was. People change and places change even when your memories stay the same. And there really is no point in ruining your memories of what you had by revisiting the people and places from your past. With the exception of seeing Jason, the entire trip was a bust. It was a goddamn bust.

"Even though we are going to be gone for only a couple of days," Jason said, finding just enough strength to speak. "I'm really going to miss Montgomery. I can tell already."

I nodded my head to acknowledge him but I kept my promise. I didn't say another goddamn word until we reached the airport, not one. It's true. It was hard as hell but I did it.

19.

The plane was barely in the air for more than five minutes and I was already regretting my choice to bring Jason along. Thankfully, our stay in the airport was pretty uneventful, which was the way I wanted it. We avoided the airport bar and I limited my conversations to just the essential personnel that I was required to interact with. After what happened at the airport in Texas, what, with the vigilante bartender and the know-it-all nose-pickers and all, I didn't want anything to deter us from getting on the plane incident-free. The only problem was Jason's incessant goddamn blabbing. He was blabbing all over the place and talking to *every fucking person* he came in contact with. He bumped into a janitor in the restroom and went on about how he'd never been out of Alabama. When he was stopped by a security guard, he would go on about how he'd never been to New York. Then when the flight attendant asked him for his ticket, he blabbed about how he'd never been on a goddamn plane before. He was driving me crazy. He just wouldn't shut up. It's true. I bet that's why Betty wanted out of their marriage. I'd hate to be married to someone like Jason being that he was such a goddamn pig and blabbed all the time like an idiot. He should've just worn a sign around his neck that said: *Take advantage of me cause I'm a goddamn redneck idiot who has never been anywhere and will never go anywhere.*

Jason's only redeeming quality so far was his innate ability to cheerlead for me and my career. I mean, even though he was blabbing to every Tom, Dick, and Harriet about how naïve and unworldly he was, he'd end every conversation with: *And this is Simon Burchwood. He's a famous writer.* He said that at the end of every conversation, like a champ. I didn't even have to pull out one business card, not one. I was very impressed with *that*, at least. He was negating his blabbing the best he could, I suppose.

Luckily, we were seated together in first class. He was so goddamn excited to see the ground from the air and that I let him have the window seat. Traveling with him was kind of like traveling with a child; everything was so new and interesting to him. I was already a weary traveler. It's true. I've traveled all over the goddamn place. So seeing the ground from the air for the hundredth time didn't interest me one goddamn bit. All I was concerned about was landing safe and sound without incident.

Once the plane leveled out and the seatbelt sign was turned off, the flight attendant made her way up the aisle for drink orders. She had the same look to her that the flight attendant had on the plane to Montgomery, that Barbie-doll-fake-blonde look. And she responded to every passenger in the same robotic, ambiguous tone. The airline must have spent a fortune training their flight attendants to look and talk like that. Eventually, she asked for our order.

"Don't give him too much to drink," Jason cracked. "He might go crazy and black out." He thought his joke was pretty funny and he laughed his maniacal laugh, wheezing and coughing and spitting all over the place. The flight attendant chuckled too but I think she was chuckling more at Jason's demeanor than his joke. He was laughing all over the place like a goddamn idiot.

I ordered a Coke for myself and a beer for Jason and the flight attendant gave us that fake, sugary smile that she was so proficient at. I was hoping maybe Jason would drink a few beers and pass out until we reached New York. That would have been a treat. But after the third one, there was no sign of him falling to sleep. It was a goddamn shame. It's true.

I decided that since I had the time to burn, I would work through a writing exercise that I did to keep my creative mind sharp. I was really disappointed that I didn't spend *any* time writing while I was in Montgomery. But can you blame me? My entire stay there was a bust: a creative bust and a personal bust. I grabbed my backpack from under my seat and pulled out the materials I needed. Jason was surprised as hell to see what I used to flex my creative muscles.

"You have Mad Libs? What do you have Mad Libs for?" he asked. Then he started laughing like a hyena again, wheezing and coughing all over the goddamn place. It was a mistake ordering him all those beers. He was obviously getting drunk off his ass. "Those are for kids, right? We used to pass those around in school. Remember?"

"Yes, I remember. I use these to keep my creative impulses sharp. It takes a lot of work to keep the creative mind active. Here, let me show you how it works."

"I know how they work, dummy," he said, grabbing one of the Mad Lib booklets. He grabbed my pen too, the bastard. "You just fill in the blanks with your own words." He flipped through the pages to find a passage of interest.

"OK. You do one first and I'll change what you have to what I'm thinking. How's that?"

Jason selected the first passage. This is what it said with the blanks empty:

"Exclamation!" she said adverb as she jumped into his noun and took off with his adjective automobile.

He scribbled in his words, wagging his tongue as his pea-brain churned out the new phrases. When he was finished, he started laughing and wheezing all over the place. He was really starting to get on my goddamn nerves. It's true.

"These are great! You'd never think grammar would be so much fun!" he said, laughing again like a drunken hyena.

I took the booklet from him and read his selections. This is what he wrote:

"Fuck!" she said underlined-pervertedly as she jumped into his underlined-pants and took off with his underlined-fucking automobile.

He was a fucking genius, I tell you. It was obvious.

"I don't know if *that word* is an adjective," I said, trying to keep my voice down. I pointed to the word *fucking*. I didn't want to have to *say* it out loud.

"Who cares. It's funny." Jason was really amused with himself. I'm sure he thought it was the funniest goddamn thing in the world. "Let me see what you would put in there."

I accepted the challenge and erased what he had in the blanks. I racked my brain for the most creative words to put there in place of his obscenities. It took me a few more minutes than it did Jason, especially since I was trying to be creative and not amusing. This is what I eventually came up with:

"Eureka!" she said underlined-boastfully as she jumped into his underlined-seat and took off with his underlined-pristine automobile.

I handed the booklet to Jason and he read what I wrote. He looked puzzled when he was finished.

"That's not funny," he said, scratching his head.

"It's not *supposed* to be funny. It's an exercise in writing."

"But it's Mad Libs. They're supposed to be funny. You're supposed to pick words that don't *mean* anything. That's why they're funny. Your sentence is just normal."

"Like I said, I'm not trying to be funny. I fill in the blanks with the appropriate words and then I rewrite them over and over, changing the words into as many variations as I can think of. I'm trying to exercise my *mind*."

It was obvious that we weren't thinking on the same plane. In a way, I felt kind of sorry for Jason, especially since it seemed like he didn't take *anything* in life seriously. Maybe that's why his marriage was such a goddamn wreck. Maybe that's why he was such a goddamn pig. He thinks everything in this world should be a goddamn joke. And unfortunately for him, his life was a joke. It's true. Since he ruined the state my mind needed to be in to perform my exercises, I decided to put the booklets away. Jason watched as I grabbed my backpack and stuffed the booklets into the front pouch. He looked a little curious, like a child looking at something his parents didn't want him to look at.

"Simon?"

"Yeah?"

"Wha'cha got in the backpack? You hold onto it and guard it like it's filled with gold or something?" he asked. He was really starting to drive me crazy with his questions and laughing and curiosity and goddamn drunkenness. I wished that he would just go to sleep and leave me alone for the rest of the trip.

"I told you. I have my manuscript in here. It's the only copy I have. So in a way, it's kind of like gold to me."

"Can I see it?" he asked. I was feeling really reluctant about pulling it out, especially knowing how Jason would probably handle it. I'm sure he would spill something on it or drop it or crush the pages and smudge the type or something. He was like that, you know. He was a goddamn disaster waiting to happen. But he insisted. "Please? I won't ruin it. I promise."

He looked all sad and hurt like I was withholding his only glimpse at happiness. It was pretty goddamn pathetic. But I thought and hoped that maybe if I did show it to him, then maybe he would leave me alone. I conceded.

"OK. But be *careful.* I'm serious as a nuclear war." I unzipped the main compartment of the backpack and pulled out my manuscript. I held it up like it was the goddamn Rosetta Stone or something. I kept my manuscript in a three-ring binder and it was --- pages of complete literary bliss. I don't mean to brag but it's true. Why do you think there was a massive bidding war for this manuscript?

"Wow!" he said, and that's all he said. He looked at the mammoth manuscript with pure amazement. I'm sure he was thinking about all the hard work and long hours I put into bringing this book to fruition. "Can I read it?" He opened the binder to the title page and read what was there. It said: *THE RISE AND FALL OF A TITAN by Simon Burchwood.* But as soon as he read that I closed the binder as quickly as I could.

"You'll have to wait like everybody else," I said, putting the manuscript back into my backpack, where it belonged. "You'll hear an excerpt at the reading tomorrow but that's all. I'll give you a copy of the book once it's released, especially since you're assisting me this weekend. It's the least I can do."

"Thanks, I guess." Jason turned to the window and watched the ground proceed beneath us, thousands of feet down. I placed the backpack safely under my chair. I decided to close my eyes and try to get some rest. I knew I had a long couple of days ahead and this was probably going to be the only time I could get some sleep. I tried not to think about my trip to Montgomery or the impending stress I was going to face or the flight or anything. But that can last only so long sitting next to Jason. His mind and his mouth run a mile a goddamn minute. He never gives you a break.

"I saw you talking to Patty Green last night," he said, still looking out the window. "I saw you talking to her at Mitchell's. How come you didn't mention it this morning?"

"I didn't think of it, I guess. It was innocent enough."

"Really?" he asked. I sensed a tone of sarcasm in his voice. Jason was really obvious that way. He had no goddamn couth whatsoever, just like his mother. It's true.

"Yes, really."

"Then how come I saw you kiss her at her house?" he asked. The question ripped through me like a sharp steak knife. "Is that how a married man is supposed to act?"

"I didn't kiss her. She kissed *me*."

"That's not what *I* saw. It wasn't like I was that far away from you two. I could see you perfectly from the backseat of the Chevette."

"I thought you were passed out?"

"I woke up just long enough to see that. And that's all I had to see. You *knew* I had a thing for her in school. How could you do that to me?" Jason did have a *thing* for little Patty Green in school, especially after she kissed him while we were playing spin the bottle at her birthday party. He had a crush on her something bad, just like I did. We both liked her. But Jason actually *told* her how he felt. Like I said, he didn't have any couth. He just blurted things out like they were nothing. And to him, I had broken the code of male friendship: never tread on another man's girl. And even though I didn't do anything wrong, Jason was convinced that I had broken the sacred code. "That really hurt me, you know. That's why I got drunk at Mitchell's."

"You got drunk because I was talking to Patty Green? I thought you got drunk because of Betty."

"That too. I got drunk because of everything. Everything was fine until you came into town. That's when everything started to fall apart."

Unbelievably, I tried to put myself in Jason's shoes. It was hard to do but I did it. I thought about how he must have felt seeing me kiss his childhood crush. And I wondered how he would feel if he knew his wife wanted to have sex with me so she could get out of their goddamn marriage. For a minute, I felt horrible, completely low to the ground. I felt like the lowest of the lowly bottom-feeders, a catfish sucking the shit from the bottom of the Guadalupe River. It didn't matter that little Patty Green had a thing for me, a thing that lasted since the first time I kissed her. And it didn't matter what I knew about his whore wife; nothing mattered from *my* perspective. Jason didn't know these things. All he knew was that his life was falling to pieces and he attributed my arrival as the catalyst for that. I didn't know what to say. It's true. For once, I was at a loss for words.

"Jason, I don't know what to say. Really. I didn't mean to hurt your feelings. But I really didn't kiss Patty. She kissed *me*. She must have been drunk or something. We did drink a lot of beer and all."

Jason continued to look out the window at the clouds. He rested his chin in his hand and released a soft sigh.

"What does it matter anyway, right? I'm married to Betty now. I have my own set of problems. What does an old flame mean now anyway?

"It means nothing, really," I said. I placed my hand on his shoulder. I really felt sorry for him. He was acting like a really sad bastard. "And I would never do anything to hurt you on *purpose*. You have to believe me."

"I believe you. Maybe I've just had too many beers," he whispered. And with that, he fell asleep. His head sagged to the side and rested against the window. He started snoring like a goddamn monster. Normally, I would have been pretty embarrassed. But this time, I was the one that felt like a sad bastard. I really did. It's true.

The flight attendant came by with a small blanket and covered Jason. She flashed me that fake, sugary smile and said, "He's sleeping soundly, huh?"

"Yes, he is," I replied. "He's sleeping like a baby." He was out cold and honking and wheezing away in his sleep. I tried to get some sleep as well but couldn't. So I pulled out the Mad Libs and continued my exercises. This is what I wrote:

"You bastard!" she said remorsefully as she jumped into his car and took off with his friend's automobile.

My word-choices seemed better suited each time I rewrote it. I rewrote the phrase twenty two times. But it was never perfect. I wanted to rewrite the entire phrase but what's the point? Sometimes, there's just no point to anything anymore.

I stopped writing because my hand started to hurt, what, with the sore the size of a half-dollar in the palm of my goddamn writing hand. It didn't seem to be getting any better and when you feel as depressed as I was feeling, the pain seemed to be amplified. It's true. What was (at first) a little scrape burned more and more like a stab wound. And goddamn it if that didn't make everything seem that much worse.

20.

New York, New York. Before I knew it, I could see the sprawling metropolis from the airplane window spreading across the surface of the earth like a cancer. But what a beautiful cancer! The plane descended from the sky like a comet from God and I could feel the anxiety and excitement well up in me and throb in the pit of my stomach. All of my dreams were finally coming to light, finally coming to fruition right before my eyes. So many wonderful things were about to happen. Besides my literary debut at the Barnes & Noble flagship store, I was supposed to meet my editor and her staff for the first time. Through the entire goddamn publishing process, I never had a chance to meet them face to face. It's true. Everything was done over the phone and through snail mail and e-mail, from the initial submission to the first, second, and third revisions to the galley. In case you didn't know, the galley is the first typeset version of the book that the publisher sends to the author for final revisions and approval. Anyway, it was a long distance affair from start to finish. Initially, I often wondered what my editor looked like, if she was attractive or not, a blonde or a brunette, thin or full-figured, lusty or prudish, with a fair or dark complexion (don't you think of these things?). We spoke for quite some time without really knowing what each other looked like. Of course, she eventually had the advantage because I had to send a photo of myself for publicity reasons (of course). But I had the burning desire to find out what she looked like so I did some research and found a picture of her on the internet. I mean, it's pretty difficult forming a relationship with someone if you have no idea what they *look* like. It's true. How do you think all these women who write to prisoners actually get the courage to marry one of those bastard convicts? At least with a photo, you know what you are getting into. And when I found her picture, I was actually quite surprised to see that she didn't look *anything* like I had imagined. From the sound of her voice, I had imagined a tall woman who looked and carried herself like Susan Sarandon, the movie actress. You know, on the phone she seemed very smart and cunning and manipulative, logical yet emotional, and oddly attractive. But what I discovered was that my editor looked more like Aretha Franklin. I'm not kidding. From the sound of her voice, I had no idea that she was an African-American woman with a hefty frame and not a typical inflection in her voice that would have given her skin tone and heritage away. It's true. It's really strange how your mind can mold images for you from clues and tidbits of information it takes in. I guess you could say that my thoughts of her looking like Susan Sarandon could give some insight into what I think and like about women in general, what, considering that I really like Susan Sarandon's goddamn movies and all. But it's also interesting how your mind can mislead you like that. It's very interesting indeed. Not that it changed how we dealt with each other or anything. I mean, I'm not a racist or anything. It was just a tiny *revelation*. That's all.

Anyway, Jason was snoring up a fucking storm. He was wheezing and honking and snorting all over the goddamn place. It sounded like he was going to choke on his own saliva or something. I mean, even the flight attendant came over and asked me if he was all right and if I should wake him up and see if he was OK and all. I didn't necessarily want to do that. I mean, I was actually enjoying not having to listen to him talk for a while. Even though he was snoring like a fog horn, he wasn't actually *talking* to me. So I told the flight attendant that I would check on him even though I actually didn't do a goddamn thing to stop the snoring. He didn't finally start waking up until the plane began its descent. Once the plane tipped forward and started heading down, Jason woke up like someone had thrown a bucket of cold water on him. It's true. He thought the plane was falling from the sky.

"What's going on?! Is everything OK? Is the plane OK? Are we going to die?!" he asked frantically, spreading his arms out and bracing himself for a crash. His hair was kind of smashed on one side and sticking up on the other side.

"Everything's OK, Jason. The plane's just getting ready to *land*. Don't you think everyone would be screaming if the plane was about to crash or something?" He stopped for a second and listened, validating what I just said. He rubbed the crust from his eyes.

"I guess you're right." He sat up and adjusted his clothes and tried to mash down his messy hair (it was useless). Looking out the window, he discovered the city below us and marveled at its size and scope. "Wow, look how big New York is. It's *incredible*. I've never seen anything like it."

"New York is an amazing place," I said, looking out the window as well. "It's not only a big city, it's the cultural center of the world, in my opinion. Anyone who is anybody in literature or music or television or theater has to make it here. I mean, there are other cities that are important to the arts but New York's the biggest and grandest of them all. If you can make it here, you can make it ..."

"You can make it anywhere, just like it says in the *song*!"

"That's right. Just like the song." I'm telling you, Jason was a goddamn genius. It's true. He could finish my sentences without batting an eye. I guess that's why we were such good friends.

"I think the biggest city I've ever been to is Birmingham, or maybe Mobile. I don't know which city is bigger but neither of them are as big as New York."

"There's no place as *big* as New York."

By this point, the plane was in fast pursuit of the runway. Jason gripped the armrests of his seat like he was holding on for his life, clenching the plastic with the tips of his goddamn, grubby fingers. The plane hit the ground with a double *thud* and skidded its way to a complete stop, before turning to the terminal and approaching at a pedestrian pace. Jason exhaled a sigh of relief, expressing his gratitude that the plane had made it to the ground safely. It would be a short while before we got off the plane, considering that we had to wait in a goddamn line for everyone else to get their bags and their crap from the overhead compartments. And the flight attendant wasn't helping matters, standing at the front of the plane flashing her fake smile and big tits. It was all an exercise in patience that I was failing miserably.

Inside the terminal, we headed for the baggage pickup for the rest of our crap. When I mentioned to Jason that we were taking a limousine to the hotel, he about shit in his pants. It's true. He started whooping and hollering all over the place like a goddamn redneck. He was so excited his head about popped off.

"I've never been in a limousine before," he said. "I feel like a rockstar! Will they have champagne and caviar inside?" He was acting like a kid waking up at five o'clock the morning of Christmas. He just couldn't wait to see what the goddamn limo was like or if it had booze inside or not and how long it was and what color it was and if it had leather seats. He was starting to drive me crazy.

"Maybe they'll have champagne. We'll see. But I doubt it."

We picked up my milk-of-magnesia blue suitcase and Jason's University of Alabama Crimson Tide duffle bag from the baggage claim and headed out front. I was told that the driver would have a sign with my name on it. And I was right. Standing in front of a black, stretch Lincoln limousine was the driver with a sign with my name on it. The sign said: *Burchwood.* When I confirmed my name and our destination at the ----- ----- Hotel, he offered to load our bags into the trunk. He extended his goddamn meat-hooks for my backpack but I told him it was off limits.

"You can load the rest of our bags. I'll hold onto this *one.*"

"Whatever you say, Mr. Burchwood. My name is Samuel. I'll be your driver today."

Samuel was a short and stocky guy with no neck and boulders for hands. He looked like a short version of Andre the Giant, with his broad face and scraggly sideburns and stringy goddamn hair. He also looked like he could break me in half with his bare hands (if he wanted to). And he had a voice that sounded like he smoked three packs of cigarettes a day ever since he was three-years-old or something. He opened the door to the limo and motioned for us to get in. Once inside, we watched him pickup our bags like they didn't weigh a thing and fling them into the trunk.

"I wouldn't want to piss him off," Jason said, checking the limo for champagne or caviar. He looked in every goddamn compartment and even under the seat. "Hey, there isn't any champagne in *here.* What a jip!"

"I didn't promise the moon, you know. I just said a limo was picking us up."

Samuel the Giant hopped in the driver's seat and the car kind of tilted to the side a bit. He must have weighed 300 pounds or more. It's true. He was as big as a goddamn tank. He started the limo and slowly pulled away from the terminal. A small group of onlookers watched us as we drove off.

"Do you think those people back there recognized you?" Jason asked. "They were kind of staring at us." Jason always was an observant one. He noticed everything. He noticed every goddamn bit of minutiae that happened in a day. It's true.

"Hopefully, they did. Maybe those marketing people at the publishing house are finally doing their job."

Samuel the Giant cautiously pulled into traffic and once we were a ways from the airport, he rolled down the barrier window that divided his space from our space. He was an excellent driver, I could tell. He didn't rock us around or anything. He seemed like a professional.

"We're on our way to the ----- ----- Hotel, gentlemen. Let me know if there is anything you need," Samuel the Giant said, with his raspy, cigarette voice.

"Actually, I have a question," Jason said. I couldn't believe he was actually going to open his goddamn mouth. I wanted to slap him. "Isn't there supposed to be champagne or caviar or some kind of *expensive* booze in here?"

"Not necessarily, sir, but we can stop and get some if you'd like," Samuel replied politely. He really was a professional even though he was ugly as an ox. He didn't look like a professional but he sure drove like one.

"That would be *great*," Jason said, leaning back in his seat with a big smile stretched across his face. "We can't have our *famous* writer riding around New York in a limousine without champagne. Am I right?"

And for once, he *was* right. I mean, Jason was a goddamn pig and a blabbermouth but he sure was an excellent cheerleader. It's true. He obviously had a great admiration for my career and my new lot in life. I think he really respected me and the work I accomplished to get out of the ordinary path that most people choose and to follow my dreams. In fact, I think he was enjoying the limo ride more than I was. He was smiling all over the goddamn place and rubbing the upholstery and pressing every button and flipping every switch he could find. He was truly like a kid in a candy store. And for once, I was glad he was there with me. It's true.

"You're right, Jason." I directed Samuel the Giant to follow Jason's instructions. He nodded his head and rolled up the window. I noticed that we were turning on Atlantic Avenue and knew that we would be in Manhattan in less than twenty minutes. Jason was as excited as an A.D.D. kid, bouncing and singing all over the goddamn place.

"So what's the plan for tonight?" Jason asked, flipping an ashtray in the door opened and closed, repeatedly. "Are we going to be hanging out with any movie stars or TV personalities? Are you going to introduce me to anybody *famous*?"

"Maybe later tonight. The first thing we need to do is check-in at the hotel and then go by Barnes & Noble. I want to check out the reading space. I also want to make sure that they will have a microphone there for me. I hate reading without a microphone." I really *hated* to read without a microphone. It's true. Every time I read my work without a microphone, I end up raising my voice and screaming all over the place like a goddamn idiot. And that's the worst thing a writer can do. I mean, you lose all the *nuances* of the language when you're screaming your goddamn head off. Plus, the audience loses interest when I writer raises his voice like that. I guess they take it as a sign of hostility or something. At least that's what one of my writer buddies told me one time. It seemed plausible to me. It's kind of like when someone sends you an e-mail and THEIR TEXT IS WRITTEN THIS WAY AND THEY END EVERY SENTENCE WITH A DOZEN EXCLAMATION POINTS!!!!!!!!!!!! It's kind of *hostile* and all. It's true. "The bookstore isn't too far from the hotel and it shouldn't take too long. After that, we can party all night long."

"That's what I'm talking about," Jason said, dancing in his seat.

Samuel the Giant eventually pulled over to the side of the road and parked in front of a convenience store. He rolled down his barrier window and turned to face us.

"Would you gentlemen like anything else besides champagne?" I'm telling you, the guy was a goddamn professional. He really was. He didn't even ask us for money to pay for the champagne.

"How about some Cokes?" Jason asked.

"Coca-Colas coming up," Samuel replied, turning around.

"Any kind of Cokes, you know, like orange or lime or root beer," Jason added.

Samuel the Giant slowly turned around to face us again. He looked a little annoyed this time, kind of like his professionalism had just run its course. I knew it was probably too good to be true, what, with his goddamn pleasant attitude and excellent driving and his meat-hooks and all. It's always too good to be true.

"Oh, I forgot, you boys are from down *south*. You call every kind of soda *Cokes*. Up here, we *only* call Coca-Colas Cokes. Everything else is some kind of soda or pop. Got it?" He turned around and got out of the car. We watched him lumber into the store, almost too wide to fit in the door. I looked at Jason and he had a slight look of fear on his face. He looked like he had seen a goddamn ghost or something, what, with his pale skin and yellow eyes. He kind of freaked me out.

"I don't think he likes us," Jason said, looking to make sure Samuel the Giant wasn't around. "He looked pretty annoyed that I asked him to get us some Cokes too."

"I wouldn't worry about it. All New Yorkers are like that. They all act like they want to kick your butt, even the women. It's kind of *their* way up here. It's true."

"Oh, kind of like how all southern men are gentlemen? I get it," Jason said, the look of fear now gone. Like I said, sometimes you just had to lead him in the right direction. He got off the goddamn track too easily.

Samuel the Giant came lumbering out of the store with a bottle of champagne and a bottle of Coke under his left arm, some plastic cups in his left hand, and a cell phone occupying his right hand. He was talking pretty intensely into the phone, like he was upset or pissed off at the other person he was talking to. I'd hate to be that person, what, with Samuel the Giant big as hell and with fists like mountains and his awful New York attitude. He got in the front seat, lowered the barrier window, and dropped the bottles and cups into our section of the limo. Then he rolled the window back up and continued yelling into the goddamn cell phone. Jason grabbed the cheap bottle of champagne and uncorked it. Samuel's attitude didn't faze him one bit.

"Ready for some bubbly?" he asked, popping the cork and filling the plastic cups.

"I wonder who he's talking to?" I asked. I couldn't hear exactly what he was saying. But whatever it was, he wasn't too happy about it. In fact, I thought he was going to explode for a second, his head all red and puffy and sweat pouring down his neck. Jason handed me a cup of champagne and began to propose a toast when Samuel turned around again and lowered the barrier window.

"Gentlemen, I hope you don't mind but I have to make a little *detour* right up the road. It'll only take a second."

And without a response or acknowledgement from us, he drove up the road a bit and turned onto a side street. He drove down a few blocks, past a bunch of rundown buildings and lots, and pulled behind an old office building. He lowered the barrier window and I could see his eyes in the rearview mirror. They were all bloodshot and hot with anger, I could tell. He looked mad as hell.

"I'll be back shortly." He got out of the limo and disappeared into the building, right through the entrance on the ground floor. All the windows in the building were kind of foggy or dusty and I couldn't really tell what kind of business went on in there. But whatever kind of business it was, it wasn't a good business, that's for sure. Jason kept slurping on the champagne like a goddamn wino, gulping it by the glass like a goddamn pig, without a care in the world. He really made me sick sometimes, the bastard, with his nonchalant existence. Sometimes, it seemed like he didn't *care* about bettering himself at all. He was just content with being a goddamn pig. I guess deep down, that's what he *really* was. And there's no sense in trying to change a goddamn pig. It's true.

And all of a sudden, like a shotgun blast, the entrance door flew open and slammed against the outside of the building, shattering the glass to the ground. Samuel the Giant had kicked it open and was now dragging someone behind him by his hair. It was fucking unbelievable. My mouth and Jason's cup of champagne dropped, literally. Samuel dragged the guy across the parking lot asphalt, to a spot about ten feet in front of the limo. Jason and I made our way closer to the front so we could see out the windshield. The poor guy on the ground was kicking and screaming while Samuel twisted him around by his goddamn hair. And without warning, Samuel the Giant pummeled the guy repeatedly with his mountain-sized fists, across the face, on the head, around his neck, like a jackhammer. The guy eventually stopped struggling and his body went limp. But Samuel didn't stop. He pounded and pounded him for what seemed like a goddamn eternity. Then, he threw him to the ground and kicked him in the stomach. He concluded the tirade by spitting on him. He got back in the limo like nothing had happened, fixing his scraggly hair and adjusting his soiled collar.

"Sorry about that, gentlemen. It was an unfortunate incident. You'll be at the hotel shortly." He started the limo and pulled away. I looked out the back window and watched the guy on the ground as we drove off. He never got back up. As far as I could tell, he probably wouldn't be getting up at all. Samuel the Giant turned back on Atlantic Avenue and continued on like nothing had happened. Maybe Samuel was a hit man or a gangster or a drug dealer or some other shady-type. Maybe that guy owed him money or stabbed him in the back after a bum deal or something. Or maybe his buddies called him Sammie Mountain-Hands or Sammie the Bulldog or Sammie No-Neck or something like that. The possibilities were endless being that we were in New York. I immediately thought about writing a new novel about a gangster named Samuel who drove a cab or something. He was trying to leave the world of organized crime and all when he kept getting pulled back in by nickel and dime jobs from high level relatives in his family. But everyone that knew him actually knew him as a gentle person, unlike the *real* Samuel, who was obviously a goddamn monster. The ideas were pouring out and I knew that I had to at least write some of them down before I forgot them. If there was one thing I learned about writing, it was that you never let good ideas *slip* by. You always write *everything* down. It's true. You never know when the next good story idea will hit you. I reached in my bag for a pad and pen when Jason knocked on the barrier window. Samuel lowered the window and looked at Jason in the rearview mirror.

"Yes sir?" he asked, all polite and gentlemanly.

"What did that guy do to *you*?" Jason asked, timidly. "If you don't mind me asking, that is." Samuel didn't respond. His eyes alternated from the road to Jason and back. "Are you a *gangster* or something, like in the movie *Goodfellas*?"

Samuel laughed boisterously. He laughed like Jason's question was the funniest goddamn joke he'd ever heard. His laugh was low and thunderous and really scary.

"Me? A *gangster*? You watch too many movies," Samuel said, keeping his eye on the road. "That guy back there, he's my brother-in-law. He likes to smack my little sister around. So I told him to smack on someone his own size. He told me to go to hell so I thought I'd teach him a little lesson."

"He's a *relative*?" I asked, scribbling the details down on paper. I couldn't write them down fast enough. It was just too good to be true.

"Just by marriage. He and my little sis got married a few years ago. He's a real prick, you know. He likes to beat on girls. He brought it all on himself." Jason sat back down and poured a fresh glass of champagne. At the pace he was going, he'd be out cold in fifteen minutes. It's true. He was chugging that champagne like it was the last goddamn bottle on earth.

"You mind if I smoke?" Jason asked, looking for his pack of cigarettes.

"Only if I can smoke too," Samuel replied, a look of relief on his face. It must have taken a lot out of him, beating his brother-in-law and all, even if he did deserve it. Jessica has an older brother but he's a skinny little fuck. He couldn't beat me up if he tried. Jason handed Samuel a smoke and they both lit up. It was becoming a goddamn *party* in the limo. "So, Burchwood, I hear you're a writer? At least that's what the dispatcher told me. That true?"

"Yes, that is true. My new novel, THE RISE AND FALL OF A TITAN, will be published in the next few weeks. I'm reading some chapters from it at the Barnes & Noble flagship store in Manhattan tomorrow night."

"Which one? The one on ---th & ---th Street?"

"That's the one."

"That's great. You know, I always wanted to be a writer..."

It was really becoming a nightmare, what, with all these wannabe do-nothings who talk about wanting to do this and never actually doing that. It was really driving me crazy. It's true. But I didn't dare say a word about that to Samuel the Giant in fear that he would pulverize me into the goddamn ground. I just listened to him quietly as he drove us to the hotel.

I leaned back in my seat and kicked my feet up, bummed a smoke from Jason and lit up, poured a cup of champagne, and enjoyed the things that *fame* was bringing my way. With the exception of watching Samuel viciously beat his brother-in-law to the ground and Jason's goddamn incessant snoring on the plane, it was turning out to be a pretty good day.

21.

"Here we are, gentlemen. The ----- ----- Hotel, safe and sound," Samuel said. When he stepped out of the limo, the Lincoln became balanced and level without his 300-plus pound frame weighing it down on one side. Jason finished the last of the champagne and I smothered the last bit of life from my cigarette before we climbed out of the limo. The ----- ----- Hotel was a grand goddamn spectacle and all. It's true. There were dozens of valets and bellboys frantically running around, moving cars, unloading luggage, and kissing people's asses with the utmost professionalism and courtesy. It was truly a *sight* to behold. Watching the hotel employees was like watching a skilled ballet troupe performing an improvised dance. It was chaotic and breathtaking, all at the same time. Samuel the Giant unloaded our bags from the trunk and placed them on a luggage cart. I gave him a dollar and, more importantly, one of my business cards as a tip. I would have given him two dollars but watching him pulverize his brother-in-law had traumatized me a bit. He seemed genuinely pleased with the dollar and impressed with the card. It worked every time.

"You can visit my web site and read samples of my work. If you like what you read, then leave me a tip in return," I said, placing my backpack over my shoulder.

"Thanks. I don't use the Internet but I'll tell my wife about it. She loves that kind of shit," Samuel said, slipping the dollar and card in his wallet. "You know, I'm yours for as long as you are in New York. You do *know* that, right?"

"What do you mean?" I asked.

"Your company paid for full service. So, whenever you need a ride, just give me a call." He handed me a card with his cell phone number on it. It also said: *Samuel, your friendly limousine driver.* "I know you want to go to that bookstore. Call me. I'll give you a lift."

"OK. We'll do that."

"I'm going to check on my brother-in-law. Hopefully, I didn't *kill* him. He is married to my sister, you know." And with that, Samuel the Giant lumbered back to the limo, climbed in, and drove off.

"What a nice guy," Jason said, pushing the luggage cart towards the hotel entrance. And out of nowhere, like a leprechaun appearing from another dimension, a bellboy grabbed the cart from Jason, shoving him to the side. And you know, he looked a lot like our friend Stanford, what, with his skinny, lanky body and oversized glasses and goddamn bowtie. The only addition was one of those little goddamn hats with the chin strap that bellboys wear. He looked pretty ridiculous, just like Stanford. He flashed us the biggest shit-eating grin he could muster.

"My name's Carl. I'll take your luggage for you," he said, pushing the cart like it was the most enjoyable thing in the world to do.

"We'll get it," Jason said, trying to reclaim the cart. But Carl wasn't having it. He held onto the cart like it was his birth right.

"Don't be ridiculous," he said, smiling from ear to ear. "It's my *job*. But I appreciate the kindness. You boys from out of town?"

"Yep, I'm from Alabama and he's from Texas," Jason said, pointing to me.

"I knew it. I could tell, you know. You two look like southern boys. Like I said, my name's Carl and whatever you need, Carl can get. Dig?" He winked at us and pushed the cart through the entrance into the lobby. We followed behind him, watching him skip along as he pushed. He must have really liked his job, the way he was dancing around like he was the happiest bellboy in the entire goddamn city.

The lobby was just as grand as the driveway, cavernous and posh and flashy and shit, what, with tropical trees and brass tables and leather couches and all. In addition to the limo, I was really beginning to feel like I had finally made it, being there in that grand place. It's true. I felt really important and larger than life. Jason was pretty goddamn impressed too. He was whooping and hollering all over the place, blabbing about how he'd never been in a hotel like this before and how Motel 6's smelled like diarrhea and shit. He was really embarrassing me. Carl motioned for us to go to the check-in counter while he pulled the luggage cart out of the main walkway.

"I'll be here waiting for you, gentlemen," he said. Even though he reminded me a lot of Stanford the thief, he was really starting to grow on me with his kindness and all. He was happy to help us and ready to please. I liked that. I told Jason to wait with Carl while I checked in. There wasn't a line so I stepped right up to the counter.

Checking-in was a breeze. Everything was already setup, the billing, all the information was in the computer and all. I just had to flash my driver's license and sign a form. I think I barely said more than two words to the nice lady behind the counter. It went so goddamn smooth, I didn't even catch her name. It's true. It was a really professional establishment, top-notch. The publishing house did a fantastic job of booking everything. She gave me two key cards and thanked me. I quickly joined Jason and Carl. The two dildos were playing *Paper, Rock, Scissors*. I think Carl was ahead because Jason looked pretty sore and all. Jason's a really sore loser (if I hadn't told you by now). He really is. There's nothing he hated more than losing goddamn stupid games like *Paper, Rock, Scissors* or *Tic-tac-toe*. He got all red and whiny when he started to lose. And Carl must have been beating him pretty bad because Jason's head looked like an overripe tomato.

"Damn it, Carl! You're too good!" Jason said, after his paper lost to Carl's scissors.

"I have seven kids. I have to be *good*!" Carl said. "Ready for your room? What's the number?"

"We're in room 2506," I told him. He snatched the keys from my hand and started pushing the cart towards the elevators. He pressed the up button and we waited amidst a dozen elevator doors for a vacant carriage. Carl turned to me with his big shit-eating grin.

"You know, I can get you *whatever* you want." He nudged me a bit with his goddamn elbow, trying to be subtle but not doing a very good job. He was about as subtle as a goddamn explosion.

"What do you *mean*?" I asked. A vacant elevator dinged and the door slid open. Carl pushed the luggage cart into the rear of the elevator and we all climbed in. He pressed the button for the twenty fifth floor and the door slid shut.

"You know, *whatever*," he said as the elevator gently lifted us upward toward our destination. He lowered his voice and leaned toward us. "You want *girls*, I can get 'em. You want some *smoke*, I can get it. You want some *blow*, *I* can get it. Dig?" Turned out that Carl the Bellboy was also Carl the Pimp *and* Carl the Hustler. He must have had it pretty good, what, with his bellboy tips and his side-jobs doling out prostitutes and drugs and *whatever*. I mean, he did have *seven* kids to support, you know. "When I say whatever, I mean *whatever*."

Jason nudged me in the side and started whispering in my ear like a goddamn idiot. "Hey, I wouldn't mind some blow, just a little. I mean, we're on *vacation*, right?" That surprised the shit out of me, what, being that he was a goddamn pig and all and now I knew he was a cokehead too. It was un-fucking believable. It's true. Betty had married a real *mess*.

"We don't need *anything*, Carl" I said, nudging Jason back. "But I appreciate the offer."

"What? You boys aren't ...you know?" He pointed at the two of us and gave us *that* look. He stuck out his hand in a limp fashion like he was a girl or something. I immediately knew what he was getting at.

"We're not *gay*!" I said, really annoyed and all. Who the hell did he think he was?

"I didn't think so. Anyway, *everyone* eventually needs *something*. They always do. I'll be waiting, just so you know. Call the front desk and ask for me. Like I said, my name's Carl."

Our elevator arrived at the twenty fifth floor and we followed Carl the Pimp down the long hallway to our room. He opened the door with the key card and we followed him in. He briskly unloaded the luggage cart and stuck out his hand for a tip. And for a quick instant, I really thought I was standing in front of Stanford. He looked *just* like him. It's true, what, with the bowtie and the goddamn big glasses. The only difference was that Stanford was a thief and Carl was a pimp. But that was a *minor* detail. It really was.

"Anything else for you, sir?" Carl the pimp asked.

"No, that will be all." I gave him a dollar and a business card. He looked at the card like it was a crusty dog turd.

"Thank you, sir," he said, really sarcastic and all. He pushed the cart out of the room and slammed the door behind him.

Jason jumped on one of the king-size beds and started bouncing all over the goddamn place. He was acting like a little kid, a *drunk* little kid. He was really getting on my last nerve.

"This room is great!" he said, jumping so high he almost slammed his head into the ceiling. "I've never been ..."

"I know, I know. You've never been *anywhere*. I get it," I told him. I was really irritated with him by this point. He was acting like a goddamn idiot. He climbed down from the bed and placed his hands on my shoulders. He leaned in really close, like he was going to kiss me or something. His breath wreaked of cigarettes and booze and Cokes.

"What's wrong? Are you mad at me?" he asked.

"No, I just have a lot on my mind. And I don't want to be bothered with girls or drugs or *any*thing. I just need to get ready for tomorrow. Is that all right with you?"

"Of course. Sorry," he said, kind of sulking. I felt really bad for yelling at him but it had to be done. It's true. He was acting like a goddamn fool with his bed-jumping and bad breath and coke cravings and drinking everything in sight and all.

He started unpacking his duffle bag and placing his clothes in the dresser. All he had were a couple of t-shirts and a couple pair of goddamn Bermuda shorts. I unpacked my suitcase, placing my clothes in my side of the dresser. When he was finished, he inspected the room, looking in all the closets, checking the bathroom and balcony. He opened the refrigerator and discovered the miniature bottles of booze and wine and the cans of beer. He got all excited and shit, like he found sunken treasure or something. He pulled a couple of beers out and handed me one.

"I'm ready for action," he said, chugging his beer. "What's next?"

"Give Samuel a call and ask him if he can come back and pick us up. I want to go by Barnes & Noble before it gets too late. Also, make sure he isn't busy beating somebody up or something."

Jason called the number on Samuel's card and got in touch with him. Turns out Samuel's brother-in-law wasn't *dead* after all. He was helping his sister put her beaten husband in her car and said he'd be over in ten minutes. So I washed my face and changed shirts (I have to feel clean) and we headed back down to the lobby. Jason had stuffed a few beers in his pocket like a goddamn thief even though I told him he wasn't *taking* anything, that I had to pay for them when we checked-out. He still seemed really nervous and all, worried that some hotel employee would tell him he couldn't take the beers out of the hotel or some shit like that. He really was acting like a big dope.

Outside, Samuel was waiting for us in front of the limo. He was holding the door open like we were big shots, big stars. And I guess, in my own way, I was. We got in the car and he closed the door behind us. When he got in the front, the Lincoln sagged to the left again like it was going to tip over. He rolled down the barrier window and turned around.

"To the Barnes & Noble on ---th & ---th Street?" he asked.

"Samuel, you can keep the window *down*. There's no point in rolling it up and down when it just might as well be down," I told him. He looked kind of surprised that I asked him to do that, like no one had asked him to do that before. "And yes, that's the one we're going to."

"Thanks."

Samuel the Giant slowly pulled the limo away from the hotel and we nestled in with midtown traffic. For once, Jason didn't say a goddamn thing. He was mesmerized by the great city, just like I was. Even though I had been to New York several times before, it still never ceased to amaze me just how *dense* the city was. I mean, everything was on *top* of everything, literally. In Texas, everything is spread out, even in the big cities like Dallas or Houston. There is a lot of space in between everything and you never seem to feel cramped, no matter where you went. But in New York, everything is on top of everything and there isn't a horizon anywhere to be found, just sky up above tall buildings. The late afternoon sky was slowly fading into darkness and it was strange not seeing a pink and purple horizon in the distance, one like you'd see Austin or out on Lake Travis. I was really starting to miss my family. I hadn't spoken to them in quite some time and thinking about the Texas sunsets made me think of my wife, Jessica. She and I used to watch the sun set almost every day when we were dating. That was something we really enjoyed doing together, going to Lake Travis, getting a table at the Oasis, and watching the sun dip behind the horizon at the edge of the lake. The water reflected the pink, orange, and purple streaks in the sky and shimmied the reflection into a million tiny, liquid explosions. It was all very romantic and enchanting and intoxicating. It's true. I asked her to marry me out there, overlooking the water. How could I not with all that beauty around and my beautiful woman sitting across from me? And I wasn't even *high* when I asked her to marry me. It's true.

Jason crawled toward the front of the limo and handed Samuel a beer and a cigarette. The two of them started drinking and smoking and whooping it up like a couple of old buddies, telling jokes and laughing like a couple of goddamn hyenas. They seemed perfect for each other as friends, you know. Jason and I were a lot different from each other. I was surprised sometimes that we had remained friends through the years. But we had a childhood bond that wasn't meant to be broken. I guess we were lucky that way. A lot of people lose touch with their childhood friends and that's unfortunate. When you lose touch with them, you lose touch with a part of yourself, in a way. And that's a goddamn shame. It's true.

After a couple of near-fatal collisions and a few potential pedestrian accidents, we arrived at the Barnes & Noble where I would be reading the next night. Of course, there wasn't a place to park on the busy street so Samuel told us to get out and he'd circle the block until we called him to come get us. So Jason and I hopped out of the limo and made a mad dash for the sidewalk.

Inside, the store was busy with throngs of eager patrons searching for their next favorite read or looking for the book with answers to their unanswerable questions. This Barnes & Noble was no different than any other I had ventured into, the sections categorized and positioned in a similar fashion to any other store. The only difference I noticed was the actual *amount* of patrons compared to the ones that went to these stores in Texas. I guess since New York *is* the cultural center of the world, there are quite a bit more avid readers than anywhere else. I mean, the store was so full that I could barely make my way around. It made Texans seem like a bunch of goddamn illiterates. It's true. But before we got too far in the store, Jason noticed the calendar of events hanging from the ceiling. And wouldn't you know it? My name wasn't on the goddamn calendar for tomorrow night. It seemed that something *else* was scheduled.

"What's an open mike?" Jason asked, scratching his head. "What does that mean?"

"It means that *I'm* pissed off! My name should be up there in *fucking* neon!" Jason looked shocked when I said that. I mean, I wasn't one to *cuss* out loud. It was something I just didn't do very often, unless I was *really* mad. But tonight, I was livid. There should have been signs everywhere with my name on them. They should have had banners announcing the release of my book. They should have had my picture plastered all over the goddamn place. But as I quickly discovered, there wasn't a sign of me or my book anywhere. And that just wouldn't do. "I need to talk to someone about this right now!"

Jason followed me to the Customer Service counter and I waited as the employee scanned in returned merchandise and looked utterly pathetic in his apron and name tag and wrinkled shirt. He didn't even look at me while I impatiently waited, purposefully ignoring me as if his duties were more important than the feelings of this pissed-off customer. I started to glare at him in hopes that he'd see my fury and frustration but he didn't look up. He didn't move his goddamn beady eyes. He was completely engrossed in his minor duties even though my glare was burning a hole right through him. I guess Jason noticed my frustration and he tried to appease me. But it didn't matter to me. I was going to take things in my own hands.

"Excuse me," I said, continuing to glare at him. His name tag said: *CHIP.* He still didn't look at me. "Excuse me, *Chip.*"

"Yes?" he asked, still not looking at me, still with his eyes on the returned merchandise, his greasy hair tied in a bun, his sideburns growing like unkempt carpet grass. He had the phrase *eat me* tattooed on the knuckles of his left hand, each letter occupying its own finger: E-A-T-M-E.

"I'm supposed to be reading here tomorrow night and my name isn't on the calendar of events. Can you tell me *why* that is?" I was completely livid by this point, beyond the limits of my control. I wanted to grab Chip by the throat and rip his esophagus out. I wanted to jab my index finger in his eye and twist it around in the goddamn socket. I wanted to grab his testicles and yank them with all my strength. I wanted to do *lots* of horrible goddamn things to him. But he didn't seem to care at all.

"You'll have to speak to the *manager* about that. I'm kind of busy right now," Chip quipped, giving me a quick, uninterested glance. He picked up the phone and called his manager. "Jim? There's a customer here that needs to talk to you." He hung up the phone and went back to his duties. I wanted to scream.

"Hey Simon, why don't we come back later?" Jason asked. But I refused. I wanted this handled and taken care of that very minute. How were my fans supposed to know if this was the correct Barnes & Noble? Where was any promotion whatsoever of my impending book release? It was all unforgivable. It's true. The manager eventually made his way out the door behind Chip. He was a tall fucker with an unassuming face, broad shoulders, a pencil neck, and sunken eyes. He looked a little jaundice as well, like Frankenstein's monster with a name tag. The tag said: *Jim, Assistant Manager.*

"Can I help you, sir?" he asked, in his benevolent yet ambiguous, corporate tone. He looked just as pathetic as Chip did.

"I want to know why my *name* isn't on the calendar of events for tomorrow night?" I pointed to the calendar hanging from the ceiling behind us.

"I'm not quite sure, sir. What *is* your name?"

"Burchwood. My name is Simon Burchwood. I'm reading from my new novel, THE RISE AND FALL OF A TITAN, tomorrow night," I said, the rage building in me. "At least, that's what I was told by my publisher!"

"Sir, you don't have to *raise* your voice at me ..."

"I CAN RAISE MY VOICE AT WHOMEVER I PLEASE! DON'T YOU KNOW WHO I AM?!"

"Mr. Burchwood, I'm going to have to ask you to leave if you're going to continue to speak to me in that manner."

"WHO THE FUCK ..." And that was all I could get in edge-wise before a security guard came and swept me off balance and whisked me out of the store by my arm. I don't know where Jason was in all this but all I remember was my face hitting the sliding-glass door and being shoved out of the store. The guard followed me out and stood in front of the entrance with his hands on his hips, blocking any way for me to return inside. Luckily, Samuel the Giant was waiting outside and witnessed the whole goddamn thing. He stomped up behind me and placed his hand on my shoulder. I could hear him breathing and snorting like a raging bull waiting to pounce.

"You gotta problem buddy?!" Samuel demanded, his mountain-sized fists clinched. The security guard put his hands up as a sign of forfeiture. He looked like he was about to piss his polyester pants after he got a good look at Samuel. I thought for a moment that I should have taken Samuel in with me in the first place but I didn't want to *beat* anybody up. I just wanted to know why my name wasn't on the calendar. The trip was starting to feel like a bust already. "Because if you got a problem with him, then you got a real big problem with *me*!"

"No problem here," the security guard replied, scared out of his goddamn wits. He had a gun at his side but I knew he wouldn't even think of pulling it on Samuel. What was shooting Samuel going to do but really *piss* him off? It's true. "I'm just doing my job."

"Me too so fuck off!" Samuel said and the guard retreated back into the store. Samuel led me to the limo and opened the door for me. And guess *who* was inside? Take a goddamn guess.

"What are you doing in *here*?" I asked. Jason was lounging in the back of the goddamn limo, smoking a cigarette and drinking a beer. "I thought you were going to *help* me on this trip?"

"I was *trying* to help you but you didn't want to listen to me. What did you want me to do? Start yelling at people or something?"

I sat down and grabbed one of Jason's cigarettes. I figured there wasn't much else I could do that night anyway so I conceded to my defeat. I decided right then and there that I would call my publisher first thing tomorrow and demand that something be done. I didn't know for sure what *exactly* I wanted to be done. But I did know for sure that some heads were going to roll. I was positive about that.

22.

Nothing's better for a wounded heart than a big, fat, greasy, cheeseburger and a pile of salty french fries. It's true. We were eating the finest burgers, fries, and vanilla Cokes that room service had to offer. The combos had to be good considering they were *fifteen* dollars apiece. Room service was always a goddamn rip off. But these particular burgers were worth it and here's why. After Samuel dropped us off back at the hotel, Jason called Betty's sister's house to try to talk to his wife about their problems but the whore hung up on him. So Jason called his neighbor, Mrs. Burke, to see if she had noticed anything peculiar around his house while he was at work. She told him how she had been out in her garden one day, watering her petunias and watching the goddamn squirrels romp around in her backyard. A cable-service van pulled up to Jason's house but old Mrs. Burke didn't pay much attention to it since she always saw all kinds of service trucks parked in front of all the neighbors' houses at one point or another. But here's the shit-kicker. After the cable man had been in Jason's house for about thirty minutes, she heard some rustling and a small ruckus in Jason's backyard. And being that she was a nosey old hag with nothing better to do, she made her way toward the fence and took a peek. She watched as the cable man and Betty fucked each others' brains out in the backyard. But, of course, the old hag didn't say the word *fucked*. She told Jason that they were *necking something fierce*, which is a nicer way of saying they were fucking or something. Anyway, old Mrs. Burke said that they were really paranoid and looking around all over the place to make sure no one was watching. They didn't notice the old hag because she was on the other side of the fence hiding behind her bushes. The old perverted hag watched the *whole* thing. She said the van eventually left but she started to notice that the van came around a lot more often than she previously thought. When Jason asked why she didn't tell him about the cable man, she said she thought it was really none of her business. But since he *asked*, she didn't see any harm in telling him since his wife was committing adultery and all. Jason was devastated, literally heartbroken. It's true. He broke down and was crying all over the place. I felt so sorry for him. I did. That's when I decided to order room service. I thought the burgers and fries would cheer him up. And in a way, I was right. The meal at least distracted him for a while.

"This is the best fucking burger I've had in a long time," Jason said, washing his meal down with vanilla Coke. At least he wasn't crying anymore. Nothing ruins a trip to another city more than if your travel companion is balling their brains out. It's true. And I wasn't about to let Jason ruin my trip. I know that may sound selfish but this was an important trip in the grand scheme of things. I couldn't handle having to drag a sad bastard around when he was *supposed* to be helping me. Plus, I was feeling really sorry for him. I must have been really difficult for him to hear what old Mrs. Burke told him. I couldn't imagine my Jessica doing something as heartless as that.

"Hey man, it's the best thing for you. Sometimes, you just have to eat to get things off your mind, especially heavy things," I said. Jason was right about the burgers. They were fucking good.

"Sorry about not helping you out more at the bookstore. I should have been there for you but, in all seriousness, I didn't know what to do anyway. This *celebrity* thing is all new to me."

"Don't worry about it. It's all over and done with. I'm going to call my publisher first thing in the morning and get this all straightened out. They'll have that store on its knees in a matter of minutes," I said. I could see that Jason was feeling much better. The color had come back to his face and he didn't look all pasty and depressed and sad as hell anymore. I was thankful for that. "More importantly, what are you going to do about Betty?"

"Don't know yet. But I'll know something by the time I get back to Montgomery. That's for sure. Maybe I'll ask Samuel to go back with me and take care of that cable man. That'd teach him for screwing around with someone else's wife, wouldn't it?" The thought of Samuel the Giant pulverizing that cable man was pretty goddamn hilarious. I imagined the look on his face when Samuel grabbed him by the neck with his mountain-sized hands and beat the shit out of him. That would teach him a *lesson*. "Only thing is, I don't know if the plane could handle the extra weight with Samuel flying. We'd be doomed for sure!"

We both started laughing at the thought of Samuel's fat ass weighing the plane down. I laughed so hard that I sucked a huge chunk of burger into my throat and started to choke. I about died, I choked so goddamn hard. Jason pounded me on the back a couple of times and the chunk of meat launched out of my mouth. It seemed that Jason really was there to help me out. If he hadn't of come along, I would have *died* for sure. It's true. I imagined the headlines in the paper the next day: *Would-be famous writer chokes himself with cheeseburger. What a goddamn shame!*

"Man, I thought I was going to choke to death," I said, gasping for fresh air.

"Not with me around, you won't," Jason replied. He smiled a kind smile and I knew, just like always, that he truly was my *best friend*. "So, what do you want to do for the rest of the night? Wanna hit the town? Introduce me to some celebrities? Get wasted?"

"Actually, it would be nice if I could practice reading from my book. You up for hearing me read?"

"I thought you said I had to wait until tomorrow to hear your story?"

"I did say that but it's more important to me now that I know that I *sound* good reading my work. There's nothing worse than an author who stutters their own words and fouls up their work by sounding dreary and dull. You up for it?"

"You know what would be great?" he asked, standing up on the bed and jumping all over the goddamn place. The remainder of our meals flew this way and that as he bounced up and down. "It would be *great* if you had a practice *audience* as well. You know, you could practice reading to a practice audience, here in this room."

"Where would I find a practice audience in the middle of the night in New York at the ----- ----- Hotel?"

Jason knew exactly where to find an audience. He called up the front desk and asked for good old Carl the pimp, who told us earlier that he could get *anything* we wanted. Now, I'm sure Carl didn't mean *anything* when he told us he could get us anything, especially since anything to Carl meant something illegal like hookers or cocaine or guns and shit like that. But Jason figured it was worth a try and assumed that Carl the pimp would do about anything for a goddamn tip. And he was right.

"Hey Carl, this is Jason, the guy from Alabama you helped with the luggage earlier. Yeah, that's right. No, I don't need a girl," he said, cupping the phone with his hand as he giggled a bit. "No, I need something *else*. Yeah, something else. You think you can round up some people to come up to our room. Oh, I don't know, maybe a dozen. What do you mean to do what? I just need some people to listen to my buddy read some stories. That's right, *stories*. No, he's not gay. Listen, I guess it'll be kind of like a party. You think you can do it? We'll give you a nice tip ..." And that's all Jason had to say. Good old Carl the Pimp was now Carl the Publicist and Promoter.

Jason started rearranging the room, pushing the two beds apart and laying the comforters on the floor so people could sit down. He moved the dining room table and a chair to the front of the room and placed my backpack on the table.

"You can read here," he said, patting the table and pulling out the chair. He then went to the small refrigerator for a beer. It really seemed like Jason had a problem with booze, what, with his constant drinking and getting drunk and all. It seemed that he drank *all* the time. Whenever it was around, he pounded it down. It's true. He had been drunk practically the entire goddamn time I was with him, from the time I arrived in Montgomery until now. "And the audience can sit down here on these blankets."

"Who do you think Carl will find that will *want* to listen to me read from my novel?" I asked, sitting down at the table and pulling out my manuscript from my backpack.

"It doesn't matter. Think of them as potential new readers and fans. *Win* them over. You can do it." For once, Jason was right. I *would* have to think of them as potential new fans. Jason was turning out to be more helpful than I had hoped, being the champion of my work and the best cheerleader I could ask for. Maybe, when my career really takes off, I could hire Jason as my publicist or personal manager or something. He seemed capable and up for the task.

Just then, the pager in my backpack went off. It was beeping frantically like a goddamn alarm clock. It was my accountant who, for some reason, was returning my call at an ungodly hour. He worked on his own goddamn schedule, I tell you. He must have been out playing golf all day and not worrying one goddamn bit about my inadequate per diem. I reached for the phone to call him but Jason stopped me.

"You need to be concentrating on your reading, not making phone calls. Call whoever it is back later," Jason demanded. I was right, he was a great personal *manager*. I decided right then and there that when we were done with this trip, I would hire Jason as my personal manager. Of course, he'd have to figure out what to do with his whore wife first but it was decided. He was the one to manage my career. I decided to call my accountant in the morning.

A few minutes later, there was a knock at the door and Jason went to answer it. There was good old Carl, smiling from ear to ear, with his goddamn hand already out for a tip.

"I told you I could get *anything*," he said. And the people started flooding in the room. He hadn't brought a dozen; he brought what seemed like fifty loud and raucous people ready for a goddamn party or something. They poured in and found places to sit or stand, grabbing beer and wine from the refrigerator, lighting up cigarettes and cigars, filling up the balcony with smoke and conversation. "Most of the day shift was getting off so I told them to come up here to party. There's Rosita, Fred, Bob, Albert, Jones, ..." He pointed out all of his fellow employees: janitors, cooks, valets, bellboys, waiters, bartenders, security guards, they were all there. Jason slapped a twenty into Carl's hand and closed the door. "I told you I'd take *care* of you."

One thing was for sure, this crowd definitely didn't seem like they were in the mood to listen to some promising up-and-coming author read from his soon-to-be-published novel. It was going to be an uphill battle winning over this crowd of illiterate, blue collar, cigarette smoking, beer stealing, looking-for-a-good-time goddamn hotel employees. They all looked about as smart as a box of rocks. It's true. I could hear all of their goddamn conversations about hooking up and smoking dope and how they hated their jerk bosses and how they didn't want to go home just yet and how there wasn't enough beer in the room and all. It was starting to drive me crazy. Jason stood up on one of the beds and started screaming and hushing all over the place. He was waving his arms around like a goddamn idiot.

"Everybody! Be quiet!" The room immediately stopped chattering and buzzing. Everyone turned their eyes to Jason, drunk as he was, who was standing above my practice crowd. "I'd like to thank everyone for coming. I'd like to introduce ya'll to Mr. Simon Burchwood," he said, extending his hand in my direction. Every bloodshot eye turned to me. "Simon will soon be a household name like Stephen King or Tom Clancy because his new novel, THE RISE AND FALL OF A TITAN, will be out in a few weeks." My practice crowd applauded limply, half-heartedly. It was kind of pathetic. "Carl asked you here for a reason ..."

"To party!!!" some jerk screamed, and the rest of them screamed raucously in return, jumping up and down and spraying each other with beer foam like a bunch of goddamn Neanderthals. Jason started screaming and hushing again, waving his arms around like a helicopter.

"We can *party* in a little bit. But first, we need you to listen to him *read*. He's practicing for his debut tomorrow at the Barnes & Noble flagship store on ---th & ---th Street. But what we need from you *now* is your undivided attention and a little kindness. Do ya'll think you can do that?" The practice crowd mumbled a hesitant acknowledgement.

"What'll we get in return?" asked the screaming jerk, sarcastically.

"I've already asked Carl to bring up a keg of beer in return for a few minutes of your kind attention. How's that?" Jason asked. And apparently, he asked the right question because the practice crowd jumped at the chance, whooping and hollering all over the place with excitement. It was amazing. "Now, everybody have a seat and give a warm welcome to Simon Burchwood, our *famous* writer."

The practice crowd applauded kindly and quietly and took their seats on the floor, beds, and wherever else they could find an empty place. All their eyes and attention were now focused on me and for the first time, I felt pretty overwhelmed. I mean, I had read my stories in front of people before but not that *many* people. My last reading (which was actually quite some time ago) was at a south side coffee shop in Austin and I think there was probably ten people there, tops, including the coffee house server and a street bum standing inside from the rain. The coffee shop crowd was kind and appreciative but there was a big difference between twenty eyes looking at you and a hundred eyes looking at you. Plus, the coffeehouse crowd was there to *actually* see the young authors read their work. This practice crowd was here for the free goddamn beer. I had my work cut out for me. It was going to be a tough crowd to win over.

I pulled my manuscript from my backpack and placed it on the table. I turned to the first page and laid the binder flat. I scanned over the first paragraph, clearing my throat of any phlegmy obstructions, and I could feel the beads of sweat gathering at my forehead. I glanced up quickly and saw all the eyes peering at me, impatiently waiting for me to start. Jason flashed me a quick look of support and nodded his head for me to begin. I took a deep breath, pushing down any bit of stage fright I was experiencing, and I just went for it. I began to read. And I didn't even finish the first sentence before someone's cell phone beeped and squealed, abruptly interrupting my concentration.

"Sorry, sorry! I thought I turned the damn thing off!" the audience member cried, mashing all the buttons on his phone to turn it off. "Proceed. It won't go off again. I promise."

I looked down at the first page of my manuscript and the words blurred and meshed together into a large mass of jumbled letters and punctuation marks. I felt my heart pounding, harder and faster in my chest, as all the eyes peered at me, waiting for me to read. The stage fright began to engulf me in paranoia and panic. But I began to read anyway, pushing past the fear. My voice cracked and stuttered (just as I had feared it would). I heard a snicker or two from a couple of goddamn ingrates but I pressed on. My story of the unscrupulous technology tycoon who rose to prominence yet fell to scandal unfolded in staccato phrases, my intentions tripping over my fear of being looked at by a hundred strange eyes. It seemed like an eternity before I finished the first paragraph. But when I did finish it, I had had enough. It's true. My anxiety gripped me like a vice.

"I think that's all I'm going to read tonight. I just wanted a little practice," I told the faceless crowd. I closed the manuscript and placed it back in my backpack, where it belonged. They gave me some sympathetic applause and began chattering amongst themselves. The practice reading was officially over. Jason hopped down from the bed and put his arm around my shoulder.

"It was good, Simon. Really," he said, a big smile stretched across his face. "What little bit I heard was good. I'm *proud* of you."

"I get really nervous in front of people, especially people I don't know. I guess I have really bad stage fright or something."

"Maybe you should get *drunk* before you read. I'm never nervous when I'm drunk."

"I'll keep that in mind," I said, shoving the backpack in a drawer in my dresser. I was relieved that the practice reading was over and I could concentrate on getting some rest for the *real* reading tomorrow. I was certain that the pressure of the actual reading would be a lot greater than this practice one, which was only attended by a captive audience of illiterate boobs. The crowd tomorrow was certain to be a more critical and opinionated group and all. The actual idea of it made my heart feel like it was going to explode.

The next thing I knew, Carl slammed the door open and wheeled in a beer keg, a bag of ice, and a pile of plastic cups, all on my tab no doubt. The throng of illiterate hotel employees hollered and screamed with excitement. Their night was just beginning while I had hoped my night was about to end. Jason helped Carl tap the keg while the others swarmed around them like a bunch of drunken bees. It was all pretty goddamn ridiculous, if you ask me. *Not one* of them congratulated me or told me they thought the reading was good or that they looked forward to buying my book or that they were glad to meet me or anything. All they wanted was to get *drunk*, just like Jason. And that depressed the hell out of me. I was really feeling like a sorry, sad bastard.

I watched the group of hotel ingrates fill their plastic cups with beer and meander out to the balcony, smoking and laughing their lives away. This was *it* for them, this kind of night. Their hopes and dreams culminating in an evening of free beer and complete abandonment of any goddamn responsibility, for at least a couple of hours anyway. I had much different hopes and dreams. I dreamed of fame and fortune, having my name grace the covers of distinguished periodicals, my work being placed in the coffers of perpetual relevance. I ventured out to the balcony and found a seat. I gazed at the city below and imagined the reception I would receive tomorrow at the bookstore, hoping that the misunderstanding would be rectified by my publishing house. It didn't take long for the keg to be drained of its alcoholic contents and soon enough, the ingrates rolled out of the room one by one until there were only three: me, Jason, and Carl the Pimp.

"That was a fine party, gentlemen," he said, pulling a cheap cigar from his shirt pocket and lighting it. "*Quick* but fine. It was a pleasure doing business with you. If you need anything else, any *more* of the *good* stuff that is, you know where to find me." And with that, Carl was gone.

"Well, that went pretty well, I must say," Jason said, sitting down next to me on the balcony. "You got to practice your reading *and* threw a party all in one night. Not bad, not bad." It seemed that Jason had the last of the keg beer and he was sipping from his cup like it was the Holy Grail or some shit like that. He was making these loud slurping sounds as he drank his beer. With each sip, the urge to slap him grew inside of me.

"Yeah, it was OK. I'm ready to get some sleep. Tomorrow's my big day," I said, getting up from my chair.

"Anything else I can do for you?" Jason asked, a small vile of white powder in his hand. He set his beer down and tapped a small mound of the powder onto his driver's license. With a rolled-up dollar bill, he snorted the pile of dust like a human vacuum.

"I see you got your *wish*."

"Yes, I *sure* did."

I left Jason on the balcony with his beer and his cocaine and climbed into my bed. I climbed in fully clothed and dirty as hell. I was too tired to wash up or put on my pajamas (weird, huh?). All I could think about was sleep. I closed my eyes and listened to the night breeze come in from the balcony. The sounds of the city quietly lulled me to sleep.

23.

I know you won't believe it but I took the most glorious crap of all time this morning. It's true. I practically sprinted to the bathroom, grabbing the first magazine I could find, and it slid out faster than a greasy, intercontinental ballistic missile. And when I mean glorious, I mean it was absolutely *glorious*. It was one of those craps that made you feel like you actually *accomplished* something when you were done. It took a lot out of me. I was a little sweaty and pretty fatigued by the time the first log came out but it was worth it. Anyway, as I sat in there, I read the copy of People Magazine I picked up on the way in. It was this year's issue of the best and worst dressed celebrities, with pictures of television and movie stars at various red-carpet events gracing the cover. And wouldn't you know it but there was a picture of Edward Norton and Selma Hayek on the cover. They were a celebrity couple that I truly *admired*. Not only had they made some of the best movies of my generation, but they actually reminded me of Jessica and myself. It's true. Edward is brilliant, intense, intelligent, and goofy-looking. And so am I. And Selma is beautiful, graceful, fiery, and Mexican. And so is Jessica. It was like we were the same couple but in alternate, parallel universes. I flipped through the magazine, looking for the article with the picture of our twin couple, when I heard a loud banging at the door. I mean, it was loud as all hell. And normally, I would have pinched the loaf, wrapped a towel around my waist, and quickly informed the visitor that I was taking a dump and to kindly wait or come back. But since *this* particular dump was so glorious and satisfying, I decided to let Jason answer it. But for some reason, he didn't. I mean, they started banging loud as hell again and I couldn't understand how Jason couldn't hear it. He must have been passed out cold, what, with all the beer and cocaine and cheeseburgers and French fries and vanilla Cokes he gorged himself with last night. Maybe his body shut down or something. But I wasn't going to get up. I just wouldn't do it.

"Jason?! Get the door, would you?! I'm in the bathroom!" I screamed. "Jason? Are you going to get it?"

But the banging continued. Frustrated, I went for the toilet paper but wouldn't you know it, it was gone. An empty paper roll hung there, useless, depleted. I grabbed a goddamn towel and wrapped it around my waist and went for the door. When I opened it, ready to bark at whoever it was, there was nobody there. But they left behind a tray at the foot of the door, covered with a stainless-steel dome lid, left by room service no doubt. I looked around for any onlookers (I was practically naked as a goddamn jaybird), picked up the tray, and slammed the door shut.

I wanted to finish my crap but it was useless. It's time had passed, unfortunately, because once you interrupt the flow of a glorious crap, it's over, the glory is gone. Since there wasn't any toilet paper, I decided right then and there that I would jump in the shower and rinse myself off. I paid close attention to my ass, scrubbing it thoroughly with a wash cloth. When I was done, I threw the stinking goddamn wash cloth away. There was just no point in keeping it anymore. It's true. No amount of bleach and detergent would restore it to its original, fresh and absorbent state.

As I got dressed, I realized I was right about Jason. He was passed out, snoring up a storm and wheezing all over the goddamn place. He laid there like a lump of shit, the sheets and the comforter disheveled at the end of the bed, drool draining from the side of his mouth onto his pillow. He was a *sight* to see. I finished getting dressed and left him there, undisturbed.

Room service had left breakfast for me in that covered tray, though I wasn't quite sure who ordered it because I most certainly didn't. It was a pathetic excuse for a goddamn breakfast too, with crusty, cold scrambled eggs, limp wheat toast, and warm orange juice. Right then and there, I decided to go downstairs and get a decent breakfast, one that would keep me through most of the day, since it was an important day indeed. Besides, the room was an absolute disaster from the reading and party last night. There was no way I was going to enjoy a good breakfast there, in the middle of a goddamn *mess*. Now Jason, he was used to living like that, so I'm sure he was comfortable as hell. But me, I just couldn't take it. So I left Jason there and went downstairs for a decent meal.

* * *

I asked the nice lady behind the counter in the lobby if the hotel restaurant was still serving breakfast, and she said they were, though it was close to being over since it was so late in the morning and all. She was such a nice young woman, kind and courteous. I looked around for Carl but I didn't see him. He was off somewhere, probably hustling someone else, trying to get them to order hookers or buy drugs or some shit like that. It's true.

"Is Carl around?" I asked. She looked at me kind of funny.

"I don't know of any *Carl*. Are you sure that is his name?"

"He told me his name was Carl. He helped us with our bags last night."

"Maybe you heard his name wrong because I'm not aware of a Carl that works here. Sorry sir," she said, smiling sweetly.

She asked me if there was anything else she could help me with but I said no. I thought it was strange that she didn't know who Carl was. But I didn't dwell on it. I was hungry and my stomach was ruling the moment. So I walked across the goddamn grand lobby to the restaurant, a snazzy place called Crumpet's.

Inside, the restaurant was posh as hell, velvety reds and dark woods and goddamn leather chairs everywhere, just like the lobby. Potted palm trees lined the walls, placed symmetrically from each other, framing the views of each window to the shimmering pool outside. The restaurant was practically empty, with a few patrons here and there and the remnants of a busy staff mulling around with little to do. I wasn't used to this kind of place but it was something I knew I could easily get used to. I sat down at an empty table with a pretty good view of the pool and waited to be served, laying my napkin across my lap to prepare myself.

***

For some reason, I thought about that picture of Edward Norton and Selma Hayek on the cover of People Magazine and I thought about how nice it would be if I was actually in the back of a limousine with my wife Jessica and how great it would be if we were on our way to the Oscars or the Emmys or some shit like that. It was a *fantastic* thought. It really was. The only thing I would have done differently was wear a different *color* tie. The tie Edward was wearing was the worst shade of purple. Personally, I would have worn a black tie. You can never go wrong with black. Black is classic. It's true.

I snapped out of my goddamn fantasy when I realized I had been sitting at the table for over fifteen minutes, and no one had acknowledged my presence, not even with a smile or a simple *hello*. My stomach was grumbling loud as hell, and I couldn't think of anything else until I put some food in it. There wasn't a single waiter in sight, but I noticed some busboys lurking in a corner, behind the buffet area, looking bored and disinterested and unprofessional. I waved my arms, back and forth, to get their attention. When one finally noticed me, he looked at me and then quickly looked away, as if I didn't exist. I decided, right then and there, that I wasn't going to be overlooked anymore, that I wasn't going to be ignored anymore, because this was much too important of a day for me to tolerate this shit anymore. So I stood up, throwing my cloth napkin on the table with a loud thud (to show my annoyance and frustration, no doubt), and made my way over to the busboys, weaving through the maze of tables and chairs. They eventually saw me coming, and in an attempt to rectify their lack of professionalism, began straightening their bowties and adjusting their aprons. I was really going to let them have it.

"Hey!" I said, sternly. "Can't you see I'm sitting over there?! Doesn't anyone work around here?! I'm hungry and I expect to be served, by someone!"

They looked at me like I was from Mars, which really pissed me off. It's true. But before I could say anything else, one of them opened his goddamn mouth.

"Breakfast is over, sir. It's been over for a little while. All the waiters have gone home until lunch."

"And when is lunch?" I asked.

"Noon."

It was ten thirty and I was starving and angry and all sorts of pissed off, but you can't argue with that. I mean, what am I going to do, change their serving hours? It seemed hopeless, and I was still hungry and feeling defeated. It's true.

"But you can finish the breakfast buffet. We weren't going to clear it away for a few more minutes," said the other busboy.

He pointed to the buffet tables and I noticed that there still was some breakfast food there. At closer inspection, it was in no better shape than the breakfast delivered by room service earlier, cold, limp, uninviting. My stomach grumbled uncontrollably, loud as all hell. The busboy noticed when I covered my stomach, and looked to have sympathy for my situation.

"Maybe I can see if the chef will cook something up for you. Would that be OK?" he asked.

I nodded. He indicated that I take my seat and the two busboys disappeared through the door to the kitchen. I sat down at my table and reset the cloth napkin on my lap and, glancing outside at the glistening pool, waited for the chef to hopefully make me some breakfast, something, anything edible. My day, it seemed, was getting off to a little better start, very little anyway. It's true.

* * *

As I waited for my breakfast, I strategically planned my day. I would need to call my publisher, call my accountant, fix the Barnes & Noble bookstore dilemma, smack the hell out of Jason (drug intervention maybe?), take a nap at some point, eat a good breakfast, finish taking a dump (hopefully), get more toilet paper from room service (a top priority), take another shower, call Samuel the Giant to prepare the limo, etc. It was all coming together, with a lot of effort, of course, but it was worth it. I can't think of a time when I didn't want to be a famous writer. It seemed, at least as far as I could remember, the focus of all my dreams. It's true.

As I sat there waiting for some breakfast, staring out at some kids playing and splashing in the pool (what are Sammie and Jessie doing right now?), I thought about when I was in college, a few months before graduation. I had been studying literature and preparing myself to receive a degree in English and I knew, more than anything, that what I wanted to do was to write novels and be famous. I had considered, rather briefly, doing something more practical, like teaching English to high school brats or writing technical copy or some shit like that, something my father pushed me towards. See, my father was a goddamn practical kind of man, or to be more frank, not one to reach for his dreams. I had learned from my mother that he was accepted to a prestigious art school out of high school but his parents refused to pay for something ridiculous like going to art school, so he ended up joining the military because the government was going to pay for his college, as a form of protest against his parents stubbornness, I guess. Well, the military wasn't going to pay for something ridiculous like going to art school either, so they sent him to an engineering school to learn about technical drafting or mechanical engineering or some practical shit like that, and he found himself in a practical career with practical goals and he was practically content. And I truly believe that he wanted me to make the practical choice as well, like he did, finishing college and settling into a practical goddamn career. I knew this because he asked me a few months before graduation what my degree was going to be. And when I told him English, he said he thought I was going for a Business degree or an Economics degree or some type of *useful* degree, even though I had been telling him throughout college that I was getting an English degree, proof that he hadn't listened to a goddamn word I had said at all. But ultimately, my father was never really a very happy person, a sad bastard that let the military-life wear on him, wear him down, and though he never mentioned anything of the sort to me, I knew, deep in my heart, that he truly was disappointed with his practical choice, and that he wished he'd attended art school instead. It was pretty obvious to me. He was never allowed or encouraged to follow his dreams, so why should I? There is nothing more painful than *regret* after all those practical years pass you by.

One time, when I was an impressionably young teenager, my father sat me down and told me that he wanted to give me his *insight into life*. He said, "Son, life is nothing but a series of disappointments. Sure, there are moments of happiness here and there, there are times when things are good, or seem good. But they are brief. Your life will always swing down, the good times never last, and the only thing that is a sure thing is disappointment. Someone or something will always let you down. Don't ever forget that." And he smiled at me after he said this, like it was a goddamn gem of knowledge or something. I remember thinking to myself, that's a pretty goddamn depressing thing to say to a kid, especially an optimistic kid like myself. But I never took him serious, even at thirteen or fourteen or however old I was at the time. It's true.

I wasn't going to let my father discourage me. Even though I had a difficult time finding a publisher, and I had to find a practical job at TechForce to pay the bills while my writing career flourished (I had to feed and clothe the kids, you know), I continued to chase my dream. Sorry, dad, but I had to go for it. Even back then, I knew I had to go for it, forgetting to be practical, always striving for my dream, my dream to be famous. There's nothing more in this world that I wanted. It's true.

I was snapped out of my daze by the hotel chef. He appeared from nowhere, stealthily sneaking behind me, then dropping the plate of breakfast on the table. It scared the shit out of me, literally, and I thought I might have to rinse myself off again in the shower after this fright. My poor boxer shorts were being tested to their limits. It's true.

"I'd like to remind you that breakfast ends promptly at ten o'clock," said the chef, devilishly. He was a menacingly tall fellow with a bald head and a pointy, black goatee. He had one of those heavy, thick, Eastern European beards, the kind that are as thick and dense as a dark rain forest, the kind with the stubble that reappears ten minutes after you shave it. Something wasn't quite right about the color of his beard, though, as well as the color of his eyebrows. They were so black, as pitch as the black of the darkness in a cavern, that it was unnatural. Maybe he colored his beard and eyebrows that shade of black. He did have some freckles perched on his nose, the remnants of his natural hair color, no doubt, maybe it was red at one point. With the combination of pitch black hair and red freckles, he looked like El Diablo himself, in the flesh. "But I wouldn't want to tarnish our excellent reputation for five star, quality service, would I?"

"I guess not," I said, cautiously. He looked like he wanted to gut me, then prod me with metal pokers and sauté me in olive oil and pesto, I could see it in his red goddamn eyes. One thing I learned a long time ago is to never, and I mean *never*, fuck with a person serving you food. You never know what they could have done to your food on the way to your table. He looked serious as all hell, too. It's true. "But I appreciate it. It's an important day for me and I was pretty hungry. This will sustain me until dinner, no doubt."

"You're welcome," he said, walking off abruptly, to chastise a busboy or yell at the wait staff or to conjure Satan through a séance.

But what a chef he was. He had cooked me up a beautiful omelet with sautéed red onions, mushrooms, and honey ham, served with hash-browned red potatoes, and crispy turkey bacon, garnished with a lemon wedge and parsley, and a croissant with apple butter. A feast for a king. It's true. My stomach was grateful. I grabbed my fork and knife and dug in, and the very second the first bite hit my stomach, the grumbling and the tension disappeared. I was beginning to feel like a new man, ready to conquer the day ahead. And then El Diablo reappeared. He sat down at my table, still uninvited.

"I must apologize," he said, rubbing his forehead nervously with his hand. "I don't know what got into me. But for all its worth, I'm sorry for snapping at you. It was rude and very unprofessional of me." He genuinely looked sorry. I could see it on his face. He looked like a really sad bastard, for sure, a devilishly sad bastard. He extended his hand to me for a shake. "I'm having a bad morning. Will you accept my apology?"

I decided it wouldn't hurt to shake his hand, since he did make me breakfast on the fly and all, even though he was freaking me out with his goddamn bald head and dense pointy goatee and his fiery red eyes. I grabbed his hand and shook it and immediately noticed the immense amount of heat his hand was generating. It was hot as hell, literally.

"Apology accepted," I said, releasing his hot hand, trying to finish chewing the food in my mouth as quickly as possible.

"It's hot in the kitchen," he said, blowing into his cupped, hot hands. "It's like a big oven in there."

"I see."

"It's hot in the kitchen *and* I'm having a bad morning. What can I say?"

"Well, you know what they say?"

"You mean, if it's too hot in the kitchen..."

"That's right."

"Sure. I shouldn't be in there, right?"

"That's right."

"I see."

It was one of *those* conversations, the ones with no point but were civil and polite and completely worthless, and they always ended in the worst way because you don't know how to cut off a stranger, trying to be polite and not hurt their feelings. I shoved some more food in my mouth and acted busy and hurried and all kinds of disinterested. It didn't work. He wouldn't leave. It's true.

"You ever have one of those kind of mornings?" he asked. "The kind where it seems like your life is just completely out of your control?"

"Yes," I said, my mouth full of egg and bacon. "I'm having one of those mornings right now."

* * *

El Diablo's real name was Ken, as indicated by a white rectangular name tag on his shirt, with red-stitched border and red cursive letters. He was bald and mean-looking, like I said, but actually, he was just a sorry, sad bastard. His exterior may have been ugly and threatening, but his insides were soft and gooey, filled with all kinds of sorrow and regret and pain and delicate emotion. Turns out, he was cuddly as a goddamn teddy bear. It's true.

Ken had one of those kind of mornings that you see in a convoluted, ridiculous, romantic-comedy movie, a series of events so coincidental and cliché that they bordered on ridiculous. But his morning actually *happened* to him, so it wasn't so much ridiculous as it was just kind of pathetic. It was one of those goddamn mornings that was completely out of his control, for sure, where his dog ran away and his water heater exploded and drained 40 gallons of water through his apartment, and his girlfriend (already upset with him about his affinity for red wine and supposed-drunken philandering) told him she was leaving and not coming back, and the hotel called him and demanded he be in to work early this morning, and to top it all off, he found a parking ticket on his windshield when he got in his car before driving to work. Then, on his way to the hotel, he shot the bird at an erratic driver who almost side-swiped his car and that crazy driver, so enraged from Ken's profane middle finger, followed him all the way to the hotel and confronted him in the parking lot, spitting at him and waving his fists for a fight, threatening to kill him. The poor chef, by that point, was so worn down from the morning's events that instead of fighting back (he looked, to me, like he could rip you to pieces), tears began streaming down his cheeks. He didn't know what to do and was so overwhelmed, that all of his natural defense mechanisms stopped working, completely withered away. He walked away from the enraged driver, teary-eyed and drained, and sat in the employees' lounge for thirty minutes, his hands over his face, his heart in his shoes. It was crazy to think that such a scary-looking guy had such thin goddamn skin, but he did. It's true.

"I tell you, after sitting in that employees' lounge for that long, all I could think about was that this was what my life had become," he said, looking me right in the eye with his goddamn red eyes. He looked like he was going to crack, crack right down the middle. "All my work, all my training, all my recognition, had culminated into a bout with road rage with a fool from Brooklyn who wanted to kill me for shooting him the finger. I was so fed up. I thought, my morning couldn't get any worse than this."

"You're right. It can't get any worse than that," I said, finishing the last of my exquisite omelet. "By the way, you wouldn't happen to have any more of this breakfast, would you? It sure was delicious."

* * *

Chef Ken took me on a tour of his kitchen, a fantastic, stainless steel place that looked as sterile as a hospital operating room. It's true. It was so goddamn clean in there that the reflection from the fluorescent lighting off the metallic counters and shelves about blinded me, almost like staring at the sun. He was as proud as a goddamn peacock about his goddamn kitchen. Turns out that when I told him that I was a writer (a soon-to-be-famous writer at that), he about shit in his pants and insisted that I take a tour of his facilities, marvel at what a goddamn fine establishment it was, and gawk at his snazzy set of Ginsu Knives and over-sized Cuisinart Mixers and larger-than-life rolls of Saran Wrap. It was all just too much to take. I mean, I was still pretty hungry and all I could think about was getting my day rolling and being ready for the evening's events and eating a goddamn nutritious breakfast. If Jason was with me, I'm pretty sure that Ken would not have invited us back there, since Jason is such a goddamn pig. He'd contaminate the place, for sure, with one touch from his grubby fingers. It's true. As Ken went on and on about his fantastic kitchen and how great a chef he was, I wondered what Jason was doing at that moment. He was probably farting up a storm, lying in bed like a lazy bastard, and dreaming of vanilla cokes and room-service cheeseburgers and piles of cocaine the size of desert dunes. And I guess, in a way, Ken's morning wasn't getting any worse, at least as far as I could tell. At least he wasn't in as bad a shape as Jason. It's true.

"And this is our walk-in refrigerator, the largest in the city," Ken said, opening the refrigerator door and letting a rush of cold air out. "Would you like to go in?"

I looked in the cavernous cold room and thought of the crazy bartender from the airport back in Austin and how I was stuck in his beer cooler for what seemed like an eternity and his pot-smoking craziness and the nose-picking barflies and I felt like I was going to faint, what, with the rush of cold air and the bad memories and my grumbling stomach and all. It was all just too much.

"No, no, no, that's OK," I said. "Really, I'd rather not go in there. I'm extremely claustrophobic. But thanks anyway."

"Ok then," he said, closing the door. "Maybe some other time."

I followed him around to the cooking area and watched as he prepped the hot griddle with a large pad of margarine and a splash of olive oil. He then slid the margarine pad around with his index finger until it sizzled into a melted bubbly streak, then poured some eggs from a pitcher that was sitting in a bucket of ice below the hot stove-top. All the ingredients were separated into tiny glass bowls in a drawer at arm's length from him, chopped onions, parsley, bacon bits, sliced mushrooms, diced green peppers, grated yellow cheese. He was a goddamn professional, for sure. He grabbed a little of this and a little of that, and I noticed that he kind of danced and shimmied a bit as he cooked, a rhythm of some sort bobbing through his goddamn head as he combined the ingredients into a plastic prep bowl. He seemed to really like being a chef, bad morning from hell or not. It's true.

"You know," he said, swirling the chopped vegetables and meat with his fingers in the prep bowl. "You look very familiar to me. I don't know from where. But I'm pretty sure I've seen you before, maybe even met you before. I just can't put my finger on where or when."

"No, I don't think so," I said.

"I'm pretty sure of it. In fact, I'm more than positive."

"Maybe you saw the piece in Time Magazine about me?"

"Nope, don't read Time," he said, cherry-picking some more ingredients. "You want this omelet like the other?"

I nodded. The scent from his cooking was euphoric, the smell wafting up to my nose and dissipating my hunger pains. It was going to be another beautiful omelet, I could tell already. It's true.

"Maybe we've met in a past life," he said, completely serious. "Maybe we were friends in another age, or maybe we were mortal enemies."

"Probably enemies, I would think," I said.

"You think?"

"Most definitely."

He flipped the omelet on a clean plate with his spatula and handed me my breakfast. He then dropped all of his utensils into a bucket of water and turned off the griddle, untying the apron around his waist and dropping it into a linen bag. He was turning red again, only this time in the face. His face was as red as a goddamn beet.

"I'll have the front desk put your breakfast on your bill, Mister... what was your name again?"

"Burchwood. My name is Simon Burchwood."

"That's right, Mr. Burchwood. Thank you for dining at Crumpet's," he said, patting me on the shoulder as we walked out of the kitchen. "It's always nice to serve people of such high esteem, people like yourself. Please come again."

"Thanks."

"And please forgive me for earlier, please. I was having a bad morning."

"Whatever."

***

The sore in my palm that I got from falling in the parking lot at *Cinammon's Big Boobie Bonanza* back in Montgomery still wasn't getting any better and I worried for a bit about getting a goddamn infection of some sort. Not only was it making eating breakfast very difficult, having to hold my fork in an awkward position and all, but I think it was affecting my desire to write. I mean, I did attempt to complete my writing exercises on the plane, even though Jason was acting like a goddamn illiterate buffoon, and since arriving in New York, I had thought quite a bit about some narratives and new characters and future plots to explore and expound upon, etc. But I found my desire to get these ideas on paper to be lacking, and I felt it was on account of my sore hand. I mean, it hurt like all hell and it really was distracting me. It's true. I thought, for a second, that maybe I should see a doctor about it. But I also knew that that wasn't something I should have entertained at all until after my reading at the Barnes & Noble flagship store. So, in a way, it was pointless to even worry about it, so I didn't. It's funny how the tiny things that worry you can easily be forgotten, if you just put your mind to it. It's true.

I gobbled up my second omelet as quickly as the first, and found myself licking my goddamn fingers and smacking my goddamn lips and scraping the edge of my goddamn plate with my fork like a goddamn heathen. I mean, I was hungry as hell but I could see that the longer I hung around Jason, the more of his habits I was shamelessly acquiring. And that worried me, worried me to no end. Hanging out with a goddamn pig will do that to you. It's true. It's so much easier living life as a goddamn pig than living life as a decent human being, and I think Jason found that to be the case for him, at least. How easy is it to not worry about cleanliness and order and hygiene and goddamn manners and social skills and a healthy lifestyle in general. I decided right then and there that that, that right *there*, was Jason's problem, in a nutshell. Jason didn't want to have to work at anything, he didn't want to have to work on his career, work on his marriage, work on his house, work on his weight, he didn't want to work on anything *at all*. It's much easier that way, not doing a goddamn thing, because you find that life still trudges on, it still goes by without any effort, even though nothing much comes out of it. And he was very disappointed that nothing much was being made of his life, even though he put nothing into it, and the vicious cycle commenced. It was sad, it's true. But that was the reality of it. I kind of felt sorry for him, especially since we had been friends for so long, but you can only feel sorry for someone for so long too. Once you realize that someone has resigned to being a goddamn pig, and that they have decided not to do a goddamn thing about it, there's really nothing you can do. It's true.

I finished my breakfast and was wiping my hands and my mouth with my napkin when I felt like someone was watching me, which was weird since the restaurant was practically empty. I had that feeling, that feeling you get when someone enters a room just outside of your view, that feeling that I was being watched from behind. I could see in the reflection of one of the windows that there was a figure by the entrance to the restaurant, so I turned around to catch a glimpse of someone turning around and walking out the door, someone that looked a lot like Carl the Pimp. And since the nice lady behind the counter in the lobby didn't know of *any* Carl, I decided right then and there to verify that it actually was him, for my own sanity and all. I dropped my napkin and left the remnants of my breakfast for the lazy goddamn busboys and headed for the exit.

I caught a glimpse of Carl at the other end of the lobby, way past the check-in counter, which he definitely must have walked by, which means the lady behind the counter definitely must have seen him. She was still there, behind the counter, looking busier than the busboys in Crumpet's, at least busily doing nothing.

"Was that Carl?" I asked as I walked by the counter, slowing my pace but not stopping.

"Who?" she asked.

"That bellboy, the one that just walked by."

"I told you, sir, that there is no *Carl* here. But I do need to talk to you. There was a problem with your credit card. It's not accepting..."

"I'll be right back," I said, turning my hurried walk into a mild jog. I didn't have any time to talk about credit cards, not if I was going to catch up with Carl, who by the way, had vanished from the lobby. And pretty soon, I vanished from the lobby too. It's true.

***

I made my way through the only exit at the other end of the lobby and descended a few flights of stairs, following the sound of the echoing footsteps in the corridor, and wound up in the underground parking garage, maybe three or four stories down from the lobby. I could still hear the footsteps, though they were dimming fast in the distance, and I walked around a bit to see if I could find Carl. But my goddamn luck had run out. He was nowhere to be found. The sound of his feet hitting the pavement was soon absorbed into the other noises of the city, the sound of cars running and buses stopping and jackhammers and pedestrians and neon signs and urban decay and air conditioners wheezing and spinning and cooling. It can be sensory overload, if you really listen hard, if you really let it sink in. It's true. Carl was gone and it seemed that so was my sanity and all. I mean, it didn't seem too much to ask to be able to talk to him for a minute, one goddamn minute. I'm sure he would have had a few choice words for the lady behind the counter. I'm sure of it.

I decided right then and there that it was time to forget about Carl the pimp and to get my day underway, to get dressed for the evening and call my publisher and my accountant and my wife and Samuel the Giant and all the other things I had decided to do while eating my breakfast. I walked back to the door where I came into the garage but when I tried to open it, it was locked. I couldn't get back into the goddamn stairwell. I tried to turn the knob and I banged on the door but it was no use. I was locked out. And I knew for sure that my goddamn luck had run out. I looked around for another door or set of stairs or an elevator, but there were none to be found, only signs overhead pointing to an exit that appeared to be up and around the turn at the other end of this level, *level G2*, whatever that means. It always seemed, to me anyway, that how the levels of buildings were named was a complete mystery, a goddamn conundrum for sure. I mean, why is it that some buildings call the first floor *ground*, and other buildings call the first floor *level one*? And some buildings have a *ground* and a *level one*? Without any floor-naming standards, how are you to know where to stop the goddamn elevator when you just want to get out of the goddamn building? It all was just too much to take, when all I wanted to do was get my day started. It's true.

I followed the exit signs and walked the length of the floor I was on (*level G2*), then turned and walked up an incline to the next level, *level G1*, and continued to follow the exit arrows. As I walked, I looked around at the type of cars and vehicles parked in the garage and was amazed to find so many luxury cars and SUVs, almost more than I cared to count. There wasn't a goddamn clunker to be found, not one like Jason's turd-on-wheels. I knew for sure, that once my royalty checks started rolling in, that I was going to buy my wife a new car, probably a BMW, or a Mercedes, something European and luxurious. She deserved it. It's true.

I was going to make my way up another incline to *level G0* or *level G1.2* or whatever goddamn number it was going to be when I noticed the hood of one of the cars up, and then a head popping up and looking at me. He was looking right at me, for sure.

"Hey you!" he said, pointing at me.

I looked around to make sure he wasn't pointing at someone else.

"Yeah, you," he said. "Come here, will ya?"

I reluctantly walked over to the car he was working on, a black Mercedes that looked like the ones that the goddamn Nazis used to tool around in during World War II. He was obviously a valet for the hotel, dressed in the standard maroon hotel-uniform shirt, complete with black shorts and black running shoes. He was sweating profusely, and smelled a little musty and salty. According to his name tag, his name was Mick.

"Here, hold the hood up. There isn't a support lever to hold it," he said.

"I have to be somewhere, right now," I said, holding the dirty hood with one hand.

"It'll just take a second," he said, maneuvering a wire somewhere, trying to plug it into something. "I'll give you a ride up when I'm done. I'll have you up faster than if you walk. Just hold the hood for a second..."

"OK. But I have to be somewhere important," I said.

"I heard you the first time."

* * *

It only took Mick a couple of minutes to get the old Nazi-mobile running, but those couple of minutes seemed like an eternity. I mean, I don't know a goddamn thing about fixing cars, but it seemed to me that he was just fumbling around, sticking things here and poking things there. I can't say much, though, because he got the goddamn thing running. If it was me trying to fix that car, we'd still be standing there like a couple of goddamn idiots, holding up a dirty hood in the middle of an underground parking lot. It's true. The Nazi-mobile seemed to be running pretty good, except for the smell of gasoline it was emitting.

The smell got stronger the longer it ran. I was pretty sure that if we stood there long enough, the toxic fumes would have killed us.

"Get in," Mick said, slamming the hood down. "I'll give you a ride up."

We got in the car and the smell of gasoline was even stronger inside the cab. It was so strong that I about coughed up one of my goddamn lungs. I could barely breathe in there, so I rolled my window down to let fresh air in. Mick slowly pulled out of the parking spot and drove the Nazi-mobile at a blistering *two* miles per hour.

"Open the glove box," he said, pointing to the small door in the dash. "Open it up and tell me what's inside."

"What?"

"You heard me. Open it up and tell me what's inside. Anything valuable?"

I popped open the glove box to find a pile of papers, proof of insurance, the title to the car, receipts for repairs, and some travelers' checks. Mick noticed the checks and dropped a vinyl bank-bag in my lap.

"Put the travelers' checks in the bag," he said, lighting a cigarette and taking a deep drag. "And the insurance papers too."

I placed them in the bag. The smoke from his cigarette and the smell of the gasoline was mixing inside my nose and making me a little light-headed. I turned to ask him if he could stop smoking at least until I got out of the Nazi-mobile, fearing that the cherry on his goddamn cigarette could ignite the gasoline fumes inside the car, and blow us to smithereens. But I didn't say anything, for some reason, I didn't say a goddamn word. I noticed that Mick was wearing an ear-piece, something like you see in the movies, when Secret Service agents are monitoring the movements of a president or senator or some shit like that. I could tell he was listening to somebody, because he would occasionally get that *look* on his face, that blank look someone has like when they are listening on the telephone. After noticing the ear-piece, I also noticed that he would say *ten-four* under his breath, quietly and discreetly, every once and a while. He was obviously getting direction from someone, somewhere, his manager or supervisor. I was pretty sure his manager wasn't telling him to snoop in people's glove boxes for valuables to steal. It's true.

"Is there any change in the ashtray?" he asked.

I pulled open the ash tray and he saw that it was full of quarters, dimes, and nickels. He nodded his head, so I pulled out the tray and poured the coins in the bank-bag.

"And how about in here?" he asked, tapping on the arm console between our seats.

I opened the console and he saw a pack of smokes and a Zippo lighter and a pair of Ray-Ban sunglasses and a radar detector and a cell phone. He took the smokes and left the rest.

"Thanks but I don't need any of that shit," he said, slipping the smokes in his pocket and closing the console.

As we ascended the ramp to the street level, he stopped the Nazi-mobile behind a row of cars waiting to park in the circular drive in front of the hotel entrance. I decided right then and there that it was time to get out of that traffic jam and walk the rest of the way. I had had about enough of Mick and his gasoline emitting Nazi-mobile and his death-defying cigarette smoking and his goddamn stealing and all. He really made me sick to my stomach, or maybe it was the fumes I was breathing. But no matter, I wanted to get out as fast as possible.

"Thanks for the lift but I think I'll get out now," I said, going for the door handle. But before I could open the door, he locked the power-locks. The door wouldn't open, and then he placed his goddamn hand on my shoulder.

"You can't get out now," he said, serious as all hell.

"Why not?" I asked.

"Safety hazard," he said, smiling back at me.

"Safety hazard?"

"It's the rules, buddy."

"The rules? What rules?"

"Hotel rules. No one walks on the ramp."

I sat back in my seat, resigned that I was going to have to sit in there a little longer, suck in more fumes and smoke, probably die of asphyxiation or lethal combustion, or be arrested as an accomplice to this thief, or some shit like that. It's true. He took his hand off my shoulder and finished his cigarette and flicked the butt out the window. Someone said something to him in his ear-piece and he got still and quiet, that blank look returning to his face again. He turned and looked at me, really *looked* at me, listening to someone saying something or describing something, then he said *ten-four*. He sure was quiet after that, and he didn't ask me to look in any more compartments for coins or valuables or any goddamn documents, and it made me a little nervous and all. So I decided to ask him a question, something to break the silence.

"I hope you don't mind me asking you something..."

"Go for it," he said, lighting another cigarette.

"Do you know a bellboy named Carl?"

"Sure do."

"So there *is* a Carl that works here?"

"Yep."

"That's what I thought. The girl at the front desk said..."

"Don't listen to that bitch," Mick said, exhaling a huge plume of smoke my way. "She's a liar, for sure."

***

Unfortunately for me, the glorious crap from this morning, the one that was unceremoniously disturbed, awoke like a dormant Phoenix from a sleepy volcano. It reared its ugly head and sent an unpleasant burning sensation straight from my gut to the back of my trousers. It was all I could do to keep the fiery turd from exploding, clinching my stomach with one arm and my knees with the other arm. It was a pretty goddamn inconvenient time for it to return, considering that I was sitting in a Nazi-mobile with Mick the valet, waiting in a stalled line of cars to exit the underground parking garage, without a toilet in sight. I was feeling pretty miserable. It's true.

"You all right?" he asked. "You don't look so hot."

"I have to go to the bathroom," I said, a little desperate.

"Did you eat at Crumpet's?" he asked, chuckling. "That food they serve will kill you, I swear. Five-star my ass."

"Can you let me out? I *really* have to go."

"Just one more second. Can you wait a second?" he asked. I nodded.

The traffic jam finally moved and Mick pulled the car into the circular drive in front of the entrance to the hotel. The grand goddamn spectacle continued, just like when we arrived the day before, valets and bellboys whisking here and there, assisting newly-arrived guests with their cars and luggage. I kind of expected Samuel the Giant to be waiting there for me, his limo parked with the air conditioner on inside, but he wasn't. Mick parked the Nazi-mobile at the first available space and I lunged for the door handle. The fiery turd wasn't going to wait too much longer, and it sent me an acidy warning of its intentions to evacuate my bowels as soon as possible.

"I gotta go," I said.

"Mr. Duncan will escort you from here," Mick said, lighting another cigarette.

"Mr. Who? Tell him I don't need an escort. I can get to my room by myself."

I opened the car door and stepped out, right in front of this Mr. Duncan that Mick was talking about, a seven-foot tower of black suit and black tie and black skin, standing on the curb waiting for me. I looked up at him and he looked at me and I immediately made my way around him, but he wasn't having it. He placed his goddamn hand on my chest and I knew, right then and there, that I wasn't going to get to a bathroom as fast as I needed to. It's true.

"The front office needs to have a word with you immediately, Mr. Burchwood. Will you follow me?" Mr. Duncan said. He was tall as all hell. He could play center for the Utah Jazz or the Atlanta Hawks or some crappy basketball team like that, since I wasn't too sure just how athletic he was. But he was tall enough to play, even if he couldn't dribble the goddamn ball. When you're that tall, you really don't need to know how to dribble, just look at Shaquille O'Neal. It's true.

"I hate to have to tell you this, Mr. Duncan, since I don't know you all that well. But I really have to go to the bathroom. I know that's really personal and all but it's true," I said. Then I leaned toward him a little and whispered. "I have to take a dump, really bad."

"Will you come with me to the front office if I let you go to the bathroom first?"

I nodded.

"Then follow me."

* * *

It was just as glorious as this morning, the crap that is, except for one thing: *Mr. Duncan was waiting in the bathroom with me.* He wasn't in the *stall* with me, but he was in the bathroom, waiting, listening, standing right outside of my stall door. If I didn't have to go so bad, I probably wouldn't have gone at all, since I don't like anyone in the vicinity when I'm taking a dump. I like my privacy. It's just one of those things. It's true. When I worked at TechForce, I used to go to the farthest bathroom on the top floor, the one least likely to be used because of its distant proximity to the majority of the workers. That was my favorite and most private bathroom in the entire building.

Anyway, my dump took no effort at all. After its thunderous evacuation, I sat there comfortably, waiting for the remainder of it. I could hear Mr. Duncan tapping on the tile floor with his shoe, a heavy Florsheim-model with a stiff sole, newly purchased and not yet broken in. It was so quiet in there that the sound of his shoe tapping the tile floor sounded like a ball-peen hammer hitting a nail through a sheet of steel. It was that loud and sharp. And the sound, becoming louder and louder the more I concentrated on it, started to drive me mad, what, with its deafening echo and gut-clinching intensity. He really made me nervous, standing there tapping his feet and not saying a word. It about drove me crazy.

"You might want to hurry up in there," he said.

"I could be in here for a while," I said. "You know how these things go sometimes."

"You ate at Crumpet's, I guess?" he asked.

"Yes, I did."

"That's unfortunate."

He began tapping his shoe again and I thought it pretty ridiculous that I had this seven-foot guy standing outside my toilet stall tapping his feet, asking me where I ate this morning, and I had no idea what it was he wanted with me. Normally, I wouldn't have spoken to him in the bathroom, what, going against bathroom etiquette and all. I mean, you never talk to someone in the bathroom unless it is a goddamn emergency, like there being no toilet paper or paper ass hats or a newspaper to read. But I figured I had at least another ten minutes to burn, sitting on the toilet waiting for my movement to stop, so I went against protocol.

"You mind telling me what the front desk wants with me?" I asked. His shoe-tapping stopped.

"Something about your credit card..."

"About my credit card?"

"...and your friend."

"What about my credit card?"

"I'm not supposed to be talking to you about this, Mr. Burchwood."

"Was my card declined?" I asked. Those bastards, those fucking bastards at the credit card company! I had a feeling something like this was going to happen. I mean, you plan and plan things but something always happens to throw a wrench in your best-made plans. I guess bringing Jason along was my goddamn wrench. I didn't budget bringing him along initially but I didn't think it would hurt. I didn't think I would go over my limits anyway.

I quickly pulled about three feet of toilet paper off the roll and wrapped it around my hand. I decided right then and there that I was going to call the credit card company and straighten this matter out myself, whatever it was. There was no way in hell that I was going to have a problem *today*, on this day, the most important day of all my days so far in my life. I began thoroughly wiping myself.

"But that's the least of your worries," Mr. Duncan said. "I hope you have a good lawyer."

"What do you mean?" I asked. "Whatever it is, it's probably just a simple mistake. I mean, I know I ride my card balance pretty close to the limit sometimes but..."

"When was the last time you spoke to your travel buddy?" he asked, his shoe-tapping starting up again.

"Last night. He was sleeping when I came down for breakfast this morning. Why?"

"Because he might be sleeping for a long time, a very long time."

***

Turns out that Jason overdosed this morning, brought on by the massive amount of cocaine and alcohol he ingested last night while I was sleeping. That's right: *overdosed*. It's true. Sometime after I left for breakfast, the cleaning lady entered our room and found him in bed, and she thought he was dead. He wasn't dead but he was pretty close, stiff as a board and cold as a fish. She rummaged around, trying to wake him to let him know that she had to clean the room, and when he didn't move or make a sound, she got a closer look. The sight of him made her scream, attracting the other cleaning ladies on the floor, all of them running in our room to see what the goddamn commotion was. And to think, I asked Jason to come along with me to New York because I felt sorry for him, because I needed someone to *help* me out and all. More than ever, I was really sorry I brought the goddamn pig with me. He was more of a burden to me and my trip than anything else. I wished I had left him and his goddamn problems back in Montgomery, where he belonged. I decided right then and there that he and his goddamn wife deserved each other. It's true. They were both a goddamn mess. Their marriage was a perfect goddamn disaster.

All I could think about was getting the hell out of the hotel, getting as far away from Jason as possible, getting to the Barnes & Noble flagship store, and finishing what I had come to New York for in the first place. I mean, Jason obviously didn't need me anyway, finding consolation with his drugs and his booze and his goddamn depression. He was the ultimate sad bastard. And like I said before, there was no time on this trip for sad bastards. It's true. I had my fans and the media and bookstore employees and important publishing-industry people waiting for me, counting on me, looking forward to my appearance. I wiped my ass and zipped up my pants.

Mr. Duncan escorted me out of the bathroom, walking close by me as he led me to the front office, no doubt. He was imposingly tall and lanky, his arms and legs freakishly long, like the limbs of a giant goddamn praying mantis. He walked in a cumbersome fashion, slow and deliberate. And even though I knew I was out of shape, a little pudgy and all, I had a feeling that I could outrun him. For some reason, I thought if I could just get out to the street and run up the busy sidewalk, that I could lose him. There would be no way he could find me. And he didn't know that I was supposed to be at Barnes & Noble; he didn't know who I was or where I needed to be or anything. He didn't know a goddamn thing about me. If I could just get to the bookstore, I could wait there until this evening, until it was time for my appearance. I was more than positive that they would accommodate me, surely supplying coffee and sweet rolls on gratis. I was sure of it. I decided, right then and there, that it was time for me to go.

So I kneeled down and pretended that I was tying my shoe, right in the middle of the lobby. It was a busy morning for some reason, and there were dozens of patrons checking out and dozens of bellboys assisting them while they were checking out. I peeked up a bit to see if Mr. Duncan was watching me, and thankfully, he wasn't. He was gesturing to an acquaintance of his across the lobby, another employee or someone to that effect, about meeting for lunch or some shit like that. And after a second or two, I leapt up and ran as fast as I could, out the sliding front door, across the busy circular drive, past Mick the valet and his thieving valet buddies, to the busy New York sidewalk. I ran as fast as I could, sure that Mr. Duncan was right behind me, and I pushed the pedestrians aside, the lazy bastards. I found out quickly that New Yorkers weren't very cooperative, especially if you were trying to go in a direction that was against the flow of where they were going. In fact, the last thing you want to do is antagonize a group of New Yorkers, because once they heard Mr. Duncan's pleas to stop me, stop me they did.

The next thing I knew, I was forced to the ground, like an avalanche of flesh had toppled on top of me. The last thing I remember was looking at a lady's high-heel shoes, red and shiny like the paint job on a brand new car. Her feet were literally inches from my nose and her skin was white like porcelain, so white that they were slightly transparent.

And then there was darkness, cold and still, like I was asleep. When I opened my eyes again, my head heavy and my neck limp and sore, I was in jail. It's true. I was in a goddamn jail.

24.

I told the jail guard that I wasn't going to talk to anyone until I talked to my lawyer first. Little did he know that I didn't have my own *criminal* lawyer (he was an *entertainment* lawyer) but that didn't matter. His name was Ira Lowenstein and he could make lots of things happen. He looked over my contract with the publisher before my deal went down. He was a really great lawyer and I *trust*ed him. You know, I was always told to get a Jewish lawyer because they are the best. It's true. They *are* the best. I demanded my one phone call and the guard let me use the phone. It was a goddamn payphone so I had to make a collect call. I called up Ira's office and he answered. He was always answering the phone because he didn't have a secretary. He always told me he was too cheap to hire any help. He was a really cheap bastard. He charged me for everything. And I knew he was going to charge me for the collect call I made to him. So I made it short and sweet.

"Ira, you gotta help me out. I'm in jail in New York. Can you help me?" I pleaded, whispering into the phone. I was really paranoid for some reason. I was shaking all over the goddamn place.

"I'll be up there as *soon* as I can," he told me and then he hung up. Ira was a cheap bastard but I knew he'd help me, even if it meant charging me for the airline ticket he used to get up here.

After I got off the phone, the guard pulled me into a small room where he took my fingerprints and a photo of me (for the mug shot which will appear on CNN tomorrow, no doubt). He then pulled me into a different room and uncuffed me. He ordered me to take off my goddamn clothes. I put on my orange jumpsuit and washed the ink off my hands and then he cuffed me again. He put the cuffs on tight as hell too. He led me up some stairs and down a hall lined with cell doors. The cell doors were a lot different than I imagined jail cell doors to look like. I mean, they weren't made of bars with prisoners hanging on inside with tin cups in their hands banging for food, like in the movies. They were solid metal doors with one tiny window about the size of a matchbox at eye-level. That's it. And it was quiet as hell. I didn't hear a goddamn thing. The guard took me to the last door in the hall. He pressed me against the wall as he unlocked the door. And then he threw me in and slammed the door behind me.

Both of the bunks were occupied so I sat on the floor. The cell was small as hell and obviously only made for two people. But today, it was filled with three of us. I sat next to the toilet on the floor as I listened to my other goddamn roommates sleep and snore the morning away. One of them, the guy on the top, was snoring loud as hell, just like Jason did. I mean, he sounded exactly like him, the lazy bastard. It was all just too much to handle. It's true. I closed my eyes and I wondered how I would explain all of this to my publisher. And I wondered, in the broad scheme of things, if this would effect my book launch.

Anyway, I had a blunt pain in the front of my mouth and I just knew I was sucker-punched by someone on the sidewalk or something. Or maybe I hit my mouth when I fell to the ground. I rubbed my chin and it seemed that one of my lower teeth was loose. I carefully checked each one and found that one of them was in fact loose and felt like it was going to pop out. And as if my luck wasn't bad enough up to this point, the goddamn tooth snapped from my gums and was sitting in my goddamn hand like the sad reminder that it was. I couldn't fucking believe it. I mean, what happens when I get out of this place and have to go to publicity spots or readings and I look like a goddamn redneck without any front teeth. Like I said, it was all just too much to handle. It's true.

As I examined the tooth in my sore hand, I noticed something move out of the corner of my eye. I looked over by the cell door and saw a tiny white rat sitting on the rim of the toilet. He was looking right at me with his goddamn little beady eyes and was rubbing his little paws together like he was ready to eat a big meal or something. He was making this noise, this little noise like he was smacking his lips and all. He trotted around the rim to the back of the toilet and slid down to the floor. He slowly slithered toward me, stopping every few inches to check on me, then he'd slither some more. He looked at me as if I had something to give him, some food to eat. All I had on me was my goddamn tooth but he kept staring at me with his goddamn beady eyes. I didn't know what to give him so (as a joke) I put my tooth in front of him to see if he'd go for it. And after he sniffed it for a bit, he grabbed the tooth with his little diseased hands and started gnawing on it. I couldn't believe it but he started *grinding* the tooth into dust with his little razor-sharp teeth. He flipped it around, chewing on the back side then the front side like it was a kernel of corn. And after a few seconds, he had eaten the whole goddamn thing. It's true. He ran back to the toilet, climbed back up to the rim, and jumped in the bowl. I expected him to drown in the fowl water but as I looked in, I noticed there wasn't any water in the bowl. He slithered down into the hole at the bottom of the bowl and disappeared.

The top-bunk guy was snoring his goddamn brains out. And like I said, he sounded just like Jason with his snoring and honking and wheezing all over the place. I wanted to check to see if it really was Jason until the bottom-bunk guy sat up. His eyes were practically glowing in the dark. It was kind of creepy. There wasn't a whole lot of light in the cell because we didn't have a window and the guy's eyes were as yellow as a two miniature full moons.

"He's got asthma," the guy said. "That's why he snores so loud." He was a big African-American fellow with braided hair, gold caps on all of his teeth, and the same orange fashion statement I was wearing. His arms were as big as tree trunks. He made Samuel look like a little girl. It's true. "He snores so loud sometimes I just want to kill him."

"I can see why. It sounds like he's gargling or something." The guy chuckled a bit and leaned forward like he wanted to shake my hand or something. I put my wounded hand out and he grabbed onto it like a vice. He about crushed my goddamn sore hand.

"My name's Wallace but my friends call me Mack, as in Mack Truck." He was right. He was as big or bigger than a Mack Truck. He was humongous. When he let go of my hand, it felt like all the bones had been crushed into dust. I rubbed my hand to make sure it was OK. And wouldn't you know it but the wound was gone. It was completely *gone*, like he had healed it or something. It's true.

"My name's Simon Burchwood. I'm a writer."

"A writer, huh? What are you doing in *here*?"

"I have no idea what I'm doing here."

"Then you'll fit right in. Nobody in here knows *why* they are in here. They just are. What do you write? Books?" He sat on the edge of the bed and slid his feet into the rubber slippers that the guards gave us to wear, except that the slippers didn't quite fit right. His feet were like tree stumps.

"Yeah, I'm a novelist, I guess you could say." I rubbed my hand, amazed that the wound was gone.

"I write a little myself." Oh man, it was starting again. I didn't think I could go anywhere without having to hear this crap from *somebody*. It's true. "But not books. I write rhymes, you know. I'm a rapper. Rapping is the skill that pays my bills."

"You're in the music business?" I couldn't believe it. Of all the crooks and goons and thieves and murderers I could have shared a cell with, I was fortunate enough to share a cell with someone who I at least had something in common with. It was a goddamn miracle. It's true. "Then I guess we have something in common. We're both artists, you and me."

"That's true."

"So, what are you in for? Wait! Let me guess." I gave him a good look and tried to think of what his circumstances were. I figured if he had some kind of record deal that he wouldn't be in for something petty like stealing televisions or some shit like that. "Drugs? You were caught up in a drug-deal gone bad, right?"

"Nope. They got me in here for *murder*. But I didn't shoot nobody. I'm at the top of my game. I have a three-record deal, I've been paid, I just got married, I gots two kids..." Wallace shook his head in disbelief. He really looked like he didn't know what he was doing in here. And I believed him. It's true. "I don't even own a gun."

"So what happened?" This was almost too good. I wished I had a pen and some paper to write this down with. It could be a great novel or short story or an epic poem. It's true. The ache in my mouth started up again and I felt around the space where my other goddamn tooth came out. I noticed that the tooth next to the gap was a little loose too. I poked at it while Wallace told his story.

"I was at a club, hanging with my girl, when a guy came up and started beefin'. I was just minding my own business but I guess he recognized me and was jealous or something. I told him I had no beef with him and that I'd buy him a round of drinks. But he wouldn't back down. Eventually, a friend of mine stepped in and they started fighting. Then gun shots started going off ... *POP, POP!*" Wallace pointed his finger at me like it was a gun. "And everyone ran. I grabbed my girl and we ran out the front. When the police started asking people questions, they said I was the one that pulled the gun since I was the only one people *recognized*. I don't even own a gun but since I was the recognizable one, everyone *assumed* it was me. Now here I am, sitting in jail for something I didn't do, all because I'm famous." Wallace shook his head and I poked at my loose tooth and it all seemed like a nightmare to be sure. I mean, we should have been out in the world, rapping and writing and doing the things we were meant to do. Not rotting in some goddamn cell for things we didn't do. I really felt his pain because I was feeling it too. It's true. I missed my wife and my kids and my friend Jason and my freedom. "I never thought that becoming famous would have been such a *burden*," he said, shaking his head.

"What do you mean?" I asked. "Being well-known is a gift. I'm sure you make lots of money and don't have to work a normal job, like most people do."

"Yes, I do make lots of money. But that also makes me a target. When you make it big, people want to tear you down. People only want to support you to an extent. Once you've passed that point, people don't want to see you go any farther. They become jealous. And then they start to say that you don't *deserve* that much success. You know, I didn't get into this game for the money. I got into rapping because I was into *rapping*. No matter where I went, to a party, to a club, to a friend's house, I always found myself rapping. So I figured I must really be into it. And my father always used to tell me to do what I loved to do. And I love to rap. But what I don't love is all the bullshit that comes along with it. All this stuff that comes with being famous, you can give it to the dogs."

"My dream is to become well-known. There's nothing more that I want than to be a famous writer, to write all the time and not have the burden of a normal existence. You can give a nine to five job to the dogs," I said. Out of the corner of my eye, I noticed that white rat again, popping his head up from inside the toilet bowl. He was staring at me again with his goddamn beady eyes.

"Well, be careful what you wish for. It may just come true," he said.

The rat sat on the rim of the toilet and rubbed his little hands together again, just like before. He stared at me with his goddamn beady, black eyes and made that lip-smacking noise again. I really felt like he was looking straight into my mouth for another tooth to nibble on. He had that look, that goddamn intent, hungry *look*. It was driving me crazy.

"I just *wish* my teeth would stop falling out," I said, examining the new loose tooth in my mouth. "I might have to get caps like yours."

The rat slid down the back of the toilet and was right at my foot, moving his little head around and pointing at me with his little finger. The loose tooth in my mouth popped out and the gap in my gums was now growing wider and wider. It was very strange, what, that even though two of my teeth came out, there wasn't any blood or anything. They just popped out like they were pearls or something.

The goddamn rat stared right into my eyes and he grabbed the loose tooth with his diseased little paws and he consumed the tooth right in front of me. It was the craziest goddamn thing I had ever seen.

"He's a hungry little guy, isn't he?" Wallace asked.

"He sure is."

"What do you think happened to *my* teeth?" he asked, smiling at me with his set of gold choppers. "It cost a fortune to have them replaced."

The guy in the top bunk was really starting to snore like a bastard and the rat was devouring my loose teeth and it was all just driving me crazy. All I could think about was Jessica and the kids and I couldn't wait for Ira Lowenstein to show up. He was just taking entirely too long. It's true. It seemed like I had been in there for a goddamn eternity already.

And even though I didn't show it, I was really starting to get annoyed with all of Wallace's talk about being famous and all. I mean, I didn't even *know* who the hell he was so where did he get off saying that he was *famous*. The snoring was getting louder and louder and the rat had disappeared at some point. I'm not exactly sure when.

"He does sound like a fog horn," I said, raising my knees to my chest and setting my sore chin on my knees.

"Believe it or not, you'll get used to it. I did," Wallace said, laying back down and resting his head on his arms. He didn't have a pillow and I was pretty sure that the goddamn rat had eaten it or something. It seemed like he ate everything. "Sometimes, his snoring kind of puts me to sleep, like a ... what do you call it? You know? To put babies to sleep?"

"A lullaby?" I asked.

"Yeah, a lullaby. That's it. His snoring sounds like a lullaby."

It seemed like Wallace was going bonkers too. How could you blame him, what, with the snoring and the goddamn hungry, tooth-eating rat and no pillows and the rubber slippers that were just too goddamn small and my teeth that were popping out all over the place? It was just all too much to handle. It's true.

25.

There was a loud banging on the cell door as if someone was hitting it from the outside with a metal baseball bat. It scared the shit out of me. I mean, I was about to doze off when the goddamn racket started. All that snoring and talking and the heavy thoughts weighing down my spirits, I thought I could at least try to catch a little nap. But that wasn't meant to be. The cell door slowly opened and the light from outside sliced through the darkness of the cell like a sword from God. It took a bit for my eyes to adjust to the glow. I saw a figure in the doorway, a silhouette of a short, stocky person with a trench coat and a briefcase in his hand. And I knew it could only be one person. Ira Lowenstein was here to save the day. It's true.

"Simon, you stupid bastard! What are you doing to me? Huh? What have you gotten yourself into this time, you dumb fuck?" Good old Ira, he always shot straight from the hip. No bull*shit*. He felt there wasn't any time in the world for bullshit and most people he encountered didn't like him for that. I mean, it's bad enough that the world throws you goddamn curve balls and all but to have someone acknowledge that that was just the way it was was more than most people cared to accept. It's true. He entered the cell and told the guard that everything was OK now and he sat on the edge of Wallace's bed, setting his briefcase on the floor.

"Careful, Ira. Don't wake up Wallace," I said, pointing behind him. I didn't want Wallace to wake up and find a short Jewish man in bed with him. He'd probably knock Ira's goddamn head off.

"Wallace who? There's nobody here. I thought this was your bunk?" Ira turned around and pulled back the blanket but Wallace wasn't there. In fact, he wasn't in the cell at all. Like I said, it was all just too much to handle.

"It's good to see you, Ira. Really, it is," I said, relieved that someone was finally going to straighten all this shit out. If anyone could do it, it was Ira Lowenstein. Don't get me wrong. Ira didn't look like a Pit bull but he practiced law like a Pit bull. I mean, you wouldn't have figured him for that type of demeanor considering he looked like a cross between Woody Allen and George Castanza, what, with his male-pattern baldness and pencil-thin legs and pot-belly gut and big round glasses that sagged to the tip of his nose. But you can't judge any man by his appearance alone, except maybe Edward Norton. Edward Norton wears his goddamn genius and integrity like an angora sweater. It's true. But Ira, Ira is a wolf in goddamn sheep's clothing.

"It seems like you have gotten yourself into a little bind here. You know, I'm not really the one who can help you get out of this dilemma, being that I practice *entertainment* law and specialize in business contracts and other mundane shit like that."

"I know, Ira, but you can do *any*thing. I mean, I trust you and all," I said, a little scared now. It wasn't like Ira to baulk on a request. But I knew, in my heart, that he wouldn't let me down.

"I did practice as a defense lawyer for The State of Texas for a few months after law school but that was a *long* fucking time ago. Plus, we're in New York. They do things a lot differently up *here*, you know. The New York government is like the fucking mafia."

"I know, I know."

"So, I have a lot of things to tell you. I have some good news and some bad news. Which do you want to hear first? Huh?" he asked, sort of matter-of-fact like. And this is the ultimate rhetorical question. I mean, if someone you know pretty well asks you this goddamn question, they already know the degree of what is good versus what is bad, because they *know* you. So if someone you know pretty well asks you this question, always take the bad *first*. It's pretty much guaranteed that it's going to be pretty bad. It's true. Plus, even if the good news isn't all that great, it will seem like you found a golden nugget after the bad news. Mediocre good news is still *brighter* than bad news. So, in a way, he didn't even have to ask me which I'd like to hear first. Since he knew me so well, he should have just given me the bad news. And he did. "Who am I kidding, right? Here's the bad news. You're in some shit, you know."

"What do you mean?" I asked. I was clueless.

"Credit fraud is some serious fucking shit. They claim you went on a spending spree with your employer's company card, extending your airline ticket from Montgomery to New York when you should have returned to Austin after the technology conference in Montgomery. Then you were reserving suites in expensive hotels, limousine rides, meals, the works. They said it was like you thought you were a fucking rockstar. And to top it all off, you never even went to the conference in Montgomery."

"But I'm not ..."

"I bet you're going to say you're not employed by TechForce anymore. And in a way, you are right. As of right now, you are terminated and your benefits have been suspended. That's effective immediately. You should have made your business trip to Montgomery, gone to your fucking boring conference, and returned like a good employee. It wasn't like you were going to be employed by them for the rest of your life anyway, right? Huh? We were working some things out, right?"

"Yes, we were."

"Your publishing deal was coming along nicely. You still have your manuscript, right? Tell me you have that first draft with *you*." He looked at me all cock-eyed and serious as hell.

"It's in my backpack, back at the hotel."

"Good. Now, I think you were getting just a little ahead of yourself. Huh? You should have conferred with me first. This all could have been fucking avoided, really. There was no reason for you to come to New York just yet. Plus, running from the hotel when they wanted to ask you about the credit card..."

"But Ira, I don't understand any of this. I'm a *writer* now."

Ira placed his hand on my shoulder and leaned toward me.

"You were always a *writer*, even when you were employed at TechForce. You were born to be a writer. You don't need some publishing deal and limousines and hotel suites and first-class airline tickets to fucking validate that. If you are a writer, all you have to say is: *I'm a writer*. That's it. You are who you say you are and you are who you believe you are."

"Really?"

"What are you fucking asking me for? You need to be asking yourself that, right? Huh? Now, for the good news. You ready for the *good* news?" Of course, I was ready for the goddamn good news and he knew it too because he had a big smile stretched across his goddamn face. "Well, actually, there is a little more *bad* news."

"What?"

"Your editor has cancelled the release of your book. It seems that your employer got wind of the topic of the book and the former C.E.O., a Mr. Hans Fitzsimmons, is suing your publisher. THE RISE AND FALL OF A TITAN may not see the fucking light of day."

My head fell into my hands like a rock. I really wanted to cry, what, with everything that had happened to me in the last few days. And now, all my hard work was not going to see the light of day. Like I said, it was just all too much to handle, especially now. It seemed, for a bit anyway, that my *dream* of becoming a writer had been squashed.

"How could this be? How did they find out about my book? The only person I spoke to about it was with you and my wife and my editor, of course."

"Turns out..." Ira started chuckling in disbelief and patting me on the back like I was a goddamn fool. He was really good at that, making you feel like a fool. "It seems that once you quit, they went through all the files on your computer and found a copy of your book there. Mr. Folsom, Mr. Fitzsimmons, they have all read your book. It really pissed them off. You wrote a real doozy!"

"I'm such an idiot. I'm such a goddamn idiot," I cried. I really couldn't believe it. I *was* a goddamn idiot. It's true.

"But that's all right. Really, it is. Even though TechForce is suing your publisher, that doesn't mean that the suit will *take*, or that your reputation will be damaged, or anything. In fact, your publisher is just as excited now as they were when we first submitted your book to them back then. You know why?"

"Why's that?"

"It *seems* that some tourist was watching when you were running away from that security guard. And it *seems* that he started filming the entire fucking thing with his digital video camera. And it *fucking seems* that this tourist dropped the video off at a television station here in New York, like you were Rodney King or something."

"What?"

"And that station has been showing that video *nonstop*. You couldn't have asked for better *publicity* than that, really. Huh? It's fucking genius!" Ira started rubbing his hands together in a greedy fashion. "Your publisher wants a different book now. They want your fucking memoir, how this happened, how you got here, why he was beating you, your side of the story, and they want it fast. You think you can write it *fast*? This kind of publicity has a finite amount of relevance. It could disappear in a matter of weeks. You have to act now and fast. You think you can do it? Huh?"

"Of course. I'm a *writer*, you know. I've always wanted to write my *memoirs*." Ira pulled out a pad of paper and a pen and handed it to me.

"Well, then you better fucking get started. The only thing the publisher wants now is a title. Can you come up with a title? Huh? It has to be a good, catchy title."

I didn't have to think about that one at all. I already knew what the title would be. I have always *known* what the title of my memoirs would be. It would be something majestic, something poetic, something *literary*. It was already on the tip of my tongue.

"THE METEORIC RISE OF SIMON BURCHWOOD," I said.

"Fucking brilliant! I'll get to work on this new deal and you get to work writing. I'll figure in my twenty five percent commission, of course. But that shouldn't matter to you. This is going to be a seven figure deal!"

I heard a rustling from the bunk above and a head appeared, looking down at us. It was a little difficult making out the features of the face because of the strong light from outside of the cell casting such bizarre shadows inside. But I recognized the voice. I immediately knew who it was from the voice. It's true.

"That's great, Simon. I always knew you'd make it," he said from the bunk above.

"Jason?"

He came down from the bunk and I jumped up to embrace him. I gave him a big bear hug. I was, actually, really glad to see him. It's true. I was so glad to see the goddamn pig. I hugged him as hard as I could.

"That's my name, don't wear it out," he said.

Jason pulled back a bit and I noticed a black and blue puffy spot on the side of his nose. It looked like someone had slugged him in the face with a baseball bat. It's true.

"What happened to your nose?" I asked, staring at the anomaly.

"What do you mean? Don't worry about it. Let's talk about *you* and your new deal." And, you know, it made sense to me for some reason. It's true. I didn't mention his black and blue puffy nose or how he came about being in the cell before I did or anything. It was all just *irrelevant*. All I could think about now was my memoirs and where I would start and if I would write it in the first or third person and if the title was a marketable one or not. I mean, it was a lot to take in. Sometimes, your life takes a turn for the worst but it's really just a transitional turn. Something good is *always* around the corner. Sometimes, you just have to be patient and wait your goddamn turn.

Ira patted me on the back again but this time, he was patting me in a congratulatory fashion. I mean, I always looked up to Ira kind of like a father-figure. He was always very supportive of my hopes and dreams and he always believed in me, even when my real father didn't. It was a fantastic consolation.

"Someone else is here to see you too," Ira said, pointing to the cell door. My eyes were still adjusting to the bright light that flooded in from the hallway outside. Another figure appeared in the doorway, a womanly figure. Her silhouette was thin yet voluptuous. She extended her hand towards me.

"Jessica?" I asked. I was in complete shock. Ira, like usual, never failed to disappoint. I was just so overwhelmed. I couldn't move. It's true.

"Simon?" she asked, with a sweet, soft tone. She stood there in the glow of the light, her curvaceous body calling to me. And I wanted to jump up and ravish her with kisses and hugs and take her to a field of flowers and make love to her like tomorrow was not going to come and tell her that I loved her and that all my success was for her and the kids.

"Where are the babies? I tried to call you so many times. Where were you?" I asked.

"Simon?"

"Yes dear? Did you hear the news? About my publishing deal? Did you hear it, sweetheart?" I asked. I'm telling you, it was all just too much to handle. It's true. Sometimes, when things come along, whether they are good or bad, they just come at you in droves. It's just too much to take in all at once. I was starting to feel weighed down. So much so, that I couldn't move. Jessica kept calling to me but I couldn't get up. I just sat there like a goddamn idiot.

"Simon? Are you all right?" she asked, her hand out like she really wanted me to go to her. And I *wanted* to go, really, I did. I wanted to jump into the glow of the hallway and embrace her. But something kept me on that bed. Something kept me down like a tremendous weight on my goddamn shoulders. It was weird. And she kept repeating, over and over, "*Simon, are you OK? Simon? Simon? Are you all right? Can you hear me?*"

And I kept thinking to myself, *of course I can hear you.* I'm sitting right in front of you, aren't I? It's not like I'm *dreaming* all of this.

But you know, the crazy thing was that I kept mulling over the title to my new book in my head. I couldn't stop thinking about it, like a goddamn mantra:

THE METEORIC RISE OF SIMON BURCHWOOD
THE METEORIC RISE OF SIMON BURCHWOOD
THE METEORIC RISE OF SIMON BURCHWOOD
THE METEORIC RISE OF SIMON BURCHWOOD
THE METEORIC RISE OF SIMON BURCHWOOD
THE METEORIC RISE OF SIMON BURCHWOOD

It had a really nice ring to it. I mean, I always wanted the title of my first book to be *grandiose.* And this one, it was pretty goddamn grandiose. It was a great title. My dream was finally coming to fruition. Finally.

It's true.

About the Author

Scott Semegran lives in Austin, Texas with his wife, four kids, two cats, and a dog. He graduated from the University of Texas at Austin with a degree in English. He is a writer and a cartoonist. He can also bend metal with his mind and run really fast, if chased by a pack of wolves. His comic strips have appeared in the following newspapers: The Austin Student, The Funny Times, The Austin American-Statesman, Rocky Mountain Bullhorn, Seven Days, The University of Texas at Dallas Mercury, and The North Austin Bee. Books by Scott Semegran include Sammie & Budgie, Boys, The Meteoric Rise of Simon Burchwood, The Spectacular Simon Burchwood, Modicum, Mr. Grieves and more. He is a Kindle bestselling author.

Books by Scott Semegran

Want more Simon Burchwood? Then get the next novel **The Spectacular Simon Burchwood**. Recently divorced and his writing career in shambles, Simon Burchwood's life is a complete disaster. He reluctantly finds work as a computer support technician and resigns that his career as the next great American novelist will never come to fruition. When he learns that his ex-wife abruptly moves to Dallas with his children, he embarks on a crazy road trip with a nerdy coworker and a hitchhiking punk rock girl and discovers the inspiration he desperately needs for his new literary masterpiece. Take another trip with the one and only Simon Burchwood.

Praise for **The Spectacular Simon Burchwood**:

"The author is quite funny and some of the quips are great. Simon can be hilarious and great to read about in his recaps and memories." -- 3 Stars / *So Many Books, So Little Time*

"Simon is starting to understand something, and his luck literally changes. Semegran handles this quite deftly; even though Simon keeps warbling his "It's true!" declarations at a great rate, the reader does not tire of them, because, well, some of them ARE true, and we see the progress he is making in getting a grasp of what life is about, albeit in his own ham-fisted way." -- 4 Stars / *The New Podler Review of Books*

Buy it today!

***

"Illustrated throughout by Semegran, this book is the author's best. In these pages, his steadfastly idiosyncratic style really begins to click. An unconventional, beguiling, and endearing family tale." -- *Kirkus Reviews*

From Kindle bestselling writer and cartoonist Scott Semegran, **Sammie & Budgie** is a quirky, mystical tale of a self-doubting IT nerd and his young son, who possesses the gift of foresight. The boy's special ability propels his family on a road trip to visit his ailing grandfather, a prickly man who left an indelible stamp on the father and son. The three are connected through more than genetics, their lives intertwined through dreams, imagination, and longing.

Simon works as a network administrator for a state government agency, a consolation after a promising career as a novelist flounders. He finds himself a single parent of two small children following the mysterious death of his adulterous wife. From the ashes of his failed marriage emerges a tight-knit family of three: a creative, special needs son, a hyperactive, butt-kicking daughter, and the caring, sensitive father. But when his son's special ability reveals itself, Simon struggles to keep his little family together in the face of adversity and uncertainty.

Sammie is a creative third-grader that draws adventures in his sketchbook with his imaginary friend, Budgie, a parakeet that protects him from the monsters inhabiting his dreams. Sammie is also a special needs child but is special in more ways than one. He can see the future. Sammie seemingly can predict events both mundane and catastrophic in equal measure. But when he envisions the suffering of his grandfather, the family embarks on a road trip to San Antonio with the nanny to visit the ailing patriarch.

Sammie & Budgie is an illustrated novel brought to you from the quirky mind of writer and cartoonist Scott Semegran. The novel explores the bond between a caring father and his children, one affected by his own thorny relationship with his surly father, and the connection he has with his sweet son is thicker than blood, going to the place where dreams are conceived and realized.

Praise for **Sammie & Budgie**:

"A quirky, mystical tale of a self-doubting IT nerd and his young son, who possesses the gift of foresight. Engaging and fun, with wonderfully crafted characters." –Derf Backderf, bestselling creator of the graphic novel *My Friend Dahmer*

"**Sammie & Budgie** is instantly absorbing, its affable narrator hooking you with wit and whimsy, then reeling you into the boat, where larger revelations await. Scott Semegran is a lively, vivid storyteller, and this book will delight readers of all ages, while leaving them with plenty to ponder about their own lives. I loved this book!" -Davy Rothbart, author of *My Heart is an Idiot*, creator of *Found Magazine*, and contributor to public radio's *This American Life*

"Scott Semegran's loose charm and conversational style brings his shaggy narrator to vivid life in this story of a loving, if imperfect father and his maybe-psychic son. A sweet story about an extraordinary everyday family, **Sammie & Budgie** will find its way into your heart, and stay there." -Emily Flake, *New Yorker* cartoonist, author of *Mama Tried: Dispatches from the Seamy Underbelly of Modern Parenting*, and creator of *Lulu Eightball*

Get it today!

***

If you enjoyed this book then check out **MODICUM**, a collection of short stories, musings, and cartoons by writer / cartoonist Scott Semegran. The book explores such themes as suicide, parenting, religion, masculinity, the apocalypse, and, most importantly, erections. It's guaranteed to make you laugh, cry, and pee your pants (hopefully, not at the same time).

Praise for **MODICUM**:

"Funny, sweet, dark, and sad, Scott Semegran's comics and short stories create a wholly convincing world of love, loss, and fear. His light touch with heavy subjects is a gift, and his forays into silliness are a delight. I can't tell if his kids should read it as soon as possible, or never." - Emily Flake, cartoonist and author of *LuLu Eightball*

"Hilarious, poignant, twisted... and those are just the stories. Scott Semegran's cartoons bring an added one-two visceral punch to a powerful collection of work." - Davy Rothbart, author of *The Lone Surfer of Montana, Kansas* and publisher of *FOUND Magazine*

Buy it today!

***

Mr. Grieves started as a poke at human nature through the use of talking, narcissistic animals. It has evolved into a full-on assault to your funny bone. Where else will you find rats fighting over cubicles, camels worrying about aging, a parrot talking to aliens, and a lonely water snail longing for a friend? Welcome to the world of **Mr. Grieves**!

Praise for **Mr. Grieves**:

"An animal or plant — or maybe even an ovum — talks. Sometimes to itself, but more often to another of its kind. The idea is simple, but the execution is smart and almost always funny in Scott Semegran's collection of 140 four-panel comics drawn between 2004 and 2008, **Mr. Grieves**." -- Reviewed for *Indie Reader* by Andrew Stout

Get it today!

***

Boys is a collection of stories about three boys living in Texas: one growing up, one dreaming, and one fighting to stay alive in the face of destitution and adversity. There's second-grader William, a shy yet imaginative boy who schemes about how to get back at his school-yard bully, Randy. Then there's Sam, a 15-year-old boy who dreams of getting a 1980 Mazda RX-7 for his sixteenth birthday but has to work at a Greek restaurant to fund his dream. Finally, there's Seff, a 21-year-old on the brink of manhood, trying to survive along with his roommate, working as waiters and barely making ends meet. These three stories are told with heart, humor, and an uncompromising look at what it meant to grow up in Texas during the 1980s and 1990s.

"The writing is sharp and unpretentiously thoughtful, and since each of the main characters finds solace in companionship, this is an affecting literary depiction of the comforting power of friendship. Each of the stories can be read on its own, but taken together, they make a coherent, thematic whole, skillfully produced. An endearing collection that deftly captures the need for youthful fellowship." -- *Kirkus Reviews*

"Verdict: With nary a dull moment, Scott Semegran's **Boys** features short stories filled with unexpected nuances that draws readers right into the heart of his well-developed characters." -- *IndieReader.* 5 Stars. IR Approved.

Buy it today!

❊ ❊ ❊

Find Scott Semegran Online:
https://www.scottsemegran.com
https://www.goodreads.com/scottsemegran
https://www.twitter.com/scottsemegran
https://www.facebook.com/scottsemegran.writer/
https://www.instagram.com/scott_semegran
https://www.amazon.com/author/scottsemegran
https://www.smashwords.com/profile/view/scottsemegran

Mutt Press:
https://www.muttpress.com